THE NEWSPAPER WIDOW

Cecilia Manguerra Brainard

Published by PALH
(Philippine American Literary House}
P.O. Box 5099
Santa Monica, CA 90409, USA
PALHBOOKS.com; palh@aol.com

Library of Congress Control Number: 2021905814

ISBN: 978-1-953716-14-9 (Paperback edition)
ISBN: 978-1-953716-24-8 (Hardcover edition)
ISBN: 978-1-953716-15-6 (Ebook edition)

The Newspaper Widow was first published by the University
of Santo Tomas Publishing House, Copyright ©2017
Cecilia Manguerra Brainard. All rights reserved.

Cover art and design by Felix Mago Miguel

PREFACE

I never met my maternal great-grandmother but I had heard and read about her, noting that she was the first woman publisher of the Philippines, and that her sons included a senator, an archbishop, and a congressman. Her daughter was a writer.

Remedios Dioscmito Lopez was a powerful matriarch who bore sixteen children, although only four made it to adulthood. Widowed at thirty-nine, she took over her husband's publishing business, the Imprenta Rosario, which was located on the ground floor of their home on historic Calle Colon in Cebu, Philippines. She, her three sons, and a daughter continued the publication of several daily and weekly newspapers including *El Precursor*, *Ang Maguuna*, *El Boletin Catolico*, and *La Juventud*. Understanding the financial realities of publishing, she wisely invested in real estate, and the houses that she rented out provided for her family.

Even as a child I squirreled away information about my great-grandmother. Here, for instance, is a precious image of her. It is a description by Concepcion Briones in her book, *Life in Old Parian*:

"It was here that the first woman publisher of Cebu, Doña Remedios Lopez Cuenco, lived, reared, and ruled her family and managed the family's Imprenta Rosario ... (she) used to come down very early, mornings, in saya (skirt) and kimono (blouse) to the printing press—her long black curly hair falling down to her waist, freshly shampooed and fragrant with samuyao (citrus)..."

Briones also writes of Remedios wearing a navy-blue long skirt, wide and bouffant, with an elegant top and a shawl pinned with a magnificent brooch of gold and pearls. Tucked inside the waist of her skirt, on the left side, was the goldenchain to hold her big silk fan.

My mother said that even though Remedios liked beautiful clothes and nice jewelry, she was fearless in handling the printing presses and always had ink-smeared fingers.

My great-grandmother's era also interested me. The so-called American Period in the Philippines, from 1900 to 1942, was the time when the Philippines had to shift from Spanish to American rule. The Americans likewise had to make adjustments, learning how to juggle the ideas of democracy with colonialism, for instance. In other words, my great-grandmother's era was a dynamic time of change.

These bits and pieces about my great-grandmother and her world sat and grew in my mind. They inspired my novel, *The Newspaper Widow.* I emphasize that my protagonist, Ines Maceda, is a fictional character. Even though Ines is a widow who inherits her husband's newspaper business in Ubec, Philippines in 1909, my novel is a work of fiction. I have "lied" and manipulated events and even geography to accommodate my story. But while I twisted things around in order to create this novel, I had great fun peering into what could have been the world of my great-grandmother Remedios.

My original intention had been to write a mystery, but I rely too much on character and character development more than plot, and so I present a novel that is more about Ines Maceda than it is about the mystery of the dead priest found in the creek of Ubec one summer day in 1909.

I'd like to thank my husband Lauren R. Brainard and our sons, Chris, Alex, and Andrew, for their support of my literary efforts. Special thanks also to the writer/teacher, Eve La Salle Caram, whose Algonquin West master writing workshop helped me create *The Newspaper Widow.*

Cecilia Manguerra Brainard

CONTENTS

ACKNOWLEDGMENTS

The Newspaper Widow is published by the University of Santo Tomas University Publishing House, 2017

This novel under the title, *Dead Priest in the Creek,* was shortlisted for the Cirilo Bautista Prize for the Novel

Portions of this novel appeared in:

Onyx International Journal, Vol. 2, ed. Kambon Obayani, Jasmaya, 2016

Outpouring: Yolanda Relief Anthology, ed. Dean Francis Alfar, Kestrel DDM, 2014,

Philippines Graphic 2013 and 2014

Philippine Speculative Fiction 8, eds. Nikki Alfar & Dean Francis Alfar, Kestrel DDM, 2013

Tomas 3, ed. Ralph Semino Galan, UST, 2014

PART I

CHAPTER 1

THE RATS

In the summer of 1909, Ubec was overrun by rats. Rodents larger than cats scampered throughout the seaside city, fearless of man even during the daytime when the scorching sun shone down on them exposing their hideousness—their wiry brown fur, long snouts and naked tails as long as their bodies. Brazenly, they scurried through the streets and rummaged through garbage. In the wet market, they aggressively ran through walkways, brushing their furry bodies against the legs of horrified shoppers. The rodents didn't confine themselves to gutters and dirty alleys, but they invaded houses, buildings, and even the fort and churches made of solid stone. They gnawed on the hard molave wood furniture in the swanky International Hotel; the new wooden houses and buildings built by the Americans were like candy to them. They shamelessly left their urine and droppings everywhere, even in the public health office itself.

The rats attacked cats that had never seen rodents bigger than their fathers. The domesticated cats, reared on fish bones and food scraps, took to cowering in the kitchen, hoping for human protection, although some did succumb to the rats' attacks. It had become ordinary to see rats dragging the bloody entrails of cats and other small mammals, sending pet-owners into hysteria.

The Americans, who had occupied the Philippines

since 1898, were confounded about what to do with these goliaths. They had had some experience with rats in 1901, after they established their civil government in the Philippines and a rat infestation broke out. But those rats were smaller, half-as-ugly, less destructive, and infinitely more discreet. While those had nibbled on copra and grain, and their droppings had caused coughing and sneezing, they had stayed away from homes, favoring warehouses and sewers. In 1901, the American public health officials had launched a rat eradication program, and the rat population had abated, but the giant rats of the summer in 1909 descended like God's punishment.

Ubecans speculated these came from the international ships that now docked in Ubec's piers (since Stockholm was renowned as the rat capital, the Scandinavian ships were highly suspected). The religious folks had another take, saying the giant rodents were God's retribution for the wayward women consorting with the foreign sailors.

One hot summer night, when three rats scrambled into a crib with their teeth bared, ready to bite an infant, they crossed a line—terrorizing cats was one thing, but physically attacking a baby was an entirely different story—and the fury of every man, woman, and child rose to a pitch. It was not fear of bubonic plague but pure hatred for the despicable creatures that fueled the Ubecans' desire to eradicate them. The fifteen centavos per rat-tail bounty offered by the public health department was not a necessary incentive—it was gravy. People took to carrying machetes; and children, who were on their summer holiday, made a sport of hunting rats.

The rat epidemic was what led to the discovery of the dead body in the creek near the Augustinian warehouse.

One afternoon, the Fernandez brothers hatched the plan of rat hunting. One was nine, the other eleven. The older one wanted to save money for the carnival. The younger one wanted to buy comics; he was fascinated with tales of ghosts, enchanted beings, creatures that could morph into forms of dogs and horses, and witches that could unfurl their tongues to suck out unborn babies. Their plan was to go to the warehouse where they hoped to find rats and maybe even encounter a supernatural being or two. Since the drowning of one of the local boys, parents did not allow children to wander far and the brothers had to time their outing. They waited until the grownups were busy preparing supper, and they crept out of their nipa hut and went to a shed where they picked up two machetes. Very quietly, they opened the side gate and left their house. The boys hurried through the downtown area, past the plaza, toward the San Agustin Church. They headed toward a huge ram shackled building made of stone and wood.

"What will you do with your money?" the younger one said. He was dreaming of the comics he wanted.

"Cotton candy … at the carnival," the older one said. "I'm going to eat all I want. Last year I only had one. And I want to buy tickets for the games."

They were talking about the Ubec Carnival, which was a two-week fair held in May. The Americans had started the carnival to help promote the products of their new colony, the Philippines. The festivities provided opportunities for business owners to rub elbows with the buyers, a great occasion to advertise their products in newspapers, posters, flyers. Pineapple, sugar, rice, maguey, tobacco, hard wood lumber, coal, silver, beer, rum were among the many items peddled at the carnival. The two-week event was also intended to promote goodwill, and included rides, games, dances, music, circus side acts, balls, and masquerades, all to imitate the festive atmosphere of the carnivals in Rio and New Orleans.

"I'm going to buy the witch comics, all of them," the younger one said. "How many rats do you think we'll kill?"

"Maybe a hundred," the older one said.

They were sweating profusely when they reached the warehouse, and using their shirts to wipe their faces, they stared at the door with a rusted iron sliding bolt. In the past the Augustinian friars had rented out the two-story building to a cigar factory. It sat near an embankment of a creek that was full of water during the rainy season, but which was low in the summertime. The building had disintegrated and part of it sagged toward the creek, looking as if it would tumble down into the rocky embankment at any time.

When the boys heard cooing sounds, the younger boy clutched his brother's arm. "I want to go home," he whimpered.

"Don't be a baby," said the older one, shaking off his hand. He made a sign of the Cross, took a deep breath, and slid open the bolt. He tried to push the door open, but dirt at the bottom jammed the door in place. Using their machetes, the boys cleared away the soil, and the older one jostled and pushed until to their surprise the door creaked open. The noise within grew louder, and suddenly there was a rushing sound like a strong wind as birds flew right past them. Both boys screamed.

"What was that?" the younger one said. "A ghost?"

The older one who had regained his composure said, "Don't be silly, those are pigeons."

"I want to go home. Mama's looking for us. She'll whip us if she finds out we came here. Let's go home, please," he pleaded. But the older boy stepped deeper into the dark and musty warehouse. Not wanting to be left behind, the younger one followed, hanging on to his brother's shirt.

When they heard squealing and snorting sounds, the boys grabbed their machetes, ready to strike. They traced the noise to a corner. Enough light filtered through so they could make out little shining eyes staring at them. These were rats, no doubt about it; they had found a gold mine! The swarm of rats started moving as the boys approached them. The boys swung their machetes left and right. Cold fear coursed through their veins that they may accidentally hurt each another, but the explosion of bodies gave them satisfaction. When all was still, they gathered six dead rats and brought them outside. The sun was setting by this time, and the older one said they should hurry home before it got dark.

The younger one held up his bloody hands. "I want to wash up," he insisted, and he lay his rats down and clambered over the rocks to get to the water at the bottom. He rinsed his hands and was working his way up, when he looked over his shoulder and caught a flash of white. "I see something! In the rocks, something covered by branches and leaves," he shouted.

"What is it?" the older one yelled back. "It's getting late, we have to go home."

"I see more rats ... coming out of something strange ... wait I'm going closer..."

Growing curious himself, the older one joined his brother. Gingerly, the two boys made their way along the rocks to a hulking mass that lay wedged in the rocks. Using sticks, they pushed back branches and leaves until they saw tattered black cloth that reminded them of the soutane of the priests. They stood mesmerized, their hearts pounding. When a rat darted out, they jumped back, and that's when they saw gleaming white bones ... over there rib bones, and ... oh ... a skull. "Ay-a!" they shouted, dropping their sticks. Turning around, they quickly ran back up and out of the creek. Completely forgetting about the rats, the carnival, and the supernatural, the Fernandez brothers raced all the way home and with ragged breath, gave their report to their parents.

CHAPTER 2

INES MACEDA

Rats, too, featured in Ines Maceda's dream. Over breakfast, she described rats, a multitude of them, swimming in water, their gray coats shimmering under the bright sunlight, rippling like gray sand, totally repulsive.

Andres, her son, said, "I think, Mama, you had the dream because everyone's talking about rats. It's nothing to get upset about."

Ines continued, "I am upset. The jasmine has been pruned, and not just pruned but hacked down to nothing. It makes me sad. Your father, may he rest in peace, and I planted that vine."

Ines was talking about the tumultuous jasmine vine laden with white flowers that grew outside her bedroom window. The plant had been a companion, a witness to the life she had led with her late husband—their love-making, their quarrels, their disappointments over the miscarriages, and their joy when Andres was born there in their room, right next to the jasmine vine.

"It'll grow back, Mama," Andres said, calmly, reassuringly, a tone that his father had often used. Ines looked at her son and saw traces of Pablo on his face—the oval face, the high forehead. She felt the twinge of loss once again— Pablo had passed away less than a year ago. Ines took a deep breath and told him to finish breakfast and get to work. It was his first day of work at a law firm. "You must be on time. You must show that you're interested, that you're competent," she said. The night before, she had inspected his clothes to make sure they were pressed. And having found a loose button on the right cuff of his shirt, she had brought the shirt to her room, hunted for a needle and thread and sewed the button in place. "This apprenticeship is important. It will help you get into law school," she said.

After Pablo died, Andres had floundered. His school grades dropped; he switched majors from Literature to History. But recently he started talking about law school, and he had taken the initiative to apply for the summer apprenticeship, citing what his father had said about the Philippines needing good lawyers, especially now that the Americans had made many changes. Out of six applicants, Andres had gotten the position.

"Don't worry, Mama," Andres said, kissing her on the cheek, and he grabbed his bag and left.

But Ines was worried. There was her son whom she had to raise and put through school. There was her mother who needed her help with the hacienda. The headache she had to deal with that morning was Pablo's pet project, the newspaper he had founded, *The Ubec Daily*.

The sun was blazing as she fumbled for the keys to the nearby office of *The Ubec Daily*. When she entered, the acrid smell of ink made her sneeze, and she searched for the ink bottles and made sure they were all covered. She was certain they would go blind or lose their hair from the chemicals in the office. Even the paper had a strange odor like burning leaves. She clucked her tongue at the disarray in the office—cluttered with paper, bottles of ink, metal frames, letters for typesetting, a lot of debris. She felt the urge to tidy up, but the times she'd done so her managing editor couldn't find things. It was better if she confined her meticulousness to her desk, which had been Pablo's desk and which was now hers.

She put on her eyeglasses and picked up a green ledger.

She leafed through it, the numbers looming large in her eyes—ghastly figures in red ink—and she did some addition. There was no doubt about it: the business was losing money. Sensing the beginnings of a migraine, she placed a hand on her forehead. "Pablo, Pablo, Pablo," she moaned, "I can make more money selling old newspapers and empty glass jars than this newspaper business of yours. The arithmetic of this business makes no sense at all. It should have been simple, Pablo. Even an eight-year-old knows that in a business, you put so much money in, and you make more in the end, but not this one." She was astounded that her husband, the Literature Professor, the publisher, a contender to the Philippine Assembly, could not do simple mathematics.

She pressed her hands to her forehead and, unbeckoned, a memory floated up—an afternoon, many years ago, when she and Pablo had visited the walled city of Intramuros in Manila. They were walking along a row of stone houses when they caught a floral scent, so strong, so overpowering that they stopped in their tracks and like sleepwalkers followed the perfume to an old house with a huge gate. They got inside and were mesmerized at the sight of the fountain, stone benches, and riotous plants of blue hydrangeas, red hibiscus, bougainvillea, and rangoon creepers. And on the far end, near the winding staircase, was the source of the seductive scent—a jasmine vine, with clouds of fragrant white star-shaped flowers. Pablo had cut off a branch and later planted it in the yard of their new home. The vine eventually grew tall, all the way to the side of their bedroom window.

It was the same jasmine vine that was now denuded, reduced to four pathetic branches, that threatened to die, and with it a precious part of her past. Ines sighed and rubbed her temples. To compound matters, less than a year before he died, Pablo had bought a huge and very expensive Miehle printing press on loan. The fine white paper he insisted on using came from Hong Kong. Her mother had repeatedly warned her that Pablo did not have a good head for business. "Let him teach, let him discourse with the intelligentsia, but you handle the money in your family," was her advice. Her mother was right; her mother was right. Here she was stuck with this newspaper business and a huge loan.

She had a way out. If she wanted to, she could end it all, she could sell the business. Pablo's publishing rival Santiago Echeveria had offered to buy her out. But even the memory of Santiago made her skin crawl. There he had stood in front of her, on the pretext of giving his sympathies. "If the business is too much for you, Ines, let me know, and we can talk," he said in a soft voice, but oily with condescension.

Santiago Echeveria was the publisher of *The Light*, the only other newspaper in Ubec. Three months after Pablo had founded his paper, Santiago founded *The Light*. It was the periodical of a copycat, a man so lacking in imagination, all he ran were Ansel N. Kellogg's syndicated materials. Occasionally, Santiago would write editorials to air his political views, one-sided unfair thoughts by someone who had no idea what "balanced news" meant.

Ines had skewered him with a look. He was plump and dapper, all in white, holding a cane, like a caricature of a colonial. All he needed was a Panama hat. "Talk about what?" she had asked.

Santiago shifted his weight, "That is ... that is..." He lost his words.

"What are you trying to say, Santiago?"

He lifted his cane and pointed it at the Miehle. "I ... That is ... I ... I ... can buy the Miehle ... from you. I can assume the loan."

Ines narrowed her eyes and struggled to control herself.

"What I mean is, I'll buy not just the Miehle, but the whole business. Everything. I can buy you out." He made a half-turn, as if doing a quick inventory of the place.

"Buy me out? I am not selling even a pencil eraser, certainly not to you. How did you get so interested in publishing, Santiago? You couldn't even spell when we were children," Ines said. "All you're good at is collecting rent from your tenants and checking on your hacienda now and then."

"Well, I ... what I mean is ... since *The Light* is Ubec's Number One Daily, I can afford a good press like the Miehle."

Her ire had risen to her temples, giving her a thunderous headache. "Santiago, who on earth said your paper is Number One? You? Your paper has nothing new in it; it's mediocre. It's only good for one thing—the outhouse. Just because it looks good doesn't mean you have a good paper, Santiago. It has no meat. You have no point of view. When you do have one, you're so off-based, even children know so. Please leave, I will never sell to you." Ines had led Santiago to the door where she gave him a little push to send him on his way, and she locked the door.

Her anger against Santiago had been seething in any case.

Santiago had gone out of his way to write scathing editorials against Pablo when he had wanted to run as a candidate for the Philippine Assembly, the gist of which posed the question: What does a Literature Professor know about legislation and government? Ines had suspected Santiago's attacks contributed to Pablo's ill health; she knew that those editorials hurt Pablo deeply. His heart stopped not too long after those editorials. Here in this very office, he had taken his last breath.

"Pablo," Ines now said, "Pablo, I have enough money to keep your paper running for another month. That's all. I have no idea what to do. I know you believed in truth, but I can't pay for your Miehle and your beautiful paper with air." She paused, before she continued her monologue. "I need your help. If things don't improve, I'll be forced to sell."

She slumped lower into the leather chair that had been Pablo's and was too big for her, and she waited for some sign from Pablo, some message from her dead husband.

CHAPTER 3

MELISANDE MOREAU

Nothing happened; no voice from the other world gave her advice. Pablo was on the other side where he belonged. Ines was alone in this matter. She turned her attention to the press that he loved, but which was now her responsibility—how huge it was, how powerful. And how expensive. A horrible truth lodged inside her gut like a painful thorn—only Santiago would be interested in buying the Miehle, and she would rather cut off her right hand than sell it to him. She pushed the hated ledger away, not knowing what to do.

Outside, the sounds of the working day had picked up as pedestrians and carriages bustled down Cristobal Colon Street. The heat of the morning carried smells of horse manure and rotting fruit. She closed the window and resumed work, counting the money in the cash box this time, to see if there was enough to pay her managing editor, Felix Santa Maria, and the contributing writers. A knocking on the door reminded her of Felix and she wondered why he didn't use his office key—perhaps he misplaced it. Ines opened the door. "Felix—" she began, then stopped. There standing in front her was her neighbor Melisande Moreau, holding out a paper bag.

"I came from the bakery; here are some rolls for you and Andres," she said in a voice that sounded happy and which made Ines feel more depressed.

Ines paused, not knowing what to do. This was the first time Melisande had visited her. She knew Melisande, but she was not a close friend. Melisande was also a Frenchwoman, and, therefore, an outsider. Like other Ubecans, Ines never fully trusted someone different. Melisande had a dress shop, Printemps, very popular among the wealthy wives of officials and merchants. When Ines had a few dresses made by Melisande, it was all business. Ines walked to her nearby shop with four meters of cloth. They discussed the design of the dress, how much it cost, and a week later Ines picked up the dress. Melisande had attended Pablo's wake and funeral, as everyone in Ubec had done. That was the sum total of their contact.

With her hand frozen on the door, Ines stared at Melisande who wore a frilly Parisian-style dress, bright yellow, with the long skirt ending in generous flounces, which fluttered with the warm breeze. Her face was powdered and rouged, her lips red, and her reddish-brown hair swept up, with a few errant tendrils bouncing around her face. Melisande's brightness made Ines feel self-conscious about her simple black dress and hair confined in a tight bun. Timidly Ines extended her hand to accept the bag, which was still warm to the touch.

"It's delicious. Walking here, I had one roll, the sweet kind—" Melisande chattered, then suddenly stopped. "Something is wrong. You are upset." Her smile vanished; she gave Ines a hug and quickly led her to some chairs. "Come, sit down. It is difficult, of course, you miss him. Everything will be all right."

Ines would never have discussed her financial situation, especially not with someone she hardly knew, but she found herself blurting out, "I'll have to sell everything. The newspaper's not making money."

"Don't worry about those things, now," Melisande said in a soothing voice.

"It must at least make enough to pay for itself. It makes no sense to keep it going." Ines had not meant to cry but tears formed in her eyes. Melisande held her hand and said, "I know how you feel. I felt desperate once, and I thought it was the end of my life, but no, it was the beginning of an adventure. Wait and see, things will get better."

Melisande pulled out a roll from the paper bag and pinched off a piece. She held it near Ines' mouth—"You must try it," she cajoled. "Go ahead, it's very tasty." Like a bird, Ines opened her mouth. Melisande proceeded to feed her warm bread with a hint of anise. All Ines had that morning was a soft boiled egg and she was now quite hungry. Since Pablo's death Ines had been stumbling through meals, not paying attention to what she ate. She had no appetite for her favorite foods chicken soup with fideos, fish relleno, or pork ribs. It didn't matter what succulent herbs and spices were included in her cook's concoctions, everything looked dull and uninviting. But now she found herself enjoying the soft sweet bread that seemed to melt in her mouth.

They were seated near a big table with newspapers on top, and just as Melisande placed the last piece into Ines' mouth, a gust of wind blew through the window, knocking off yesterday's edition. Pages scattered on the floor, and Melisande got up to gather them. She placed them on the table and swept her hand over the front page. "It looks nice. Did Felix do this?'

"Felix did most of the work."

Melisande turned the page and singled out an article, "This one is about American rule, about the plusses and minuses of being under American rule." She looked up at Ines. "Are you interested in politics?"

"Yes, I am. In history, too." Even as a young girl, she read her father's history books. He had a well-stocked library at their home. Ines glanced at what Melisande pointed out; it was written by one of their contributors.

"I'm afraid it makes me sleepy," Melisande said, and she pretended to yawn. "And here's one about the Liberal party and the Nationalista party. Well, that is important." Then she frowned. "Ines, what does 'antediluvian' mean?"

Before Ines could answer, Melisande continued, "Here are more hard words: 'ineluctable,' 'procrustean,' 'autological'—do you know what they mean?"

"Ineluctable means inescapable, but I'm not sure about the others," Ines confessed. She knew exactly who the writer of those highfalutin words was—a retired stuck-up professor from the university where Pablo had taught. "I have wondered about the use of big words," Ines said.

Melisande shrugged her shoulders. "If you and I don't understand them, why are they in the newspaper? What I mean is, you and I are not stupid and yet we don't understand these words. That means a lot of people won't understand them either."

Ines had known, from the time Pablo came out with his first issue, that his readership was limited to what he called the intelligentsia. But the newspaper had been his creation and she had left him alone to make decisions about it. But now, studying it with Melisande, she felt as if she were seeing it for the first time, and yes, Melisande was right: the articles with bombastic language were not interesting at all. In fact, they were simply boring.

Melisande flipped to the back page. "Do people pay for these?" she said, pointing at the few advertisements, pathetically clustered at the bottom of the page.

Ines remembered the figures in the ledger. "The advertisements don't make too much, not even enough to pay the salary of Felix. Pablo and Felix worked to have a good newspaper; they never really looked at it as a way of making money."

Melisande lifted her head to indicate she understood. "But people pay to buy the newspaper, correct? And some subscribe?"

"It can earn more money than it now makes," Ines admitted.

Melisande started tapping her forefinger on the table. She closed her eyes, deep in thought. "Why not try to get more people to advertise? Are they expensive? They should not be too much. You have to think like the clever Chinese merchant who can be satisfied with a small profit per item, unlike the

Spaniard who wants a one hundred percent markup for every chorizo he sells."

"If the newspaper includes other articles, not just politics and serious matters, do you think businesses will buy advertisement?" Ines asked.

Melisande opened her eyes wide. "Oh, yes. Do you know what my clients talk about?"

Ines thought of the women who flocked to Melisande's shop—young, old, wealthy, middle class. "Dress designs? Their families?"

"Yes, and about shoes and bags and their looks. Women are very vain, and they love gossip. In short, they want to have fun. Don't you like to have fun?"

"Well, I ... I..." Ines had no idea how to answer this question. She married Pablo when she was eighteen, and had a couple of miscarriages before she had Andres. She had taken care of her husband and son, and she had always helped her parents run their hacienda. Even then, she found time to do gardening, and, of course, now her fingers were smeared with ink. She did not think of life in terms of "fun." "Fun" was for children; grownups lived life doing what they had to do.

Melisande threw her head back so a tendril of hair quivered above her forehead. "It's good to have fun. We're not here in this world for a long time you know." She leaned forward, smiled briefly, but quickly became serious. "The other week, a new client saw me to have her measurements taken for a carnival dress. She never came back." She paused, widened her eyes and slowly enunciated, "She died in her sleep." She paused to let her words sink in before continuing, "The women who come to my shop like to enjoy life. The newspapers in Paris have articles about society and what the wealthy women wear to this and that, and there are also gossip columns—this actor was running around with the wife of so-and-so—and there is also a cooking section with recipes—all quite—how do you call it?—alegre."

"Do you have some of these French newspapers?" Ines asked. "I would like to see them sometime."

"I have *Le Continental, Le Petit Parisien, Le Figaro,* and others. You will get a lot of ideas and you will know how to make your newspaper popular."

"Pablo's newspaper," Ines corrected her.

Melisande smiled. "Ines, I know he started the paper. He was very smart and well-read. Everyone adored him, but unfortunately he's no longer here with us." She paused before adding, "You are."

Ines swallowed hard, uncertain about how to react. She thought she should have been offended, but she wasn't. Melisande was right. Pablo was dead and she, Ines, was alive. Here she was with Pablo's newspaper, which from a business point of view, she ought to get rid of, and yet she recalled Pablo's passion for this newspaper and for Truth. He used to go on about how important it was for Filipinos to have their own newspaper to document their own Truth. She didn't fully understand his idealism, but she didn't want to destroy his creation. More importantly the thought of selling the equipment to Santiago Echeveria turned her stomach.

Melisande continued chattering. "You do not know this, but your husband lent me money. He and Mr. Fitz helped me to start my business."

Mr. Fitz was the manager of the International Hotel. Ines nodded. "Pablo was always helping people." Ines recalled the host of students, academics, merchants, even street vendors who had shown up at Pablo's wake and thanked her for what her husband had done to help them.

"They were very kind to me. I had nothing, you understand, when I first arrived Ubec. You are probably wondering why a Frenchwoman would leave France for Ubec. I will tell you. I left Paris because of a man. A beautiful man named Samir." She paused and crinkled her nose in a charming way. "It's always about a man, isn't it?" She gave a quick laugh before continuing, "I had heard about Ubec at the Exposition Universelle, and when I needed to leave him—Samir, that man—I told myself, 'I will go there.' And so I came. When I arrived, I stayed at the International Hotel, paying weekly. I wanted to open a dress shop but had no money, no contacts. Once I overheard the hotel people talking about me. They said things like, 'She appeared in Ubec like a mushroom that sprouts after a thunderstorm.' Have you heard of the saying? There were other stories, that I lived here and there, Paris, Athens, Constantinople. A lot of gossip."

Ines nodded, knowing Ubecans liked to sit and talk about other people. She had heard people suggest then that Melisande was working as a highly-paid prostitute in the hotel. Proper ladies simply did not live in hotels, certainly not by themselves. "It is not very nice … People are sometimes cruel … They say things that are crude."

"I did not care, really. What I was worried about was not having money and I did not know what to do with myself. I was young and alone in another country—I was frightened." Melisande folded the newspaper and returned it to its place. "Mr. Fitz was an angel." Her face brightened. "He knew my predicament, and one day he brought me to a fiesta celebration and introduced me to your husband. Mr. Maceda was the quintessential professor, very serious, and he asked what I did. I told him I was a dressmaker and that I wanted to open a shop. He asked what kept me from doing so, and I told him I needed two Singer Sewing machines and enough money to rent a place for three months, but that I didn't have the money. Without knowing me, without a fuss, he asked how much I needed, and I told him. A few days later—voila!—he and Mr. Fitz had the money for me. I was able to open Printemps. I paid them back in six months. It's not difficult to make money. You use your head and you work. And you have to be a bit lucky."

By now, Melisande was standing next to the Miehle press. Gingerly, she lifted her skirt to one side to avoid the oil and ink. "It's really very big!" she said, eyes widening, voice lilting with undertones. She giggled at her double entendre. She stood there for a while with her big eyes sparkling, and she bit her lower lip and shook her head as if overwhelmed.

Ines felt amused at the Frenchwoman's antics.

Twirling around to face Ines, Melisande declared, "I

should go. I have to finish the mayor's wife's gown. She's in the Maria Elena Procession of the carnival. You know she is big-boned and it took me a while to come up with the right design, but finally I discovered that the accent has to be on her big bosom. She has beautiful breasts, so we have some cleavage, and we have to tell all eyes to look there—" Melisande was pointing at her own buxom breasts—"and not elsewhere." Melisande laughed and Ines had to smile.

By the time Melisande picked up her purse to leave, the heat of the day had risen from the cracks of the dry earth and cobblestoned streets. Melisande kissed her on the cheeks. "Now, be sure and eat a good lunch. And don't worry. I'll buy advertisements and tell my clients to do the same. You can do it, you know," she said, and the Frenchwoman traipsed out of the office, leaving Ines alone.

Ines sat in Pablo's chair for a spell, mulling over Melisande's words: "You can do it."

Such words were easier said than done. Ines knew that Melisande's start in Ubec hadn't been a snap. Printemps hadn't blossomed overnight. Ines had seen the dress shop empty and bare for months. Then indeed, bit by bit, via word of mouth, clients started appearing, and more dresses hung on the racks, and the single mannequin that graced the picture window became two, and the women who worked in the shop multiplied, and then it seemed that every woman in Ubec yearned to own a Melisande gown. Yes, Melisande's Printemps was now very prosperous, but it had not started out that way.

Ines came from a long line of merchants on her mother's side, and she had a good head for business. She knew that if she redid things, the newspaper could make enough money to pay for itself. Her only other major hurdle would be Felix Santa Maria, Pablo's former student and assistant, the newspaper's managing editor, who was also the reporter, typesetter, bookkeeper, buyer, deliverer—Felix did whatever needed to be done to keep the newspaper rolling.

Felix would be difficult to deal with. From the time Felix sat in their Smoking Room with the other students of

Pablo, clutching a La Corona cigar and sipping Boutrand cognac, Felix had echoed Pablo's ideas and vision exactly. He would want to continue running a newspaper that catered to the small elite group of intellectuals who did absolutely nothing to support the publication of the newspaper—tired, old professors who enjoyed seeing their names in print and who covered up their insecurities behind big words.

The more Ines thought about it, the more piqued she became by such snobbery. Well, if it came to that, she concluded, she would have to close the newspaper. She would inform Felix, the contributors, the handful of advertisers that that was the case. The question then would be: What would she do with all the equipment?

CHAPTER 4

FELIX SANTA MARIA

It was almost ten when Ines heard the ringing of Felix's bicycle, an old Gazelle bicycle that he had bought with his first paycheck. He had named it Rocinante, after Don Quixote's horse, and had declared, "I too want to fix the ills of the world. My windmills are American imperialism and exploitation." He shared Pablo's dream of complete independence from America, not statehood as others wished.

The plump young man burst into the office, sweaty and out of breath. "I'm sorry I'm late. A dead body was found in the creek."

"A body?" Ines asked, surprised. She shared the opinion of other people that nothing ever happened in Ubec.

"Just the remains," and Felix began his story, starting with shopping at the wet market with his grandmother and finding great deals for bitter melon, sayote, papaya, bananas, because even though his grandmother served fatty pork and innards, she believed people should eat fruits and vegetables to keep healthy ...

"Get to the point, Felix," interrupted Ines, drumming her fingers.

Felix lived with his grandmother, Mercedes, who ran a small eatery at a wet market. She was famous for food she served at the cemetery during All Souls' Day, when people visited their dead. Felix's grandmother always made sure their

20

family crypt was scrubbed clean and decorated with flowers. She invited everybody to stop by their crypt, where, in front of the tiered crumbling structure, she had a table laid with platters and tureens of food, swimming in fat. She fed all who took the time to remember the dead. She was often seen at church having Masses for the dead said. If anyone died in Ubec, there Mercedes was at the wake and funeral, sobbing loudly and teary-eyed, like a professional mourner.

Felix continued his story of how he and his grandmother came across a group of people talking about the Fernandez brothers who had disobeyed their parents and had gone rat hunting. The boys had returned utterly flustered and they were barely coherent as they confessed that they had gone to the abandoned Augustinian warehouse and later discovered human remains at the nearby creek. The parents led the brothers to the police station to report the matter.

"Could it have been a dog? Or goat?" Ines always suspected that Felix's tragic background colored his vision of the world: a pile of dog's bones could suddenly be human bones.

"They saw a human skull, Ma'am. And rats." Felix was rummaging through the archive file, when he looked up and said, "I think it's Father Zafra. He went missing last January."

"The Augustinian priest? Ah, yes, nativity sets were still up, but it wasn't Three Kings yet. A fire broke out in the rectory—what a commotion there was in church. Father Zafra was last seen on January 3." Like other Ubecans, she had noted the disturbance. Ines remembered the tall Spanish priest at San Agustin Church. Some people found him handsome and charming, and people praised his community programs. Father Zafra appeared in Ubec less than a decade ago, during the time the Americans took control in the Philippines.

Felix pulled out a back issue of *The Ubec Daily* and laid it on a table. "Yes, Ma'am. Here's the article I wrote about the incident: Father Zafra ... 55 years old ... Augustinian priest ... had said the evening Mass on Sunday ... missing the next day."

"I believe he had supper with Mr. Dela Cruz," Ines

said, looking over Felix's shoulder. "Didn't they have a quarrel that night?"

"Yes. Zafra left the music composer's house, headed toward the San Agustin rectory, but never made it home. The police interrogated Mr. Dela Cruz, but his Catalan friend vouched they were together all night. The police released Dela Cruz." Felix furrowed his brow. "Two months later, the priest's remains are found."

"Didn't people look for him last January?"

"They did, but they found nothing. The remains are wedged into a crevice."

"The creek is low now, which would explain why the remains are exposed. But something feels strange, Felix," Ines said.

"I feel it too. I'm going there to investigate. Someone from *The Light* has already interviewed the Fernandez boys."

"Santiago," Ines murmured. "Do you mean *The Light* will have an article about this tomorrow?" She felt a tightness in her chest at the thought that Santiago Echeveria's newspaper would beat them to this news.

"Yes," Felix said, and lifting an eyebrow added, "We should too."

"I'll walk with you. I have something to discuss with you."

"Sure, Ma'am," he said, and they set off.

***

The sun was high and people held umbrellas over their heads. Exhausted dogs lay under the shade of trees and houses. Ines and Felix cut through the part of town called the Ciudad, the old section built by the Spaniards, which was right next to the sea, and which had haphazard clusters of structures from the days of the Spanish—the fort, the Plaza Independencia, the port area and wet market, two churches, the government offices, and two- and three-story stone buildings that had stores on the ground floor and residences on the upper floors.

The Americans had respected the Spaniard's invincible stone buildings and had constructed their new buildings on the outer fringes of the Ciudad—government buildings that echoed Thomas Jefferson's Monticello, and whitewashed wooden two-story buildings with charming patios in front. They were also busy paving roads, building bridges, putting up electric street lamps, and constructing railways.

It was during their walk under the sweltering heat when Ines broached the financial condition of *The Ubec Daily*. She stated the newspaper had to make more money than it did.

There was silence for a long time. Felix lowered his head and stared at the ground as he walked.

"Felix?" she prodded.

"Well, Ma'am," he finally answered, lifting his head, "Professor Maceda was not a business person like Madame Moreau. *She* is a couturiere, a high class dressmaker—" he paused to let that statement sink in, before continuing, "—he was an intellectual, one with a huge vision. He thought of educating and changing the minds and hearts of people. Professor Maceda's goal had been to tell our own Truth, the Filipino's Truth that is. He often said Truth has power, and that we, as newspaper people, have the obligation to publish the Truth. He wanted to create a newspaper that would be as important as the *New York Tribune* or the *Faro de Vigo*. One of his proudest moments was when Mark Twain quoted something he wrote."

It was true. Everything Felix said was one hundred percent correct. Ines had watched Pablo frame and hang Mark Twain's editorial with his quote. Pablo had been a visionary, an idealist; and his thoughts were good; his newspaper was important. But businesswise, it was a disaster, and if she let the matter drop now, the newspaper would have to close and Pablo's vision would fritter into thin air. Taking a deep breath, she said in the calmest voice she could muster, "Felix, vision is one thing, survival is another. The newspaper is losing money. I'm still paying for the Miehle, and the paper and ink, everything adds up. I can't keep it going."

Felix did not answer. The city sounds retreated as they walked across the grassy area of the plaza toward the San Agustin. They passed a group of women with their babies in prams. A balloon vendor approached the group; one woman bought a red balloon, which she tied to the handle of her baby pram. Ines and Felix continued in silence, past thick bushes and colorful flower beds, until they caught sight of the Augustinian complex—the San Agustin church and rectory, the warehouse, the cluster of eucalyptus trees, and beyond, the creek. Felix then said, "I'll look at the books carefully and let you know."

Ines understood that what Felix had said, in the Ubecan way, was "No."

All the talk about Mark Twain and Truth were just words to sugarcoat his resistance to the changes she suggested. She would have no choice but to sell the equipment to Santiago Echeveria.

And then as if she had summoned him, there in the distance, in front of a group of people clustered near the creek, beyond the cluster of tall trees, was the hulking figure of a man who looked familiar—Santiago Echeveria. "What is he doing here?" Ines whispered.

"He has a photographer with him," Felix said.

Indeed a man brandishing a Sanderson Tropical camera in a shining teak case stood beside Santiago.

Ines and Felix exchanged glances—they did not have a photographer; they had not interviewed the Fernandez brothers.

Santiago strode up to them. "Ines, I'm surprised that you're here. I didn't think you did this. You're looking well," he said.

Ines lifted an eyebrow. "And I see you are here, Santiago."

"This is a very unusual case. I knew the people involved—the good priest, the flamboyant composer and his Catalan boyfriend. It's a very colorful story, haw-haw-haw— one that people have been following and will continue to do so," he said, laughing. Then in a more formal demeanor, he continued, "My photographer will take pictures for tomorrow's issue."

"That's good, Santiago, and I have my writer and editor so we can have a real story tomorrow."

Santiago winced. "Ines," he said, in a contrite voice, "I realize how difficult it is for you, a woman, to continue Pablo's business."

"There is no reason to feel sorry for me, Santiago. I assure you completely that my womanhood is not a handicap," she said, her voice rising a few decibels. "Felix, don't we have work here?"

"Yes, Ma'am, let me check." Felix excused himself and approached some policemen.

Santiago said, "By the way, we took a picture of the creek earlier. We'll be taking a picture of the remains as soon as these people leave."

Ines held her tongue and waited for Felix to return. "The police have cordoned off the area. They're not allowing people near the remains," the young man reported.

"Is that so?" Santiago addressed Felix.

"Yes, Sir," Felix replied, pointing at some policemen who guarded the area.

"Well, I need more pictures." Santiago beckoned his photographer and they elbowed their way through the crowd to the front where a broad-shouldered policeman stopped them.

Ines and Felix listened to what went on. "Sorry Sir, but you can't get in," the policeman told Santiago.

"*I* am the owner of *The Light*," Santiago declared.

The policeman blocked his way. "I'm sorry, Captain Borja's orders."

"I'll talk to Captain Borja myself," Santiago huffed, and he and his photographer retreated.

"This officer wasn't here earlier. I know him," Felix whispered to Ines. "Wait here, Ma'am." Felix approached the policeman and in an affable way said, "How's your daughter,

Officer. My Lola Mercedes asks about her all the time."

The policeman stared at Felix, blinked several times and said, "You're Mercedes's grandson?"

"Yes, Sir. That was a terrible accident your daughter had," Felix said.

The officer shook his head. "I could wring the neck of the carriage driver that hit her. But it was Suerte—Fate. I know it was meant to happen to Alicia, but it's hard to accept."

"Lola says the bitter melon is good for her." Felix was talking about the vegetable dish that his grandmother liberally gave to those who were sick, believing the bitter vegetable had medicinal powers.

"Alicia enjoys the food that your grandmother sends. We are grateful to her," the policeman whispered, as he ushered Felix and Ines past his rope blockade. "Over there," he pointed out, "be careful because the rocks are slippery."

Ines and Felix walked to the berm of the creek, and looking down, saw a swarm of policemen and friars working amongst the rocks and debris. The two descended the steep creek side. The policemen and friars were laying what they found on a tarpaulin: skeletal remains and a skull caked with mud, some tattered black cloth, and a pectoral Cross that gleamed under the hot sun. Ines and Felix exchanged glances: there was little doubt that the remains belonged to Father Zafra. The sight of the bones in particular perturbed her, but Ines pushed back her feelings and focused on what needed to be done.

They tried to get confirmation about the body's identification, but the policemen and friars kept directing them to their superiors. Ines asked if they had found anything unusual and got nowhere. One policeman offered that the unfortunate person had fallen further upstream, and his body had gotten caught in the rocks at the creek's bend.

Ines and Felix climbed up and looked around. They were in the corner of the backside of the church and rectory, quite a distance from the servants' quarters and the arbor. For the most part, this section of the Augustinian complex with the abandoned warehouse was undeveloped, with trees, shrubs, and plants growing wild. "What was the priest doing near the creek?" Ines wondered aloud. "When he returned from the composer's house, he would have been over there, making his way toward the rectory."

They walked along the side of the creek toward to the warehouse. "So the Fernandez brothers were here catching rats," Ines said.

"Yes, Ma'am," Felix said. "The younger one went to the creek to clean up."

"Let's take a look," Ines said.

The policeman who guarded the warehouse gave them permission to look inside. It was dank and musty, with a bit of light filtering through cracks and holes, allowing them to make out old implements, broken furniture, and piles of coconut husks.

Felix started fidgeting and breathing heavily. Ines touched his arm and offered "Do you want to rest?"

"We-we-we should go. There's a lot-lot to do," he said.

Outside, beads perspiration dripped down Felix's face. They were both quiet for a long time until Felix said, "I apologize for my behavior, Ma'am. You know what happened to my parents, do you not, Mrs. Maceda?"

"Pablo told me."

Felix's parents had been massacred in Balangiga, a town in the island Samar. This happened in 1901 during the height of the Philippine-American War. In retaliation for the attack and killing of forty American soldiers by Filipinos, General Jacob H. Smith had ordered the killing of all civilians ten years and older. "Make the island a howling wilderness," Smith said, which earned him the name of "Howling Wilderness Smith." Over 2,500 Filipinos were killed. The Americans also took the church bells that had signaled the attack and shipped them to Wyoming as war trophy. A military trial had been held for the American officers involved in the massacre, but in the end, all Howling Wilderness Smith got for punishment was early retirement.

"Terrible thing to be buried in a mass grave—thrown into a pit along with the others." Felix shook his head before he continued, "I was a child when it happened. The priest hid me and two other boys in the attic ... We had to be quiet ... I heard a lot of shouting and crying, and later gunfire ... that is all I remember." Felix had grown pale.

In the office of *The Ubec Daily*, right above Felix's desk, a poem written by him was framed and hung. It was about the Filipino revolt and subsequent massacre of the residents of Balangiga by the Americans:

The Bells of Balangiga
By Felix Santa Maria

The bronze bells ring at dawn
How they swing and clang
Calling all to freedom
They rise, machetes in hand
Defying the new invaders

The bronze bells toll at noon
How they throb and sob
When blood is spent
Dreams cut short
By guns and cannons
A common grave
Resting ground for all

The bronze bells descend
How they weep,
As they are exiled
to a distant wilderness
Howling silenced

But only for now

Ines remembered that poem and understood the

feeling behind the simple words. She wanted to say something to comfort Felix but was unable to find the words. She knew grief and she reached over to pat his arm.

"I'm all right now," Felix said. "When Professor Maceda was alive, he found out that I'd spent fourteen months tracking the military trial of the American officers involved in the massacre. When I discovered that Smith's punishment was nothing more than early retirement, I almost went crazy. I started stut-stut-stut-tering…" He paused but later managed to continue, "Mr. Maceda ordered me to write a two-part series about the massacre and military trial. To our surprise, *The New York Tribune* quoted my articles. I do not mean to sound prideful. The reason I mention this is that Mr. Maceda believed in the miraculous powers of self-expression. After I wrote those articles, I could speak properly."

"Pablo was a good man, Felix," Ines said. "We were both lucky to have known him."

"Ma'am, forgive my presumption in saying so but Mr. Echeveria has no idea what a newspaper is about. He tries to compete with us; he has attacked us; he has attacked Professor Maceda. The Professor didn't know how to fight dirty politics. He thought Echeveria's editorials ended his bid for the Philippine Assembly. The Professor was very discouraged … I don't believe you should sell to Mr. Echeveria, Ma'am."

"I don't want to, Felix, but … but…" Ines did not complete her sentence.

Felix lowered his eyes and became pensive. They were near the city center and it was getting to be high noon. People were hurrying home for their lunch and siesta. A rat skittered along the side of the gutter. Finally, Felix said, "About the newspaper, you are right of course: *The Ubec Daily* will not be able to continue without money. Perhaps it's all right to publish the Truth and also make some money. We should give it a try. But our standards must remain high."

CHAPTER 5

―――――⟨⟩―――――

BISHOP LOGAN

I f I could bilocate like San Francisco Javier, I would interview the American Bishop and Captain Borja at the same time," Felix said, rubbing his forehead. He and Ines were standing under the shade of a mango tree.

"What do you need from them?" asked Ines.

"From the bishop, we need confirmation that the remains are those of Father Zafra, and from our Police Inspector, we need to know if he agrees it's Zafra and what he thinks the probable cause of death is. Any other additional information about the deceased are welcome."

"I'll talk to Bishop Logan," Ines said, knowing Felix was not fond of Americans. After the words rushed out of her mouth, however, she was sorry she could not swallow them back. She knew some of the technical know-how about newspaper-making from Felix, and she was proud that she could set the type and run the printing press by herself. She was a good reader, and in fact, in her younger days when she had time, indulged in reading history books and crime stories by Pedro Antonio de Alarcon and Emilia Pardo Bazan. She was good with grammar and spelling, although numbers were her strength. But she'd never interviewed anyone, and she wondered how to go about getting what Felix wanted.

Felix looked relieved. "Thank you, Ma'am. You just have to ask him some questions and act like a reporter. Keep in mind, Ma'am, that the bishop will protect his own kind. In other words, he may lie or give half-truths. If you sense he is not telling the truth, be sure and let me know so we can corroborate his statements. And by the way, Ma'am, you are the first woman publisher, not only of Ubec but of the entire Philippines. And Ma'am," he added, "I should get the written report before six tonight." And off he went.

First woman publisher, indeed—she inherited the title of being a publisher—that was all. Ines had gone to the Colegio Inmaculada Concepcion, an all-girls school founded in 1880, where the nuns taught the 3 Rs—Reading, Writing, and Arithmetic, plus cultural subjects including Home Economics, Fine Arts, and Music. It was like a finishing school. Many of the graduates never worked in an office, although Ines had worked for her family's hacienda, traveling from the city to Carcar once a month. Before there was a train, it took her half a day to get there; when the train was running, a mere two and half hours. She had learned the business of growing sugar cane, converting it into sugar, and selling it from her parents, not from school. Aside from that she had been a housewife and mother, and she took meticulous care of their home, which ran like a Swiss clock—or so people said. The notion of interviewing Bishop Logan made her dizzy. "Pablo, look at me," she muttered under her breath as she walked toward the Bishop's palace. "I have no idea how a newspaper person should behave. Help me out, Pablo. Pray that God will give me the words and the courage."

Ines had seen Bishop Logan in his elaborate purple robes and mitre when he said Masses, and now and then Pablo had invited Bishop Logan and the American judge for dinner. Ines was present for the chit-chat while eating, but after that, the men retreated to the Smoking Room, where they smoked cigars, sipped liqueurs, and spent hours discussing politics, sometimes disagreeing, but in the end still slapping one another's shoulders as they said their good-nights. Ines had never understood how Pablo could talk against the American government and policies but still get along with these

Americans. She asked him about this and he said. "It's not personal. They're victims of the errors of their government as well."

Now, here she was, about to try her hand at—what did Felix call it?—being a reporter. This was a different role she had to play.

"Palace" was too grand a term for the residence of the bishop. It was a stone and wood structure from the Spanish times, massive, but stark and plain. She knocked and a dour nun opened the door, stared at her with rheumy eyes, and silently led Ines to his office. The nun failed to inform Bishop Logan that Ines was there, and Ines had to rap on the glass door. A heavy chair was pushed back; there were heavy footsteps. The door opened, and there stood Bishop Francis Logan, round and ruddy-checked, in his flowing white cassock with purple buttons. His Excellency, a forty-five-year old native of the New Mexico Territory, had been assigned Bishop of Ubec right when the Spaniards were being eased out of power in the Philippines.

"Your Excellency," Ines said as she bowed to kiss the bishop's ring.

The bishop's salt and pepper hair looked mussed. His eyes were beady like the eyes of the fish; put simply, he looked tired and harassed. He blinked several times before he said, "Do you wish to confess?"

"Confess? Oh, no, Your Excellency. It's me, Ines Maceda. I'm here on behalf Pablo's paper, *The Ubec Daily*. We're running a story tomorrow about the body, and ... and ..."

"Pablo Maceda's widow. Of course. My mind's in a fog. Dreadful news, isn't it. I've been dealing with it since this morning. The police were here. The friars as well. What can I do for you, Mrs. Maceda?"

"Could I ... that is, I have to get confirmation ... could I interview Your Excellency?"

He turned to look at his desk piled high with folders and books. He sighed and, opening the door wider, beckoned her in. "I've been trying to dig up information about this matter. Unfortunately a lot of documents have been destroyed by rats. Those miserable creatures are all over the place. What a mess. Come in, Mrs. Maceda, come in."

Once they were seated, the bishop, who knew the gracious ways of the people, small-talked, "You've done a good job keeping up the newspaper, Mrs. Maceda."

"Felix is my managing editor, Your Excellency. He was trained by Pablo. He was one of his students."

"What about your son? How is he? Nineteen now, is he not? Graduated from the Normal School, am I correct?"

"Andres helps when he can. He just started working at Attorney Vargas's office for the summer. He's talking about going to law school. I'd like him to attend the Ateneo."

"Jose Vargas ... yes, a fine lawyer. He'll learn much from Attorney Vargas. He's had a series of misfortunes, hasn't he?—Vargas, I mean. The child drowning, and the wife leaving him. Such is human drama." He sighed and was momentarily lost in his thoughts before he recovered and said, "The Ateneo is a good choice. It has a fine law school ... run by the Jesuits. Oh, those Jesuits are good educators, but troublemakers ... yes, the Black Robes were booted out of the Philippines—" he laughed, before continuing, "Now, let's see, were they expelled in 1768 or '69? It was '69 I believe. I had considered being a Jesuit myself, but ended up a secular priest."

"They were expelled from other countries, as well, Your Excellency. They had to leave France, Parma, the Portuguese Empire, as well as the Spanish Empire."

"Ah," he said, looking pleasantly surprised, "you know your history well, Mrs. Maceda. Not too many women do, but my mother understood the value of knowledge. It's good to know history, is it not?"

"It gives one a broader perspective on life and the world, Your Excellency."

With a few more sentences, the requisite social banter was sufficient and Ines began, "Your Excellency, *The Ubec Daily* will be running a story on the body. May I ask you some questions? Do you believe the remains found belonged to Father Zafra?" she said, getting to the point. She pulled out a pencil and notebook.

He wrinkled his brow and paused for a long time.

"Your Excellency?"

Bishop Logan sighed. "So everyone knows. I had foolishly considered keeping it quiet, but it's impossible, isn't it, in a small place like this? It would have been the same in Santa Fe—that's where I grew up—news like this would have spread like wildfire." He ran his hand through his hair. "I am uncertain about what to say, Mrs. Maceda, but ... well, yes ... the Augustinians have confirmed the remains are Father Zafra's." He rose from his chair and walked to the window to peer out at the street where people were rushing home. A warm breeze wafted into the room.

"We suspected the same thing, but my editor, Felix Santa Maria, wants confirmation of all facts."

"Oh, yes, Mr. Santa Maria ... still more human drama. I know about his parents and that massacre of Samar. We all experience it, Mrs. Maceda, human drama. Oftentimes it is perplexing and we wonder if God is in the midst of terrible events."

When he spoke again, his voice sounded as if it came from far away: "A long time ago, in Santa Fe, a woman with four children lost her husband during an Apache attack. My mother was that widow and I was one of the children. With sheer grit, she continued running my father's ranch. My mother was once beautiful, but in no time her skin looked like leather from that intense desert sun. She sent us all to school. It was important for her that we were properly educated. We were never really hungry because we always had milk, cheese, and so on, but our clothes were patched over and everyone knew we were hard up. Because of her strength of character, her tremendous will power, she succeeded."

He smiled as he continued, "I became a priest, a brother became a doctor, a sister became a nun, another sister got married and raised her family in Santa Fe. The married one took care of my mother until she died peacefully in her bed." He returned to his seat. "I sometimes think of her conversation with Our Lord when they finally met. He must have congratulated her: 'Job well done, Martha.' And she must have replied, 'That was a helluva ride, Lord.' I can discern the same Spirit that guided my mother in you, Mrs. Maceda. Your widow's mite will go far. You may quote me unless I tell you it is off-the-record."

"Certainly, Your Excellency. Father Zafra went missing last January—what do you think caused his death?"

"I'm not entirely sure of course. The Augustinians say he took a walk and accidentally fell into the creek."

Ines wrote that down. "Can you give me some information about Father Zafra, Your Excellency? Do you know anything of his background, when he was born, what his family life was like?"

"I looked at his files ... here it is ..." He leaned forward, pulled a folder with its corners in tatters. "As you can see, Mrs. Maceda, the rats have been feasting on this." He rifled through the damaged papers. Ines caught sight of a daguerreotype photograph and made a note to ask the bishop about it later on. "There's not very much here, but let's see, he was born on March 15, 1853. He became a priest in 1878 in Sevilla and served there for six years." The Bishop's eyes lingered on the files before he closed the folder.

"Do you know where else he served, Your Excellency?"

He adjusted his eyeglasses on his nose and cleared his throat before saying, "All I know is that he was in Iloilo and Carcar."

Ines looked up from her notes. "My family has a hacienda in Carcar, but I don't seem to remember him there. Do you know when he was in Iloilo and Carcar? And here in Ubec?"

"He started working in Ubec in 1902, but I regret I don't have the other information. Most of these papers are unreadable." He proceeded to arrange the papers and folders on his desk. "I did not know him well, Mrs. Maceda. He answered to his Augustinian superiors. I oversee the diocesan priests. My predecessor, the Spanish bishop, said Father Zafra had good programs—food and health—that sort of thing. That was all he said about him."

Ines took notes then continued, "Last January, there was a church fire. Do you remember that, Your Excellency?"

The bishop paused before answering, "Oh, yes, the rectory fire, at the San Agustin."

"It happened the day before Father Zafra disappeared."

"Indeed, it was so. First the fire, then the disappearance ... that is the drowning of Father Zafra. What a strange coincidence."

"Presumed drowning, am I not right?"

"The creek runs along the boundary of the San Agustin grounds—what else could it have been, Mrs. Maceda, if not the unfortunate priest slipping off the edge that rainy night?"

"Was it raining, Your Excellency?"

"The friars said it had rained and the creek was high and moving swiftly. To be honest with you, Mrs. Maceda, I had a difficult time getting the story from the Augustinians. They reported the matter to me, but they did not—how do I put it?—relish talking about it. As you can imagine, Mrs. Maceda, the Spanish religious are not fond of an American bishop like myself. Sometimes their hostility is downright palpable."

"Change is always a challenge, Your Excellency." Ines was well aware of the tension between the Spaniards and Americans in all aspects of Philippine life. The old order had to give way to the new. People had to deal with changes the Americans had made in government, religion, education, laws, and so on down to the less important matters.

The Bishop continued, "Hundreds of the Spanish priests have been sent back to Spain, and they blame us. I can understand why they're upset; after all, many of them have lived here for decades. The Philippines is home to them. But in fact, their religious superiors were the ones who recalled them." He lowered his voice when he added, "There is also the matter of the Friar Lands. People are unaware that the Dominicans, Augustinians, and Recollects owned about one-tenth of all the improved land in the Islands. The current government instituted a land reform program, taking back the Friar Lands from the church. Something had to be done: the religious were extremely wealthy, while the people remained poor."

Ines knew that the American government paid the Vatican seven million dollars to buy the Friar Lands. She was aware of the American government's attempt to return the Friar Lands back to the people, and that the religious had legally protested the American move. "Do you know if Father Zafra was involved in any legal dispute, Your Excellency?" Ines asked.

"Mrs. Maceda, all the Spanish friars, Father Zafra included, were used to owning entire towns along with haciendas and sugar mills. They were and are unhappy about losing their properties and there are numerous legal cases going on. These will probably go on until we are dead and gone," Bishop Logan said.

Ines jotted down what the Bishop said before saying, "The idea of selling the land back to the tenant farmers is a good one, but I've heard of abuses."

"Have you, Mrs. Maceda?"

"My family grows sugar in Carcar, Your Excellency. We keep track of such news because it affects the value of sugar. I understand the government is charging more than the farmers can afford to buy the land. Huge American firms have been buying Friar Lands."

"The whole point of land reform was to return the land to the farmers who have worked on that land for generations," the Bishop said.

"Unfortunately, it's not working out that way, Your Excellency. Recently 55,000 acres of sugar land was sold to a Havemeyer representative."

"The Havemeyer ... an American company?"

"Yes, Your Excellency."

"I see, well, that's all a mess, but that's that not my business. I'm a man of God." His cheeks had turned bright red, as if he had been running. He seemed relieved when the nun whom Ines had met earlier, knocked and entered the office. Beside her was a young girl holding a tray with two cups of hot chocolate. The nun directed the girl to place the tray on the Bishop's desk. After bowing to the bishop, they left.

"I see that Sister Dolores has hot chocolate for us. Her order grows their own cacao and makes their own chocolate. It is not often that the sister is so kind, so please help yourself, Mrs. Maceda."

Ines set her notebook and pencil down and reached for a cup. The chocolate was lukewarm and too bitter, but she carried on chatting with the bishop about the forthcoming carnival, while taking obligatory sips.

Later, Ines asked the bishop if he had any other statements regarding the discovery of the body of Father Zafra. The bishop said no, and then gathering her courage, Ines asked, "Your Excellency, I happened to see a photograph. Is that Father Zafra?"

The Bishop got the folder and pulled out the picture. He turned it over, paused for a moment, before handing it to her. "The rats have spared this, Mrs. Maceda. Yes, it's Father Zafra."

Ines glanced at the image of the tall Spanish priest, around forty years old, standing in front of a church. "This looks like Santa Catalina Church in Carcar, Your Excellency."

"Is that so? These stone churches all look the same to me, Mrs. Maceda. The picture must have been taken when he was in Carcar then."

"It will mean a lot to us if we can borrow this? May we print this in our *Daily*?"

Bishop Logan waved his hand. "Return it at your convenience, but I do want it back for my files that are shrinking because of these infernal rats."

CHAPTER 6

NEWS ARTICLE

FRONT PAGE ARTICLE OF *THE UBEC DAILY*,

Tuesday, March 30, 1909

BODY OF MISSING PRIEST FOUND
by Ines Maceda

A body recovered from Mabini Creek has been identified as that of an Augustinian priest, Father Nicolas Zafra, who went missing after a Sunday dinner last January 3, 1909.

The Fernandez brothers, Marco and Lorenzo, eleven and nine years old respectively, made the grim discovery of the priest's remains, while hunting for rats in the Augustinian warehouse.

Ubec's Bishop Francis Logan and Police Inspector Antonio Borja, who is a candidate for the Philippine Assembly, confirmed the identity of the deceased. Father Zafra was last seen alive leaving the home of Mr. Juan Dela Cruz, composer and choral director, at around ten p.m., January 3, 1909.

A native of Sevilla, Spain, Father Zafra, 55, was a member of the Augustinian community and also an ordained priest. He took his religious vows in 1878 in Sevilla where he served for six years. In the Philippines, Father Zafra served in Iloilo, Carcar, and Ubec where he met his untimely demise.

Known for his community feeding and health programs, Father Zafra, along with many other Spanish priests, was involved with legal disputes regarding their Friar Lands.

While Police Inspector Borja declined to cite the cause of the priest's death, Bishop Logan stated that Father Zafra accidentally fell and drowned in Mabini creek, near the San Agustin Church. Fiscal Ariston is currently reviewing the case and will release the official cause of death when his investigation is concluded.

The picture here published, courtesy of Bishop Francis Logan, shows Father Zafra in front of Santa Catalina Church in Carcar, Ubec.

CHAPTER 7

THE ARREST

Before Police Inspector Borja showed up, Ines and Melisande had been sitting on the verandah, sipping cups of chocolate, and watching the pedestrians on Cristobal Colon Street.

"I stayed up last night wondering why I don't remember Father Zafra in Carcar. Maybe it was because I went to school here and visited Carcar only on weekends—I'm not sure," Ines said.

Melisande straightened up and put her cup down. "Some of my clients talk of how wonderful he was, but Juan Dela Cruz dislikes that priest intensely. He and Father Zafra had that ugly fight, you know."

"What about?" Ines asked.

"Something about a land deal," Melisande said. "I don't know much about it."

"I'd like to talk to him about that."

"You are becoming more of a newspaper woman, Ines," Melisande said, her voice lilting in admiration.

Ines smiled. That morning, she had woken up feeling a lightness that she hadn't felt since Pablo died. She had asked the maid for gugu bark, which she soaked in water and used as a rinse for her hair. It gave a nice wholesome scent. She had thought of asking the maid to cut the ends of her hair, but the morning had begun, and so her freshly washed hair hung streaming down her back.

"Juan Dela Cruz wants to know if Andres can be one of the escorts for the carnival princesses and queen," Melisande said.

Ines had seen some billboards and posters about the carnival, but she had been so busy, she hadn't kept track of carnival developments.

"We're working on the theme for coronation night and we're trying to decide between Egyptian or Greek. The gowns will be lovely, either way—flowing robes, headdresses, a lot of flair. But our young ladies will need escorts—and handsome ones at that. Andres would be perfect. You must say yes."

"He's too busy for such nonsense." She understood it was an honor for Andres to be invited to be part of the coronation night event, but Ines didn't see much redemption in these social events. It seemed as useless as the fluffy mounds of pink cotton candy sold at the carnival, all sugar and air.

"Ines, remember, we talked about fun. This is fun. All of Ubec will be there. Dignitaries from Manila, politicians, the Americans, will be present. So there you are, if you want your son to have connections, he ought to attend."

The sound of young men's voices interrupted them. Felix and Andres had climbed the stairs and laid out newspapers on the dining table. "Good morning, Madames, please come and take a look," Felix said, holding up, not only their newspaper, but an issue of *The Light* as well.

Ines and Melisande left the verandah to join the young men. Melisande ran her finger over the front page of *The Ubec Daily*. "Look at this—your name. Ines, you can write."

"It's a good article, Mama, but perhaps it can be longer next time," Andres said.

Ines scowled. "There was a lot information but Bishop Logan kept saying, 'Off-the-record.' It's very short, but the picture is effective. I got that from the bishop. Felix had to transfer the picture to a coated metal sheet in order to get the image on the page."

"You did a good job, Mrs. Maceda, given our tight

deadline," Felix said.

"However, Felix, I'm not at all happy that you insisted we mention Tonying Borja's candidacy," Ines said. "That's free advertisement for Tonying. I'm not really fond of him. When he was a boy, he used to catch coconut beetles and pluck off their wings and six legs, just for fun."

Felix winced. "Mrs. Maceda, Borja has not forgotten the editorial we ran in 1907 when he ran for the Assembly and lost. It's best to let bygones be bygones. He is the Police Inspector, after all."

"His wife comes to my shop," Melisande said. "Many times, she has bruises on her face. I never ask. We never say a thing. All of us pretend there is nothing wrong. Twice she said she fell down, but how often does one fall down?"

Felix pointed at their rival newspaper, *The Light*. "Here is Mr. Echeveria's front page. His article is based on an interview of Captain Borja."

"Look at this," Ines said, "There's one paragraph about the dead body and the rest is about Antonio Borja, how long he's been in the force, his life story basically. And here's a huge picture of Borja at the creek. Instead of providing unbiased news, Santiago has publicized Borja. He wants Borja to win a seat in the Assembly. The whole thing leaves a bad taste in my mouth." Ines pushed the newspaper away.

Andres, who had to get to work, said his goodbyes, but Melisande kept him to ask if he could participate in the May carnival. "What do you think, Mama?" Andres said.

"It's not up to me, it's your decision," Ines said.

"I'll be happy to do so," Andres said and just as he picked up his bag, the maid appeared to announce that Police Inspector Antonio Borja was there.

"Tonying? What does he want?" Ines asked, surprised.

Felix peered down the stairs and whispered, "He has two policemen with him." Ines said, "Ask them to come up, Felix."

When Police Inspector Borja and his companions were there, Ines asked, "Tonying, would you like some hot chocolate?"

"No, thank you, Mrs. Maceda, we're here on business," Borja said, his voice terse.

Ines glanced at his crisp white captain's uniform. Indeed, he looked businesslike. Everyone knew that Antonio Borja had been an orphan who used to roam the streets of Ubec, barefoot and clad only in a shirt. After his parents died of tuberculosis, he was raised by an aunt and uncle with ten children who had not wanted another mouth to feed. The child Borja grew up in extreme neglect, and Ines recalled seeing him near Iyo Titi's bakery, looking hungrily at a pile of soft sweet bread. Ines, ten years old at the time, could not bear seeing the child so hungry, and she had reached into her pocket and pulled out a silver coin, which she handed to the boy. Even though Borja had gone on to become the Police Inspector in Ubec, Ines could not erase the image of that needy child.

"Tonying," she said, calling him by his pet name again, "what can I do for you?"

"I'm here to talk to your son, Mrs. Maceda." Borja nodded toward Andres. "I have to ask him a few questions."

"What about, Tonying?" Ines continued, still in a buoyant voice. "Sit down ... and your friends too."

The men did not budge. Borja said, "Just a few questions, Mrs. Maceda, about what your son did last January."

"January, Tonying?" Ines asked lightly, although she felt unease in her gut.

"Mama, if they have questions for me, I can answer them," Andres said.

"What questions?" Ines said, looking first at Borja then at her son who had turned pale.

Borja said, "Andres Maceda, on the night of January 3, where were you?"

"January?" Andres furrowed his brows, then shrugged his shoulders. He ran his hand through his hair.

"Let me help you: on the night of Sunday, January 3,

were you not at the Plaza Independencia?"

"I was with my friends," Andres replied.

"Could you give me their names, please?" Borja asked.

"Mario Jacobo and Jesus Celdran. May I ask what this is all about, Captain?"

Ines, who was losing her patience, added, "I'd also like to know what is going on, Tonying. We are busy, as you can see."

"It's about Father Nicolas Zafra. Fiscal Ariston determined that he died from unnatural causes," Borja said.

"Whatever are you talking about, Tonying? The priest drowned. The bishop said so," Ines said.

"Unnatural versus natural, Ma'am," Felix said. "Excuse me, Mrs. Maceda, I'll will be going back to the office."

Felix was heading down the stairs when Andres called out, "Please let Attorney Vargas know I'll be late this morning."

"What is this nonsense, Tonying? If you'll excuse us, we have a lot of work—" She took Melisande's arm, and they stood close to Andres.

"Mrs. Maceda, it's murder we're talking about."

Ines sucked her breath in. Melisande, who had been struck dumb since Borja appeared, turned as white as the cotton dresses her mannequins sometimes wore.

Antonio Borja addressed Andres, "Your friends said you got into an argument with Father Zafra that night."

Andres kept silent.

"The three of you were at the gazebo at the plaza, were you not? When the priest walked by, you exchanged words with him."

"Father Zafra accused us of drinking and he said foul words at us."

"And were you drinking?"

Andres cast an apologetic glance at Ines and Melisande. "We had a bit of Ginebra, but that has nothing to do with the priest," he said softly.

Ines placed her hand on her brow. The vein on her

forehead was throbbing. She couldn't believe that Andres had been drinking with his friends. She had taken excellent care of her son. When he was a boy, if he had the smallest scratch, she treated it; if he sneezed, she gave him a handkerchief. In her mind's eye, she had accompanied him when he walked to school, when he sat in his classrooms, when he ate and played during recess, when he returned home for lunch, and later after school, when he played ball with his friends. She knew what books he read, what time he went to bed, but some time, somehow, he grew up, and then she didn't know everything Andres did. It was not that she was oblivious to what he had been up to, or that he hid information from her, but her son had simply developed his own life.

"And what time did your fight with the priest occur?"

"It was not a fight, Captain." Andres remained calm and reasonable.

"The exchange, what time?"

"Ten, ten-thirty, eleven, I'm not sure." Andres got up. "Listen, Captain Borja, I have to go to work now."

"You're not going to work this morning, Andres Maceda. You're going to tell us what happened after you got into an argument with Father Zafra."

Ines protested, "Tonying, wait a minute. First of all, I have no idea what you're talking about, and second, I'm not a lawyer, but I'm one hundred percent sure you can't barge in here and harass us." Her voice was strong and clear.

Andres said, "Mama, please, let me take care of this. When the priest left, we also left. We serenaded a girl, and then we went home."

"And who was the girl? The name, please?"

"Is that any of your business, Captain Borja?" Andres asked.

"A man was murdered, it is my business, Mr. Maceda."

Andres glanced at Ines before saying in a soft voice, "Pilar Echeveria."

Ines felt her legs go weak. Pilar Echeveria was Santiago Echeveria's seventeen-year-old daughter—her archenemy's child.

Andres continued, "The three of us sang to her. She came down to talk to us, and then we said good night and left. End of story."

Ines felt her son's betrayal right there in her gut. Despite her feud with Santiago; despite all the talk of the rivalry between their newspaper and Santiago's newspaper—Andres and his friends had socialized with his daughter after all! While it was true that she had never instructed Andres to harbor a grudge against the Echeveria family, she had assumed that Andres knew of the harm that Santiago had inflicted on Pablo and on her, and that he, Andres, would avoid that family.

Ines tried to remember what the girl looked like, but the only image she conjured was that of a sickly child. When Andres was around two years old, Santiago's pregnant wife, Aphrodite, had gone into a prolonged labor. After twenty-two hours, totally spent, Aphrodite gave birth to a premature baby girl. Shortly after, Aphrodite hemorrhaged, slipped into a coma, and died, leaving behind a premature infant that had to be kept warm in the incubator like baking bread. Santiago named the puny baby Pilar after Our Lady of the Pillar of Zaragoza, and for once Santiago humbled himself and begged Mother Mary who had appeared on the Ebro River to the apostle St. James, to take pity on the infant and make her live. Pilar survived although she remained frail and prone to asthma attacks.

From infancy, Pilar had been treated like a hothouse orchid, doted upon by her father and grandmother. For one thing, Pilar was rarely seen outside the house. Ines could count with her fingers the times she had seen the girl in public. During a Fiesta de Mayo festival, Pilar—ten years old at the time—wore a white gown with wings attached, a slight little creature that looked more like a ghost. Pilar was pretty enough—and thank God she did not have her mother's jaw that jutted out like a brick wall—but she was as thin as a toothpick and gave the impression that the slightest breeze could knock her over. As the years passed, Ines would see her now and then with the other girls, but the gaggle of girls all looked the same. Although Ines had heard people praise Pilar's beautiful large eyes fringed with long eyelashes and her winsome smile, Ines found Pilar quite plain.

Andres faced Ines. "Mama, I'm sorry," he said, but Ines waved her hand to indicate this was not the time to deal with this matter. There was something more serious confronting them at that moment. Something more dangerous.

With a matter-of-fact voice, Ines said, "And what is wrong with young men serenading a young woman, Tonying? Surely you must have done that when you were nineteen."

"The problem here, Mrs. Maceda, is that your son and his friends are lying," Borja said. "Their stories have a lot of holes. I'm sorry but we have to take Andres Maceda to the police station." Antonio Borja waved his hand and a policeman approached and grabbed Andres by the arm.

Without thinking of the consequences, Ines pushed the policeman's hand away.

The policeman reached for his baton and raised it above his head, poised to strike Ines. Andres pushed her out of the way and started dancing on his feet, ready to punch the policeman. The situation would have exploded right then and there if Felix and Attorney Jose Vargas had not at that instance rushed into the dining room.

"Please put the baton away, officer. What's going on here, Captain Borja?" Attorney Vargas said in a calm, commanding tone.

Borja thrust his head forward and said, "I'm arresting Andres Maceda."

"On what grounds, Captain Borja?" Attorney Vargas said.

"On suspicion of killing Father Nicolas Zafra," Borja said, and his two companions took Andres by his arms and led him away.

CHAPTER 8

THE PASSION OF INES

For most of the night her heart skipped beats and her hands turned cold.

Her son was in jail.

Unable to sleep, she lingered in his empty bedroom. Afterwards, she went to the kitchen, and using a wooden stick, poked the cooking hearth, making sure the glowing embers were safely covered by a thick blanket of gray ash. In the morning, the cook would clear away the ash and blow on the embers to bring them back to life. It had always been that way, but tonight Ines remembered the neighbor's house that had burned down in fifteen minutes.

Anxious at the memory, she walked through every room, scanning everything, looking for something that might be amiss: she straightened the errant drapes, removed a forgotten plate and fork on the verandah, closed cupboards, watched out for signs of rats or cockroaches. She checked and double-checked the locks on the doors and windows.

When the church bell rang once, she went to her bedroom, the room she and Pablo had shared for over two decades. She walked past their four-poster matrimonial bed to the windows. Once again, she missed the heady scent of the jasmine, and her forehead tightened in pain, and she felt the wild knocking of her heart against her ribs.

Her son was in jail.

A low chatter started in her mind, and to try and silence this, she opened her armoire, took out clothes, shook them out, and folded them to perfection. She walked down the hall to take a second bath, washing away the sweat and grim of the day, scrubbing her skin raw. She asked God to still her mind. "Lord," she says, "if I but touch the hem of Your clothes, I shall be cured."

She slipped on her long cotton nightgown with crocheted edges and returned to her room to arrange her toiletries and knick-knacks on the dresser table, measuring perfect equidistance between objects. When the church bells tolled twice, she felt panic rise from her gut to her throat. She hunted for her silver rosary and went to bed. Earlier that evening, the maid had arranged the mosquito net so the gauzy net flowed around the edges of the bed, glowing stark white, a beacon. Ines parted the mosquito net and climbed in. She tucked the netting around the mattress, leaving no gaps, so mosquitoes would not feast on her. In bed, she stared past the canopy at the ceiling with wavering shadows. She listened to the scurrying of the rats, waited for the dragging of something large that thudded its way across the broad expanse of the ceiling above her.

The noise in her mind grew, and she felt as if she were on a mound of sand and was sinking into it. She was a ghost in a crowd of people: no one could hear her, nor see her—no one.

Saying the rosary gave her peace. Instead of whipping around, her mind anchored on the Hail Marys and Our Fathers, and she imagined Mary and Joseph in Bethlehem when Jesus was born, and she was also in Jerusalem for Jesus' Passion. The Sorrowful Mysteries were her favorite, and when she was saying them and picturing Jesus rejected by His friends in the Mount of Olives, when she saw Jesus arrested, accused, scourged at the pillar so His flesh was in tatters, when she saw the Roman soldiers take away His cloak, shove the crown of thorns on His Head, spit on Him, ridicule Him, when she saw Him pick up His Cross and stumble His way up to Calvary— she wept with abandon. When He is crucified, she moaned in agony.

Ines was experiencing her own passion and crucifixion.

***

Later, Ines walked to the carcel to see her son.

She had five minutes to see Andres. That was the best Attorney Vargas could arrange. Five minutes, in the damp stone carcel that had been built by the Spaniards in the sixteenth century and which the Americans also used as their jail. The latter had scrubbed the coral stones and whitewashed the interior, but the place remained foreboding, as if the centuries of misery could not be erased.

The garrote, an all-time Spanish favorite, was used for capital punishment during the Spanish time, and for a few years, the American military government availed of the garrote for executions. The principle behind garroting was simple: crush the larynx while applying pressure to the victim's back. All you needed was a chair with a back rest and a neck clamp which could be tightened by crank, wheel, or hand, thereby strangling the victim. About garroting, Antonio Borja was said to have claimed, "It's an art not to kill someone too fast."

The carcel was also famous for the waterboarding that took place there. This was a form of torture that the Americans had learned from the Spaniards. Laying a prisoner on an inclined board, with cloth over his face, jailers poured water over the prisoner's face causing immediate gagging and discomfort as the prisoner felt he was drowning. With water torture, Captain Antonio Borja was reputedly able to extract a prisoner's confession in a matter of a few minutes. He was fond of using water boarding because it left no marks on the body.

"Are you all right?" Ines asked her son.

Andres looked pale and disheveled. A policeman stood beside him. "I'm fine, Mama," he said in a weary voice.

She saw his handcuffs and said, "Is that really necessary?" Ines pointed at the cuts on her son's wrists.

The policeman muttered, "I'm sorry, Ma'am. Captain's orders."

"And where is your captain?" Ines asked.

"I'm sorry, Ma'am, he's not here."

"This whole thing is outrageous," Ines said. "Your captain picks up my son, throws him in jail, and isn't around to explain to me how long he will hold my son. Andres has done nothing."

The policeman lowered his head.

"Mama," Andres said, "Don't worry too much. I've done nothing. They can't hold me forever. Attorney Vargas will know what to do. Talk to him."

And then the five minutes was up.

CHAPTER 9

ATTORNEY JOSE VARGAS

Soon after the arrest of her son, they were back, the dead babies who sometimes fooled Ines into thinking they had left for good, especially after Andres was born and filled her soul with delight. But her dead babies never really left. Their memories floated up unbidden whenever she was tired or discouraged. She would feel them near her, little ghost babies, hovering about, keeping her company. They were both boys—her sons—and she had no fear of them.

With the first miscarriage, Ines had been three months pregnant. She was young then, just eighteen. Her mother's disapproval of Pablo made Ines determined to show her and the world that she, Ines, was the happiest woman on this planet. She and Pablo threw themselves into fixing the rundown house they had bought. Ines rightfully discerned that its downtown location would make it a good investment. They hired a carpenter and two painters, and to save money, Pablo and Ines did the landscaping themselves. Thank God the place didn't have much of a yard to speak of! There was a bit of land in the back with overgrown trees and bushes, and there were planter areas alongside the building. Pablo and Ines decided what plants to keep, what to discard, and they hired a young man to do the grunt work. They did some planting themselves, including the jasmine vine near their bedroom window.

One late afternoon, Ines was repotting bandera

española plants in two blue-and-white Chinese pots for the entryway. It was the best time to plant because the heat of the day had subsided and could no longer suck the moisture out of the delicate starter plants. So there Ines was, expecting and happy, digging and shoveling the soil into the second pot when she felt a leap in her belly, then a bitter iciness sweeping over her, an opening, and the gush of something warm and slippery down her legs.

Less than a year later, when Ines learned she was pregnant again, happiness and terror swept over her, swirling within her. She was certain she'd lose the baby once again. For most of the day, she lay petrified in bed, listening to the hourly ringing of the church bells. Rigid as a molave plank, she feared making any movement at all; she was even afraid to breathe. She would touch her belly a million times, squeezing here and there, trying to feel the baby. During this period, she first experienced night terror, although it wasn't as terrible then because Pablo was there to calm her down.

Her round belly was showing when she discovered red-brown stains on her underwear. The midwife came, checked her, and heaved a long sigh. Stay in bed, the midwife said. Elevate your feet.

Not too long after, Ines dreamt she was walking along the seashore, and the sea subsided, exposing a huge expanse of sand with fish flopping and crabs and other creatures skittering about. She ran to pick up some fish, but when she looked up, there was an enormous wave curling above her. She awoke before the wave hit, and she felt blood oozing out of her and a fully formed baby slipping out of her womb.

That second miscarriage convinced Ines that she'd never get pregnant again. Aside from praying, she visited the Chinese herbalist who made her drink concoctions with crushed bones of a flying lizard.

When she became pregnant the third time, all kinds of emotions roiled up inside her. She felt joy and hope, but there was this ball of terror in her gut like she was walking on a tightrope. Sometimes, afraid that the child would slip down and away from her, she held her breath until she almost passed out.

Ines's mother convinced her and Pablo to go on a pilgrimage to Manila and ask for the intercession of San Andres, the apostle saint and brother of San Pedro the Rock. On their knees, the couple crawled the full length of the San Andres church aisle, begging the apostle to convince God to grant them a child.

During the last two months of her pregnancy, Ines stayed in bed with her feet propped up on two pillows. In the early mornings and evenings, if a slight chill crept into the bedroom, she covered herself with a colorful woven blanket from Northern Luzon. Eventually, the sight of the blanket and the crocheted edges of her pillowcases made her feel like an invalid and depressed her. She spent her time reciting the rosary and praying to the good apostle.

As she approached nine months, her panic attacks became more intense; she had palpitations and difficulty breathing. She was afraid the baby would be born breach or have the cord wrapped around its neck. She never prayed as hard as she did then.

On a November night when the moon was full and a multitude of stars studded the sky, her bag of waters broke, and Pablo sent for the midwife. To Ines's surprise, the birth pains felt no worse than a bad indigestion, and after three hours, she gave several pushes, and there Andres came, a writhing little creature covered with slime and blood, sliding out into the world, and working up his lungs with his robust crying. Pablo, who had been present, said the birthing was the most magnificent sight he had ever witnessed.

When the infant was placed in Ines's arms, she counted his fingers and toes, and she pored over his tiny body to make sure he was flawless. The baby was pink and long, with a little pug nose and he never even squalled. When he was hungry, he rooted around. When he was dirty, he whinnied a bit, and that was the limit of his fussing.

It was November 30 when the baby was born, the feast

day of the apostle, San Andres. It was clear what Ines and Pablo had to do. They named their son "Andres" and offered him up to the good apostle. They always lit a candle in church on November 30, to thank the saint once again and to celebrate the birthday of Andres Maceda.

***

Ever since Andres's arrest, Ines had felt the two dead babies hovering beside her, but walking toward the office of Attorney Vargas, toward his hopeful sign that read, "Jose Vargas–Attorney at Law–We Fight For You," she sensed the presence of *another*. Her babies generated a lightness in feeling but the third one who popped up that morning seemed older and had a heaviness and hunger for stroking, cuddling, and lullabies. She couldn't put her finger on it exactly. The problem was that Ines never actually saw these little ghosts. She had vague feelings about their presence, and only when she was in a state of disequilibrium. In other words, she was a little crazy when the dead babies presented themselves. Even she knew that her mental state then was unreliable, and she treated these sentient manifestations as figments of her imagination. At best they were like an itch on one's palm that came and went. She never told anyone about the dead babies, lest she be locked up in the insane asylum.

Before knocking on the office door, Ines said a quick prayer for the stranger-ghost, and took a deep breath. Ines caught a whiff of a pungent smell like something fermenting when the door opened. There the secretary stood, a large curvaceous woman with rouged cheeks. After greeting Ines, the secretary led the way to Attorney Vargas's office.

Her heart beat faster. Ines did not actually know Attorney Vargas. She only knew of him. People, including her son Andres, swore Vargas was diligent and hardworking and that he devoted an inordinate amount of time and attention on his clients. Ines had also heard bits and pieces about his son's drowning and his wife's abandonment soon after the tragedy.

Attorney Vargas's office was dim and Ines could only make out gloomy shadows. She heard rustling from a corner and a raspy shrill voice said, "I remember ... I remember..." To her horror the person proceeded to make awful weeping sounds. Ines made the sign of the Cross. From another part of the room, a man's voice said, "Gracula religiosa palawanensis ... a hill mynah." The person pushed back a chair and walked to the corner.

By now Ines's eyes had adjusted and she could see that Vargas was near a black bird that was perched on a table. It had been the bird talking and weeping after all. "His name is Yuyoy," Vargas said, stroking the black bird's head. "Yuyoy was found in a forest area that had been cleared for a pineapple plantation. He's lost part of a foot, but he manages to hop around."

She knew about the American corporations cropping up all over the Philippines, with investments in gold, silver, copper, tin, coal, sugar, coconuts, pineapple, logging and other ventures. The corporate managers and their top executives lived in huge airy houses in gated compounds with armed guards. Pablo had often said that the Americans increased the gap between the rich and the poor in the Philippines.

Attorney Vargas lifted the bird and gently placed it inside the cage. He clucked at it and stroked its head before closing the cage. Once it settled on its perch, the bird proceeded to preen itself. The bird was around a third of a meter long, and its feathers had a green gloss. Its beak was bright yellow, and it had a yellow wattle that curved around its neck to the back. It was a handsome bird.

"He talks; he sings; he whistles. It took me a while to get used to his nonsense." Vargas picked up a banana from a side table, broke off a part, and placed it inside the cage. "Yuyoy is a good companion. The only thing he hates is to be left alone for long. The woman I got him from warned me that these birds will kill themselves if they're lonely. This is why I keep him in my office." Attorney Vargas closed the cage, and turning to Ines, he said, "Come, let me show you Andres's office."

He brought her to a small office, where Ines saw her son's brass name plate on the desk. How important it looked with bold black lettering—it made the pit of her stomach quicken—her husband would have been proud to see this. Books and folders were stacked up in an orderly fashion on his desk. One cup held half a dozen pencils; another cup had a lace handkerchief arranged to look like a flower. Near the window was an Underwood typewriter with documents beside it. Ines imagined her son working in this office, and it frightened her once more to think he was in the carcel.

As if reading her thoughts, Attorney Vargas said, "I hope you are holding up all right. I am sure this is all confusing to you, but I promise you that I will do everything in my power to get Andres out of jail," he said.

There was something about the timbre of his voice, a wavering, that made Ines look him straight in the eye. "During the time of prayers for my dead husband, my son told me he wants to be a lawyer. He wants to be like you, Attorney Vargas. He looks up to you. Keep in mind that Andres is all I have," Ines said.

"I understand, but here are the facts, Mrs. Maceda. Your son, Mario Jacobo, and Jesus Celdran not only had an argument with Father Zafra, they had a scuffle with him."

"I have not heard of this," Ines said, alarmed.

"There was a witness who reported the fight to the police. It was apparently a nasty fight. All three say that after the priest left, they went to Pilar Echeveria's house to serenade her. The young lady served them some cake and juice, after which Jacobo and Celdran left, leaving Andres in the Echeveria home. The timing of the priest's death comes into play here. The police say they have incriminating evidence," he said.

"I thought my son would be released after questioning," Ines said.

"It's more complicated now. Jacobo and Celdran have an alibi; Andres has to account for his time after they left him,"

Vargas said.

They had returned to his office and now Ines straightened her back against the chair. She didn't want to hear of complications. She wanted assurance that Andres would soon be free. As firmly as she could, she said, "I know my son like I know the back of my hand. He is innocent."

"I agree completely with you, Mrs. Maceda. I'll file the writ of habeas corpus as soon as possible."

"What does that mean?" Ines thought the words "habeas corpus" had a lovely sound and could have been the name of an orchid. But Attorney Vargas was not talking about plants, and she bent forward to listen more carefully.

"Habeas corpus means produce the body," Vargas said. "It protects the person under arrest so he or she can't be detained indefinitely. The person must be brought before a judge or court, and the judge or court must decide on whether the person can be rightfully detained."

"Shouldn't you be filing the Amparo de Libertad?" Ines asked, remembering the Spanish document filed to release those detained unlawfully.

The lawyer said, "The Americans introduced the Philippine habeas corpus in 1901. I will file it as soon as possible."

Through the years, during the Spanish regime and now the American, Ines had seen boxes of legal documents stacked along the walls and corridors of the city hall. She had never understood until now that each document may have meant the release of a son from jail.

Attorney Vargas went to a side table to search for sheets of paper. "Unfortunately, next week is Holy Week. The judge is away on his Easter holiday. I was in court so I know this for a fact." He furrowed his eyebrows. "It's a disruption, Mrs. Maceda. Basically the court shuts down. He's going to Manila, and then on to Baguio where it's cooler. This summer heat of ours is too much for Americans. He won't be back until after April 15."

"That's over two weeks away!" To consider her son in

jail for even a day was terrible, two weeks was unimaginable.

"And even when the judge returns, it may still take time." He returned to his desk and started writing.

Ines had heard stories of torture and cruelty, of people dying in jail, of people unjustly detained for years. She had thought the situation had improved with the American regime, but evidently she had been wrong.

When Vargas finished writing his notes, he called his secretary and handed her the piece of paper. Soon Ines heard the rapid metallic clickety-clacking of the typewriter. The sound prompted the bird to flap its wings and cry some more, "I remember ... I remember."

Vargas ministered to the bird until it became quiet. "My son wanted a bird like this, but I didn't get him one. It's something I regret." His voice cracked and he was silent for a while.

"I heard about your son, and I'm sorry," Ines said.

Vargas picked up the bird and allowed it to perch on his left arm. "Right now, all we can do is file the writ and wait. My secretary will get it done soon so we can get the process started. Borja is talking of charging him with the murder," Vargas said.

Ines stood up. "Murder? Can Captain Borja accuse my son of this crime?"

"As you know, Mrs. Maceda, our Police Inspector does pretty much what he wants to do." Vargas gave a wry smile but quickly became serious once more. "I know the charge is unfounded, Mrs. Maceda. The problem is our system that's very slow. Sometimes suspects are detained for over a year—"

Ines clutched the table. "A year! No, that cannot be. He has school after the summer holiday. He's going to the Ateneo. There must be something we can do."

"I know how it is to be a parent, Mrs. Maceda. Unfortunately, sometimes, matters are in the hands of others or Fate itself. Suerte, Mrs. Maceda. You have no choice but be patient. I will make sure he is all right at the carcel."

With that, their meeting ended.

While Ines's mind swam with fear and foreboding, there was the wonder too of the stranger-ghost that had come to her that day. Could the stranger-ghost have been Vargas's child? But what a puzzle because ghosts are restless spirits with unfinished business in the earthly world—everyone knew that—so what sort of unresolved matters could a child, a seven-year-old boy, have?

CHAPTER 10

JUAN DELA CRUZ

The strangeness of Ines's visit with Attorney Vargas lodged within her, and the more she reflected on it, the greater her disconcertion. Her only son, her precious Andres, was in jail and she was relying on this peculiar man to get him out—what folly that was!

After hearing Ines's account of her encounter with the lawyer, Melisande did not hesitate in casting her verdict. "Ines, he is not trustworthy," she stated, voice trembling with conviction.

Ines had to agree. Her mind clicking, trying to make sense out of matters, Ines asked about Juan Dela Cruz. "He was jailed by Borja, was he not?"

"That horrible man picked him up for interrogation. Poor Juan was in jail for a long time. His mother helped him get out. We can see him, Ines. We are working together on the carnival. Juan and Esteban are my good friends."

"I've heard Esteban Magri is very talented," Ines said.

"He is famous. If he wanted to, he could have joined the St. Petersburg Company, but he chose to be with Juan," Melisande said.

Ines recalled how surprised Ubecans were when, at the turn of the century, the composer and dancer who moved into the mansion near the Plaza Independencia turned out to be two young men. They had assumed the couple would be husband and wife, and there had been a collective hush when the newcomers moved in, one Filipino and the other a Catalan. But times were difficult then, with the Spaniards going and the Americans coming, and with more pressing things to worry about, Ubecans shrugged and decided the two were business partners. Besides, the two men were accomplished and contributed much to Ubecan culture. There the matter had ended.

People learned that Juan Dela Cruz was the only son of the owner of Sandoval Rum and that father and son were like oil and water. His father had wanted Juan to go to business school, but Juan preferred fine arts and music. His father had pressured him to marry the daughter of his business partner, an unacceptable situation for Juan. Juan's mother finally sold some of her jewelry to finance her son's studies at the Reial Academia Catalana de Belles Arts de Sant Jordi in Barcelona.

"That was where Juan and Esteban met, in Barcelona," Melisande explained. "It was very romantic, Ines … at the Plaza de Catalunya, while Juan was walking to his boarding house, a flock of pigeons suddenly rose up to the sky—" Melisande fluttered her fingers in the air. "Juan stopped dead in his tracks to watch them flutter up. 'The sky turned gray,' he told me. When the birds were gone, there in front of Juan was Esteban. Like an apparition. And Esteban was staring back at him."

It was an interesting, if unconventional love story, Ines thought as she listened carefully. She was in fact trying to understand how a composer/artist like Juan Dela Cruz, a man highly respected in Ubec, ended up a suspect for the murder of Father Zafra. Juan seemed an unlikely candidate for a murderer.

Melisande continued her account of how Juan and Esteban were very happy in Barcelona because, as Juan said, "they could walk down La Rambla without people staring at them." Eventually, Juan's mother convinced Juan to return to the Philippines, saying he was still his father's only son and heir. Juan and Esteban chose to live in Ubec to spare Juan's parents the embarrassment of having to listen to the Manileños gossip about their son and Esteban. Juan and Esteban realized that a smaller place like Ubec could offer them some measure of freedom and acceptance that Manila could not.

***

One morning soon after their talk, Ines and Melisande made their way to Juan and Esteban's mansion. When they entered the gate, a free-standing wall with elaborate carving blocked their way, and they had to go around the structure. The garden was filled with plants and flowers that grew in a haphazard but pleasing way. Colorful song birds flitted about, lured by the flowing fountains and watermelon seeds on hand painted trays.

"The place looks different," Ines told Melisande. "The house used to be gray-white ... well, dingy-white is more accurate. But this terracotta with blue trim is attractive. The garden was more formal, with flower beds in one section, bushes in another, fruit orchard in the back, and a vegetable garden near the kitchen."

"Was this before Juan and Esteban moved in?" Melisande said.

"Many years before. Two unmarried sisters lived here and I used to come here with other children. Somehow we knew we were always welcome here," Ines said.

"The ladies sound very nice," Melisande said.

"Oh, yes, they were," Ines said, and she told Melisande of the time she and five other girls had stopped by sweaty and thirsty. The youngest among them had curtseyed and held out a bunch of magnolias, recently picked from someone else's garden. The spinsters accepted the magnolias, invited them in, and handed them tall glasses of cold tamarind juice, which the girls gulped down shamelessly. The girls then turned the glasses in their hands to study the animal they got that day. Each glass was hand-painted with the picture of an animal. "I loved the tiger," Ines said, "I used to run my finger around the outline of that beautiful striped tiger!"

Ines continued her story of how the sisters sent the girls up to the verandah with instructions not to fall off the railing. It was a bit of paradise there, with tenacious succulents in Chinese blue and white pots, a moss-covered fountain, three plantation chairs, and most important, the tambis tree that hung over the back portion of the verandah. They didn't even have to climb. All they had to do was reach out and pluck all the fruit they wanted. They ate while they gathered fruit and Ines remembered the pleasant feel of the waxy cover and the delight of sweet juice when her teeth sank into the spongy pulp. When their stomachs felt like bursting, they rolled out rainbow-colored woven mats, which the sisters also kept upstairs, and the girls lay on the floor to watch the clouds floating by. "Look," they cried, "there's an elephant; look, a giraffe, and over there, a zebra, and oh look, there's an angel!"

Melisande asked, "It is a lovely memory, Ines. The women who lived here, the sisters, were they happy? They were not lonely in this big house?"

Ines thought of the sisters with their quiet lives that ebbed and flowed with the rainy season and dry, meaning, they went to church, they helped their neighbors, they were kind to children, and they followed the seasonal rituals of the community. They lived their lives and then they died. "Yes, I think they were happy," Ines said.

***

A young woman dressed in a flowing white dress welcomed Ines and Melisande. Barefoot, she quietly led them to a room that looked like a greenhouse filled with potted orchids. Ines and Melisande were studying the impressive orchid collection when Juan Dela Cruz appeared, a slight man wearing red silk pants and a homespun white top that tied in front. His hair was long, and he wore six rings. He held copies of *The Ubec Daily* and *The Light*.

Melisande said, "Before you say anything, Juan,

Captain Borja arrested Andres Maceda."

He raised his eyebrows, kissed Melisande on the cheek, and gave Ines a peck. With theatrical flair, Juan said, "Dust off the Judas cradle and iron maiden! Bring out the rack, the chair of torture, the breast ripper, and the head crusher—the Grand Inquisitor, the Dominican, Tomas de Torquemada, lives! When I read the newspapers, I knew the Inquisition would start all over again. I told Esteban, we'll soon be lacerating flesh and crushing bones so the marrow gushes out. Beat, suffocate, strangle, burn, mutilate—"

"Stop it, Juan! This is not a laughing matter," Melisande said.

"Forgive me, Mrs. Maceda, I did not mean to sound flippant. As you may know, last January, after the priest disappeared, the police interrogated me. Our Police Inspector was rough, and not the way I like rough to be." Juan rolled his eyes up.

"The Inquisitor would have used water torture on me if my father were not Rum King. Borja had two men ready to pin me down. Usually, I like men near me, but they had buckets of water with them, and I was terrified! I told them, 'Gentlemen, my father is the owner of Sandoval Rum! If you inflict even a little scratch on me, you will pay dearly!'" Juan crossed his legs, picked up a fan from a chair and proceeded to fan himself.

"You are too dramatic, Juan. Calm down and talk to Ines. She needs help. I'm going off to see Esteban. Where is he?" And turning to Ines, Melisande said, "Talk to him. I'll be back."

"I have a simple question," Ines said, "how did you get out of jail? My son is there now and I have to get him out. He is innocent."

Juan cleared his throat. "I was innocent but that didn't stop our capitan from picking me up. To answer your question, Mrs. Maceda, my lawyer, the best Manila has to offer, thanks to my mother, got me out."

"May I ask what your lawyer did?"

"I am a composer, Mrs. Maceda, I do not understand legal matters. I was in jail, and then I was out. About your son, why would Borja have him picked up?"

"It's a misunderstanding, Mr. Dela Cruz. He has done nothing wrong. His lawyer is doing what he can, but unfortunately the courts are closed because of Holy Week."

"You say he is innocent. Can he prove this?"

"He was with friends."

"In that case, your lawyer should be able to get him out." He leaned towards a tray that the young woman in white had set in front of them. There were glasses of lemoncito drink and a bowl full of tambis fruit. "You must try this. This is from our tree." He selected a fruit and handed it to Ines.

Ines turned the bell-shaped fruit over in her hand to study its pink hue. "When I was a girl, I used to visit the sisters who lived here. There was a tambis tree in the back. Is it still alive? It would be over thirty years old now." Ines bit into her fruit. It was crisp and juicy and sweeter than she remembered the fruit to be.

"The tree is thriving. We can take a look," Juan said.

They left the greenhouse and went up wide stairs to the verandah. Ines discovered with relief that the fountain and tambis tree of her youth were still there. The tree had grown taller and bigger and its branches were studded with fruit. They sat under the shade and soon Juan beckoned Ines to look down over the railing. Juan waved at Melisande and a lithe, muscular man who were dancing the fandango. Melisande's partner was humming a tune and now and then he called out, "Step, step, twirl the hand, turn. One, two, three, twirl the hand, turn."

"That is Esteban," Juan said, proudly. "Is he not a beautiful man, Mrs. Maceda? Look at him—tall and strong and agile." The two dancers switched to a lively jota, which had a faster rhythm than the fandango; beads of perspiration shone on their faces.

Juan continued, "I can see from your widow's clothing that you are conservative, Mrs. Maceda, so I will not bore you with the details of our romance. I don't want to test your limits."

"And by the way, Mrs. Maceda, if you wore some color and did a little something with your hair, a few wisps here and there to soften the face, you'd look as fantastic as our beautiful Melisande down there. It's a waste when a handsome woman chooses to be drab." He flicked his fingers to indicate where the locks ought to be.

Ines felt her face flush.

"I didn't mean to embarrass you. You are our dear Melisande's friend and are therefore our friend."

"Thank you, Mr. Dela Cruz," Ines said.

Juan plucked some fruit, which they ate in comradely silence. Later, Ines asked, "Mr. Dela Cruz, can you tell me what happened the night Father Zafra was here? The last time you saw him alive, I mean."

"He had supper here, as you may know. He usually had supper with us on Sunday nights. That night, Father Zafra asked us to do something that surprised both Esteban and me." Juan looked away and crossed and uncrossed his legs.

"May I ask what that was?"

Juan's demeanor had changed. His eyes glinted with anger when he said, "Father Zafra wanted Esteban and me to participate in a land deal. It was illegal. He asked us to lend our names as buyers of the Friar Land near the church. He did not want an American firm buying Augustinian church land."

Ines said, "Can you tell me more about the land deal?"

"It was a very complicated matter. An American firm had its eye on Augustinian land, and Father Zafra wanted us to get the land before they got it. He wanted us to hold the land until such time when he could switch the title back to them. It was an impossible proposal, and illegal. I told him Esteban and I were honest people, but then he started screaming. This is what he told Esteban and me, 'You call yourselves honest people? And you dare talk of fraud. *You* are fraud. You and your Spanish friend here are frauds, masquerading as friends when everyone knows what abomination is going on.' He hurled ugly words at me and Esteban." Juan had gotten up and he started pacing back and forth.

"Do you remember what time it was when this happened?" Ines asked.

"Time? It must have been before ten o'clock. I am not sure. His words stung. You see, Esteban and I had always welcomed him to our Sunday dinners. We treated him like a family member. My anger percolated until it boiled over and I threw him out of my house. I told him he was no longer welcome here. I didn't care that he was a priest; he could have been the pope himself, I didn't want him in our house. I said things that I shouldn't have, but I was very angry and I wasn't thinking properly."

Juan had gotten hold of a long stick, and in his anger, broke it in half. "The truth is this: when Esteban and I were in Carcar, we heard complaints about that priest."

"People seem to admire his programs. Can you tell me what the complaints were?" Ines asked.

There was a long pause before Juan spoke up, "The programs are a sham, Mrs. Maceda, but I've had to live with gossiping all my life, and I'm not going to repeat the stories about others. If you believe in truth and justice as your newspaper motto states, 'Veritas Aequitas'— you will find ways to get information about that priest."

"I can tell you this, Esteban and I are guilty of covering up for him. Before we knew what kind of man he really was, we helped propagate the idea that the Father made great sacrifices to serve Filipinos. We praised his so-called excellent programs, and so on, ad nauseam. We protected that demon. I would not be surprised if his murderer was one of those he had wronged."

Juan was breathing heavily. It wasn't until they heard sounds of Esteban and Melisande making their way to the patio, before Juan collected himself. In a calmer voice, he said, "Be sure and bring tambis home with you. Come help me pick fruit, Mrs. Maceda, your childhood fruit." They stood on chairs to pluck the fruit, and they quickly filled two woven baskets, one for Ines and one for Melisande.

Esteban and Melisande appeared, perspiring but happy from their dancing. Esteban strode to Ines, gallantly bent over, and kissed her hand. He had yellow hair, and his skin was as translucent as pure beeswax. Unlike Juan, he was soft-spoken and reserved. Esteban pressed the women to stay for lunch, but the women excused themselves saying they had work to do. He told them that he made callos and paella the way his Catalan grandmother did, and that they should come over one Sunday night for dinner. They did not have to worry, he assured them, because Juan and he had already put up the wall in front of the gate. "That is what the Balinese build to prevent evil from entering their homes. Evil is blocked off at the entrance. We put it up after evil entered our house and took away the priest last January," he explained.

PART II

CHAPTER 11

CHRISTMAS EVE, 1908

Time had taken on a rubber quality, stretching here and there, never fixed despite the insistent tick-tocking of the grandfather clock in their living room. Jose had lost all notion of what day or time it was, and he slept and awoke at strange hours. It was Fernanda who announced that they should "join the world." Earlier that day she had taken out her pearl jewelry and gold hair comb and she had put on a black satin skirt and blouse of gossamer fabric. He was surprised by this, her vanity, her declaration that she was ready to relinquish her mourning. For over four months, Jose and Fernanda had shared a cocoon of darkness and dread, confining themselves to their house, avoiding people, even his parents, sending out their servant, their sole umbilical cord to the world. During that time, they said very little to each other, but they shared a bond that was to some degree like a balm.

Before they left their house, Fernanda threw a shawl over her shoulders. She was as stark as a fruit bat, and the darkness of her clothing made her skin appear chalk-white. He had always found her fair skin attractive, but this December night, it was unearthly; she could have been a fearsome enchanted being from the forest.

In church, the sacristans scurried about, lighting the candles in the tall silver candelabras. Jose and Fernanda were early but the pews and benches were filled with women and children. The mothers, grandmothers, and spinster aunts waved at friends and neighbors, kissed relatives on the cheeks, talked about their Christmas meal which they had entrusted to their servants. They admired the altar with its seventeenth-century silver retablo that glowed pearly-gray. The children, whose skin looked raw from having been scrubbed clean, wore shiny taffetas, fine cotton, and lace. The older ones searched for their friends, arms flapping upward when they caught sight of them, and thrusting their chests out, hoped their new clothes would be noticed and admired. The young ones wriggled about near their mothers, some of them gumming homemade sweets, their attention focused on the nativity set on the right side of the altar. They stared at the manger and figurines of Mary, Joseph, the angel, the Three Kings with their camels, some shepherds with their sheep. They studied the empty crib most of all, with a hankering since they had been waiting for weeks for the Child Jesus to be placed in it.

The chattering ceased when Jose and Fernanda squeezed into a pew. Jose didn't have to lift his head to know that all eyes were riveted on them. Staring at the tiled floor beneath him, he told Fernanda he would join the men outside, and without waiting for her answer he slipped away.

The men huddled under the centenarian acacia tree, smoking their cigars to ward off the night chill. They lacked the giddiness of the women and children. They had carried the brunt of the expenses for the new clothes, shoes, decorations, food, and holiday riff-raff, and they dreaded the financial consequences in mid-January. When Jose joined them, the men grew quiet; they paused, shifted their weight, and some coughed as if clearing their throats. Finally, someone mentioned the new electric lights being installed by the Americans, what a nuisance, he said, all the poles and lines scattered on the streets, what a mess. Another brought up the ongoing legal battle between the Americans and the religious orders over the Friar Lands. The Americans are trying to get the land back for the people, he said, imagine, they paid the Vatican seven million dollars for the Friar Lands. Someone else mentioned that if you knew the right people, you could buy huge chunks of Friar Land cheap. It was all small talk to hide their embarrassment.

Jose knew it was all about him. They were saying: We don't know what to say to you; we're sorry you lost your only son, sorry that you didn't have to spend on clothes and toys for him; we have no idea what it feels to have a son drown and we are very sorry for you. To make them feel at ease, Jose joined their chitchat and threw in some remark about Father Zafra fighting the Americans over a huge track of land near the church.

He was their parish priest, this Father Zafra. Jose had gotten the information about him from Fernanda who was the bookkeeper at the rectory. Fernanda started working there a year ago, shortly after Danilo could extend his right arm over his head and touch his left ear, proving he was six years old and qualified for kindergarten. After school, Danilo walked to the rectory and waited for his mother to finish work. It was a perfect arrangement; idyllic in fact, until the body of Danilo was found on the seashore. Fernanda pulled her hair when she saw her dead son, and Jose fainted when he found out what had happened. The story that finally emerged was that Fernanda had been working in the rectory office, and Danilo had been with her, but growing bored, he went outside to play. He must have been chasing a dog or cat along the seawall when he lost his balance, fell and drowned. It was a simple story, straight to the point. People hated talking about such tragedies because they had their own sons and grandsons, and the idea of losing a seven-year-old son exceeded their imagination. A one-year-old or two-year-old could succumb to dengue or typhus and die just like that, and mothers had learned to protect their hearts by not falling too much in love with the little ones, but a seven-year-old was marked to survive. Him you could love. So beyond the official story of how Danilo died, nothing more was said.

When the church bells sounded the beginning of the High Mass, Jose returned to the side altar where Fernanda knelt. A long black lace veil covered her short hair. After the discovery of the dead child and Fernanda's hair-pulling incident, a neighbor had cut her hair to make the ends even. Her hair was very short, like the French Jeanne d'Arc haircut, new in fashion but still alien to most Filipinos.

The church had become more crowded still, but they were close to the main altar and he could see the three priests and altar boys clearly. Fernanda kept her eyes closed most of the time, and now and then, she would heave a deep sigh and, pretending she was arranging the veil on her head, wipe away her tears. He wished she would stop; he wished they had stayed home in the first place.

The people were praying, giving thanks perhaps for the good fortune that had come their way that year 1908—how fortunate for them—asking God for this and that for the coming year, communicating with God in any case, something he could not do, not now. Father Zafra was one of the three priests, all of them imposing, with elaborate vestments embroidered with silver thread. Father Zafra, with his aquiline nose and Hapsburg jaw reminded him of the Spanish conquistadores sailing on galleons from Spain to all parts of the world.

The scent of candles and incense, the rising-kneeling-sitting in church, the crush of people in that damp stone church made Jose's nostrils constrict, made it impossible to breathe. The four months since his son died was the Calvary of his life. He tried to think of the Mass, of his surroundings, but the sensation of suffocating was foremost in his mind. When Fernanda stood up to go to the communion rail, he whispered, "I'll see you back home." And he waded through the crowd and left the church. He could not receive Holy Communion. He was never particularly religious, but like other Ubecans, he went to Mass on Sundays and holy days of obligation. That night he did not want to be in that church; he did not want to be near a God who could take away a child just like that.

The cool wind on his face was a blessing, and he took

a deep breath, grateful to be rid of the cloying scent of incense and melted wax. Some candle vendors rushed to him, holding out their candles, promising to dance a prayer for him. He shook his head. He walked past an old woman with a cart selling roasted chestnuts. Two men held clusters of balloons, waiting patiently for the children to be released from the church. He hurried on, toward his house, away from the giddy happiness. But when he approached the two-story building, which was cloaked in purgatorial darkness—not a single lantern hung on the windows—his palms became damp and his breath quickened.

Last year, he and Danilo had sat at the kitchen table to make star lanterns. He guided the boy's hands to teach him how to hold the sticks together. He bound the sticks, formed the frame for the star, and he cut and glued the fine Japanese paper over the frame. Together they clipped the fringes for the bottom ends of the star. How amused he had been at the serious child who pressed his tongue thoughtfully against his upper lip as he carefully used the scissors to snip four-inch strips. When the star lanterns were hanging above the windows, the boy got candles from his mother, and he and Jose placed them inside the lanterns. Jose lit them, and they turned off all the other house lights, and they basked in pride at the wondrous stars hanging above every window of their house. They waved at the passersby who looked up and smiled and knew that a happy family lived in this house.

Three sharp sounds of a bugle startled him, and he quickly glanced at the Plaza Independencia, wondering what the Americans were up to. The American military occupied the old Spanish fort which stood at the far end of the plaza. The gas lamps were lit there and colorful star lanterns and garlands decorated the grandstand. It would be better there, Jose thought, so he walked toward the plaza. Last May, when the school children were on holiday, the American military band played in the evenings, rousing military songs, a bit of jazz. This memory made him feel hopeful, but when a gust of wind blew, bringing with it the tangy smell of the sea, he remembered once more that his son had drowned in this sea.

It was impossible. He could not think of anything else. By the time he got to the seashore, Fernanda and countless people surrounded the boy who lay on the ground looking like he was asleep, except for the God-awful gash on his head. A little boy, seven years old. He struggled not to think.

He found a bench near the fort where it was thankfully quiet. Here perhaps at least for a while, he could rest. He looked up at the stars and tried to find peace. The hooting of an owl startled him; owls were rare in the city. The owl continued with its mournful sounds and he felt his eyes well with tears. This surprised him because he had not cried for his son, for his loss, and now finally, he found himself weeping with abandon.

He was still sobbing when the wild ringing of the bells announced the end of the midnight Mass. His little bit of peace had ended. He imagined people rushing out of the church, eager to go home for their family celebration—the Noche Buena, where they would serve fish and chicken rellenos, pastel de lengua, piquant goat stew, Chinese hams, and, of course, roasted suckling pigs, and children would quarrel over who would get the ears and tails. Last year, Danilo had gotten the pig's tail and he had happily paraded it around.

"Papa," the child had said, "I want a bird. A black one, the kind that talks." They had seen a man selling a hill mynah, with lustrous black feathers and someone had trained it to say a few words. Jose had told him he'd get him one when he was older, but now he was gone.

Jose shook his head, but the bells continued ringing. He recalled the mournful tolling of these same bells at his son's funeral—how small his casket had been. The horror engulfed him once more and he felt ugly and powerless. He tried to compose himself, afraid to lose himself, afraid he'd become useless once again. He had little memory of what had happened. Someone, he could not recall who, had found him in the city hall to tell him that the child's body had been discovered. Jose was in a fog after that. People said he passed out; people talked about the wake, the funeral, the burial, the forty days of prayers. What he remembered most was the silence when he and Fernanda were in their dark house.

He also remembered Danilo's room, which they left exactly as it had been when the child was alive. Neither of them had the courage to remove a single item from the room that had assumed an aura of sacredness. It was as if leaving the room untouched kept Danilo alive; it was as if he would still come bounding in for the wooden spinning top or the mechanical monkey that played the drums which had amused him greatly.

Hands shaking, he pulled out his handkerchief from his pocket, wiped away his tears and blew his nose. When finally the church bells stopped, the sudden silence grew and tugged at his mind: there was something about his son's death that he couldn't grasp. Danilo knew never to go to the sea wall by himself. Even though he was only seven, he was like a little grownup with a lot of common sense. He was not a risk taker, and often when father and son played, Jose had to coax the child: "Come, come try out your new bicycle, you'll be fine," or "Come swim with me; I will hold you, you will be safe." But in the end the boy died of drowning. Or perhaps it was from hitting his head on the rocks. Nothing was clear. The vagueness stretched out like the long and implacable night.

Jose took a deep breath and rose from the bench. He never asked why the boy was playing alone at the seawall. He never asked why shortly after Fernanda started working at the rectory, the boy became very quiet, almost like a mute. He never asked about his wife's silence too, her evasiveness. He never asked why, when they had been happy before—their only concern had been financial since Jose was starting his law practice—why, a strange feeling entered their house like a fungus growing in the silence and quiet and dark. It was time to get answers.

He felt as if he was choking. He felt as if a void was created inside him and he had to go to Augustinian complex, to explore where his son had played, to walk on the seawall from which the boy had fallen. He found himself walking toward the Augustinian complex. But when a mangy dog crossed his path, Jose stopped, and the thought flitted through his mind: *It's not time.*

He turned back and headed home.

CHAPTER 12

FERNANDA JIMENEZ VARGAS

Jose found one solitary oil lamp lighting the living room; the room was dim, and long and strange shadows wavered on the walls. Out in the street, a group of people walked by and their burst of laughter tightened his chest, made the room seem larger. Jose stepped into the darkness and felt it enfold him. For a few heartbeats he stood still, breathing raggedly. A movement near the window startled him, made him realize Fernanda was present.

"We should have hung lanterns, like last year." Her voice was soft, conciliatory.

But the memory of the child cutting the fringes of the star lanterns rushed to him, and he wondered why she should bring up that painful memory.

"Sit down, please." She pointed to the chair opposite hers. As his eyes grew accustomed to the dark, he could make out the special chairs, raised high to allow them to view the fiesta procession. She was perched on the chair like a child. Downstairs, some carolers rattled some instruments and began singing about Mother Mary and Father Joseph watching over Baby Jesus. Jose and Fernanda remained still until they left. When Fernanda sighed he saw the glint of her tears.

He felt a sharp pain like a piercing of his heart. She was his wife, Danilo's mother, and it was Christmas, he told himself. With great effort, he rose from his chair, went to her and kissed her on the cheek. He caught the scent of something sweet in her hair. When they used to talk freely, she described rubbing crushed petals into her hair. "How was Mass?" he asked, trying to sound normal, before returning to his chair.

She wiped her tears away and blew her nose, her white handkerchief fluttering in the dark. She was five years younger and built like a waif. A friar's daughter, half-Spanish, different and difficult to understand.

Not knowing what to say, he too was silent. They sat facing each other in that somber room for countless heartbeats, his mind wandering back in time to when he first met her.

His aunt's statement, "She is not exactly beautiful," had terrified him. He had roiled the words over and over while visions of fat girls with doughy flesh and enormous dimpled thighs had populated his imagination. He disliked fat girls, and when Fernanda walked into Mother Teresa's office, Jose exhaled with relief—she was small with a scrunched up pallid face, and protruding upper teeth that made him think of a mouse. Underneath the stiffly starched uniform, her slight frame suggested crooked bones. She tilted her chin toward him and their eyes locked for a millisecond of a lifetime—her pupils were black as ebony. She curtsied at the doorway before gliding toward them like a white lily, just like a nun. He remembered glancing down and being surprised that her worn leather shoes were planted firmly on the tiled floor. Her best feature was her single heavy braid, as dark as her eyes, which hung down her back and swung as if it had a life of its own.

"Where did you go?" Her words startled him. "The Mass was too long. Some children started crying. I left early." She spoke in a monotone. The long hair was gone, and the short hair altered the proportions of her face so that her head seemed smaller, her eyes larger, and her buckteeth more pronounced.

"To the plaza, to get some air." Suddenly, it seemed to him that the air in that room was thin and stale.

She lowered her head so her face was shrouded in shadow. "There's a note from your mother. It's on the dining table. It says we should get there before noon. I won't go, but you go, they're your parents."

The thought of being with others, even his parents, frightened him, and he shook his head.

She slid off the chair and stamped her feet. "No, you must go!" Facing him, hands akimbo, she continued. "This must stop! We'll turn into lunatics. Don't you see? He's gone. Nothing we do can bring him back. We are acting as if we are dead too, like him. It's wrong. We have to live again. We have to try … I have to…"

Her outburst surprised him; but when he recovered, he felt angry. He wanted to shout: How can you want to live? How can you want to go on? But the words that escaped his mouth were soft … benign, "Then you should go. Tomorrow you must have lunch at my parent's house. With me."

As quickly as her defiance flared, she turned docile. "I hate how they look at me, especially your mother. She, more than your father, blames me."

"No one blames you. It was an accident."

She did not reply. A breeze blew through the window and stirred the crystal prisms hanging on the oil lamp. He recalled how people talked of a quiet before a big typhoon. He felt as if a storm would rush into the room any minute now. The tinkling was the only sound for a long time.

When she spoke again, her voice had a steely quality. "You blame me too."

At some point, Jose had learned that the Sisters of Charity had tried to marry Fernanda off to a fifty-five-year-old widower with six children. Fernanda had taken one look at him, then walked out, leaving the humiliated man with Mother Superior. Later Mother Teresa had scolded Fernanda, "Are you disobeying me, child? Do we not abide by our vows of obedience, chastity and poverty? You are almost seventeen. Most girls your age are gone, married. What will happen to you if you do not find a husband? You will have to leave the orphanage, you understand, when you turn eighteen." Her glassy gray eyes pierced through the girl.

Fernanda had stared right back: "I am not a sister, just a poor orphan, Reverend Mother, I am not bound to your three vows. When I have to leave, I will do so and find work somewhere. But I will not marry that man."

Fernanda was small but incredibly tough.

Jose slid off the high chair and faced the window. He gulped down the fresh air, felt his chest expand and contract. His childless aunt had some blame for this tragedy, he was certain of it. She must have colluded with the sisters to marry off Fernanda before her eighteenth birthday. He, Jose, had not been given a chance to consider the matter. The very day they met, Mother Teresa had announced, "Tomorrow morning, the priest will be here to marry them."

"Do you remember—" he said suddenly, "— the name of the galleon that carried the gown of Mother Teresa to Manila? Was it the *Nuestra Senora de las Mercedes*?"

She blinked, not comprehending him. She was still wallowing in her self-pity.

"It's not important," he said, with a wave of his hand.

Fernanda had often told him she was a favorite of the sisters, and on her wedding day, instead of wearing the cotton and lace communal gown, she had the privilege of donning the gown that Mother Teresa had worn at the Grand Debutante Ball in Sevilla, the same gown that had elicited praise from the Duchess of Alba herself. The gown was made of expensive silk bobbin lace, like Chantilly, and by some miracle, Fernanda and the sisters had been able to tuck the seams to make the dress fit the diminutive bride-to-be.

He could imagine Fernanda a long time ago, waking up at 5:30 in the morning, having a cold bath, and using the communal toothbrush to clean her teeth. She slipped on the precious gown and white satin slip-ons, and she gave away her few belongings to the older girls who had presented her with a spray of lilac cattleyas from Father Blanco's nearby garden. Because Fernanda was virtually out the orphanage door, the sisters had set aside their modesty rule and allowed her to have her hair down, and this cascaded down her back past her waist, a mass of black hair that overwhelmed her little white face. One by one, Fernanda had kissed the sisters and orphans goodbye, and by six in the morning, she and Mother Teresa glided down the chapel's aisle toward the anxious Jose who wore an American-style suit, ordered by Ignacia from Trinidad and Tobago Tailor, right after she had written the letter saying, "It is time for Jose to get married."

Fernanda's cracked voice cut through his reverie. "All of you blame me."

"No one blames you," Jose said, feeling tired. He ran his hand through his hair. It was almost two in the morning and the street was finally deserted.

"I can feel it. The way you look at me, the way you treat me. You've changed, you know that? You used to be good to me, but then you became too busy with court hearings, with clients, always something ... and when this happened you started looking at me in a strange way. Even the people in church look at me that way."

"And what look is that?"

"As if they know something."

"What is there to know? The child is dead. There is nothing more to discuss. No one is blaming you. You're tired, come, let's go to bed."

"Even before this happened, they have been gossiping about us. They talk behind our backs, do you know that?" She wore an ugly scowl.

"Go to bed, you're tired."

"They've always been jealous of me, jealous that we can live here, that I have my own money. It's been that way, always, people jealous of me. At the orphanage, some girls resented me because the sisters favored me. If I hadn't worked, we'd still be living with your parents and you'd still be notarizing documents for farmers and fishermen. They gossip about us, our success." She paused and checked to see if he was listening. "Have you noticed the smirk on their faces when they look us up and down?"

He did not answer.

"Well, I have. I know they blame me for Danilo's death. They say I should have stayed home and taken care of him. But you know, don't you, that I had to work to help make money? Besides, it's not true that I didn't watch him. I knew he was fine. He was always with somebody."

He leaned forward to listen carefully. She was breathing rapidly.

"There was always the cook, or the handyman, or the maid. Even Father Zafra allowed him to help him take care of his orchid garden. They were always there to help watch the boy. Danilo was never alone. Someone was always with him."

He straightened his back, tried to make sense of all of this. He felt as if he'd slipped down a dark pit. "If someone was always watching him, why did he drown? What happened?"

She wrung her hands. "I don't know ... I don't know ... I've asked myself the same question over and over. I was working; there was something I had to finish. That afternoon, I had difficulty balancing some figures; I had to ask Father Zafra about some numbers. Father and I were out in his orchid garden when Danilo arrived from school. He waved at me. He entered the office, and later I saw him seated at the small desk near mine. He was working on a paper boat. I heard him singing the ditty about a fisherman catching a tambasakan fish. Do you remember the song?" She started humming.

"I don't care about the song. What happened?" His voice had turned loud, sharp. It pained him to imagine Danilo's last moments, but he wanted her to continue talking.

She stopped, looked up at the ceiling, and spoke slowly as if choosing her words. "Time went by so fast. The next thing I knew he was gone. I didn't think anything of it. It was past five when I noticed that he wasn't around; I went looking for him. The cook said she saw him near the orchid garden." She paced back and forth as if reliving the experience. "But he wasn't there. We searched everywhere: the church, the rectory,

then I remembered his paper boat so I went toward the sea
When I found his toy on the seawall, I knew something was
wrong. I ran up and down, asking the fishermen and their
families to help me find him. I asked everyone. That was all
there was to it. They should not blame me. Can they not see
that I am suffering, that I'm his mother and I'm suffering? I
carried him in my womb for nine months, I'm the one who's
in agony. They have no right to accuse me. No right at all!"

She had made her way to the oil lamp and she turned
up the light so that the darkness receded and a harsh light
shone on the things she had bought: the expensive furniture
and Italian porcelain knick-knacks, the heavy drapes on brass
rods, the Austrian china in the cupboard, the gold-leaf mural
she had painted on the ceiling. Two years ago, when they had
moved into the city, she had bought a four-poster matrimonial
bed made of ebony, with a thick mattress, and she returned the
simple bed which his parents had given them. She ordered
from the French seamstress expensive linen sheets with their
initials monogrammed on the edges—J.V. and F.J. His parents
never had linen sheets; they had slept on woven mats laid on
bamboo-slatted beds.

She continued talking: "I have gone over this matter
over and over again. In my head, I see everything all over again,
and I've tried to rearrange events, but it's no good. What
happened, happened. I will go mad if I continue doing this ...
if I continue hanging on to him. I have to let him go ... I must
... I must allow him to die..." She collapsed on the floor on
the Persian carpet that had a garish floral design; this she
acquired in the past year.

The "I's" and the "me's" in her monologue echoed in
his head. He had followed his aunt's lead in praising Fernanda
for her hard work, for the sacrifices she made to advance his
career and their family, but now he saw her as if she were
stripped naked—she was selfish and greedy. She had a
voracious and insatiable greed larger than both their sorrow,
and he felt like ripping off her expensive clothes. He felt like
coupling with her—not the romantic lovemaking they had

indulged in—but he wanted to force himself into her, fill her with his anger and hate. At the orphanage, she had once said, she used to have a feeling akin to hunger when she had seen wealthy girls in the parks and churches, girls who wore shimmering silks trimmed with fine Belgian lace, the ones who wore rich leather shoes with large round buttons. Fernanda had so many yearnings, he wanted to fill her hunger, her unfathomable emptiness.

He wanted to silence her, to punish her.

He took her there on the floor of their fashionable home surrounded with the things she loved, took her as a dog would couple with a bitch, by force, although he felt her yielding, felt her own hunger, and sensed her body quiver when he was inside her.

It was dawn when they staggered to bed. Jose had another fitful night. He dreamt of being chased by giant rats in an underground tunnel. The rats were lunging at him when the ringing of the church bells rang as if from the distance. Bit by bit his awareness filtered back. He felt the warmth of the sun slanting in through the windows. The sweet smell of baking breads and cookies wafted up from the nearby bakery. It was Christmas morning. He stirred, felt hope rising within him. He remembered how as a child, he and his father used to climb coconut trees to get tuba, and after, sweaty and tired, they sat in the kitchen to take in some of the sweet heady drink. He could hear people moving up and down the street outside. It was the sound of a firecracker that reminded him of last night's sad coupling and he experienced deep shame. He had hurt her, he knew that, and he wanted to explain to her his anger, tell her he had not meant to harm her, tell her that he too was grieving, that sorrow had consumed him to the marrow.

He reached out to touch her, only to discover that she was gone.

CHAPTER 13

THE INCIDENT

The soft movements and muted sounds made Jose feel as if he were underwater. "He's back ... he's awake," a voice said. Through blurry eyes, he saw a woman bending over him. Rough fingers rubbed cool salve smelling of coconut oil on his forehead. It was Fernanda, he thought, and he opened his eyes wide only to see his mother. He turned away, curled up like a fetus, and started sobbing.

"Hijo, hijo, that's enough now, you must stop," his mother murmured.

"Leave him alone." It was a man's voice, filled with so much sadness he thought it was his own.

"Arturo, he hasn't moved in a day. Should I call the faith healer? Maybe someone has placed a curse on him."

"Let him rest." It was his father. For a moment, he thought he was a child again, sick with a fever or cold. His mother used to massage his chest with homemade balm and she fed him chicken soup tangy with ginger. She used to call the fat girl next door to keep him company, and the girl would waddle into his room with a book in her hand. After ordering him to lie still, she used to read fairy tales to him. The fat girl's voice was soothing, and she smelled of vinegar.

He surrendered to his mother's ministering and fell in and out of sleep.

At some point, he sensed the presence of another

person who mumbled some prayers. Later he felt the quick movement of a blade on his belly—it was a superficial cut and not painful—then something warm as a clot of blood oozed out of him. The man said, "There are spirits in this room … Don't be afraid, they are not bad … but they are restless as they want something … continue praying. I will make an offering in church later." It was the faith healer. Jose had seen this man—old, with a crucifix hanging around his neck. The priests spoke of him in their sermons, warning people to stay away from him, not to believe in sorcery and witchcraft, but his mother said faith healers had been around long before the Spaniards and Americans appeared and what was good enough for her great-grandparents was good enough for her.

It was the whispering later on that woke him up again.

"Should we tell him?" his mother said.

"No, not now…"

"He needs to know…"

He felt a cold thrill travel up his spine. What was it now? What did they want to tell him? Why could they not tell him now? "What is it?" He thought he had shouted, but his voice was a hoarse whisper. He tried to move but discovered he barely had any strength.

He struggled and managed to prop himself against the pillows. "Tell me!" he demanded. He was in his old room in his parents' house. How had he gotten there? His last memory was waking up on Christmas Day and discovering that Fernanda was not beside him.

His mother stepped back while his father drew forward. "We waited for you for lunch on Christmas, but you didn't come. We went to your house. You were not well so we brought you home. You have been sleeping all this time."

"Fernanda?" he asked.

"She's gone," his mother said, "but don't worry about that now. She was impossible anyway. Capricious, with airs."

"Nieves, don't. We talked about this," Arturo said.

His mother continued, "I heard about the complaint about the priest. She must have known, Arturo."

"That's enough, Nieves!" Arturo said. "The child is dead and let it be. Talking about the dead holds them back." Turning to Jose, Arturo said, "If you want to rest here, rest. I'll arrange things with your maid and secretary. Most offices are closed for the holidays anyway. Rest."

"How long have I been here?" Jose asked.

"Late Christmas night."

"Two days." He scrambled up. "I have to go."

Arturo held him down. "Stay here until you are better. There is no one in your house. She's gone."

"Her jewelry's gone, also her sewing kit," Nieves said. "Some spools and things were scattered on the floor. She left hurriedly. Like a thief."

He slumped back against the pillows and realized that Fernanda had left for good.

"It's just as well," his mother said. "Fernanda was never satisfied, never happy. A normal person needs a roof over one's head, three square meals a day, a place to sleep on, some clothes, a few things to make life comfortable, that is all. The important things, money cannot buy—family, health, happiness. She had everything, first our house here in San Nicolas, but no, it wasn't good enough, and you had to move to the city. She had a baby. Think of all the childless parents in the world, your aunt included. God gave Fernanda Danilo and it wasn't enough for her. There was always something else she wanted. It's impossible to be married to someone who's always dissatisfied, hijo. Be grateful she has left. It is time to pray hard that God will give you a fresh start. You are young. You have your whole life ahead of you."

His father pulled his mother away and her ranting merged with the confusion in his mind.

He slept late and ate the food his mother prepared. His parents kept conversations to a minimum and left him alone to do as he pleased. He felt like a seedling growing in the dark.

When he got stronger, he insisted on returning to his own home. Reluctantly his parents let him go. He considered getting rid of Fernanda's things, but just as he couldn't get rid of Danilo's belongings, neither could he dispose of hers. He wondered where she went and if he should try to find her, but the thought of doing so made him weary. In the end, he sulked, wallowed in a dreamy kind of state, uncertain of where the boundaries of his dreams and reality were.

He had rich colorful dreams. In one, Fernanda and Danilo were in the kitchen boiling coconut milk with sweet potatoes, jackfruit, and sago. "Come Papa, come. You must try," the child said, as he crooked his finger and beckoned him. The boy placed a bowl of their soupy concoction before him. He searched for a spoon but could not find one. "Fernanda, where are all the spoons?" he asked, but when he turned Fernanda and the child had left the kitchen and were outside heading toward a tall dark shadowy figure, leaving him breathless and terrified.

As December came to an end, he started to have dreams of twigs and mud on a dark road, nightmarish dreams of big hands with dirty fingernails, old hands reaching out to his son.

One afternoon when the New Year had begun, Jose looked out toward the San Agustin Church, rectory, and buildings that were part of the Augustinian complex. His father had explained that the Spanish friars had built churches so that they were one day's travel apart by horse to provide resting places for the Spanish soldiers and officials.

Jose noted that the buildings of the complex formed the sides of the fortified square. Beyond the square were the servants' quarters, and farther away loomed the abandoned Augustinian warehouse, which had been damaged by generations of termites, countless typhoons, and decades of sheer neglect. Beyond that was a creek that ran along the land of the Augustinians toward the sea.

The garden area fascinated Jose. It was populated by tall fruit trees, shrubs, and patches of flowers, giving the impression of being a colorful jungle. In the early evenings, hundreds of noisy starlings would alight on the tall eucalyptus trees and continue their chattering and singing until the birds fell asleep. An arbor made of wood provided a shaded walkway from the priests' quarters to the servants' area. Fernanda had told him about Father Zafra's orchids hanging underneath the arbor.

Jose started taking evening walks to the San Agustin Church on the pretext of attending the six o'clock Mass. After kneeling in church for a short while, he would leave and go to the garden.

Once, the church janitor, Macias, caught him standing behind a cluster of birds of paradise. "I'm sorry, Attorney Vargas, but visitors are not allowed here."

"I'm just admiring the orchids. I'm thinking of starting my own collection," he rattled on, then remembering that Macias had a sick wife, Jose touched his arm, "Macias—" he called him by name, "—how is your wife?"

Proud that an important man like Attorney Vargas would remember him in a personal way, Macias replied, "Still bed-ridden." Then reciprocating, he added, "I'm sorry about your son. He used to play around here. He was a good boy."

Jose's face must have shown his pain because Macias said, "Wait here." The janitor went into the greenhouse and returned with a small orchid. "Here Attorney, you can have this. It already has a flower. Father Zafra won't miss it. It's a Moth Orchid. Instead of soil, use shredded coconut husk. Make sure to place the plant in the center of the pot and cover the roots with the husk. Water early in the morning, not in the afternoon or evening. The Moth Orchid is easy to raise."

"Thank you Macias, I'll take care of it. I hope your wife gets better." His heart was beating so hard, he feared Macias heard it.

"Come around, Attorney. Sunday is best because Father Zafra has supper at the music composer's house then."

Over and over, he returned when the stars and moon were out and the servants were asleep and only the twittering of the starlings broke the stillness of the night. He learned that the priest enjoyed evening walks in the plaza; several nights a week he had supper in various people's homes; but on Sunday evenings, he dined at the music composer's house.

The composer's name was Juan Dela Cruz, who lived with his Catalan lover, Esteban Magri, although Jose didn't care about such gossip. What he was interested in was Father Zafra—what he ate, what he talked about, what kind of person he was.

Jose imagined the friar seated at the head of a long table, the place of honor. There he would have his squash soup, fish escabeche, and chicken relleno. After supper, he and his hosts would retire to the smoking room where they would indulge in premium Havana cigars and green liquors made by French monks. At around midnight, the priest would say his goodnight and head back to the rectory. It was a short walk, only eight minutes if one walked briskly, longer if one took in the sea breeze. Jose had repeatedly traced the path that Father Zafra took to and from the music composer's house, and he knew it by heart.

Late in the afternoon of Sunday, January 3, Jose visited his parents. They had supper and afterwards, he helped his mother make soap. As she heated up the mixture of lye, coconut milk, and goat's milk, she talked about the danger of lye. "It burns; you must be very careful." She added the scent of ylang-ylang, and they both admired the sweet floral smell. Shortly after he poured the mixture into the wooden molds, he said he had to leave. His parents stood by the doorway with their shoulders drooped. The flickering light from the overhead oil lamp cast shadows on their faces, deep lines etched on their foreheads and around their mouths, their expression so forlorn. How old they looked. He understood that they too had suffered and he wished he could make it up to them. But his debt was as vast as the darkness outside and he knew that even if he had two, even three lifetimes, he could never repay them. He kissed them and told them he loved them.

"Stay," his mother said suddenly, grasping his arm, pulling him back into the house. "Spend the night here. I feel a quickening in my spleen ... as if something ... something ... will happen."

His father shifted his gaze and shuffled his feet, embarrassed at his mother's burst of emotion. "She's had bad dreams, your mother. She'll be all right. Go."

When he stepped out into the night, the stars vibrated with life, studding the dark blue dome, and the moon was a huge slice of yellow. The scene was a picture from his childhood book. It was like a dream; he had lived this moment and was now reliving it again—a déjà vu. As he walked down the dirt road, the perfume of the flowers saturated the air; he listened to the sawing of the cicadas, their call for rain. He experienced a clarity that he never had before. At times, he thought he heard children whispering and rustling behind the bushes, but when he turned, he would see nothing.

Sometime during his walk, the notion to talk to Father Zafra struck him. The priest had been one of the last people to have seen his son Danilo. During Jose's confinement at home, the suspicion that Father Zafra knew something about his son's death had taken root, and tonight the idea hung full-blossomed in his imagination. He wanted to ask what the priest knew. His mother had mentioned during his time of delirium something about a complaint against the priest. Jose wanted to find out more about this.

After his questions were answered, he, Jose, could surrender his son more easily to the sea in which he drowned, to the earth that claimed his small body, surrender him to the stars and universe. And maybe he, Jose, could finally get up in the morning and put one foot in front of the other, go about his business. Continue living. That was all he wanted.

And Fernanda—what sorrow to think of his wife; what sorrow to remember what he had done to her—would she ever forgive him? He hoped she would come back; he hoped they could wake up to a new morning again. His parents doubted she would return, but who knows, perhaps if she finds her salvation as he was now trying to, then perhaps she could forgive him; because in balance, despite her greed and mistakes, he still loved her; and he felt certain that she cared for him still.

Quietly, barely breathing, he made his way down the dirt road toward the plaza. He would catch Father Zafra on his way home from supper at the composer's house. He felt hopeful that tonight he would find an end to his nightmare.

There were few people in the plaza when he got there—a handful of people promenading, three young men playing basketball, some lovers hiding in the shadows of the stone walls, the vendor of fruit and boiled bananas who never left his post under a makeshift awning under a sprawling mango tree. Jose paced up and down the sidewalk, where it was dark and he couldn't be noticed. He considered climbing the walls for a better view of the house, but they were too high. He discovered that across the street, at the edge of the park, he could catch glimpses of the priest and two men smoking cigars and sipping long stem glasses. Jose sat close to a wild oleander bush, where he could not be seen.

When it started to drizzle and a blanket of clouds hid the stars, he felt his hope wane. People scurried about, finding safety from the rain, but he continued to wait. He was drenched when the church bells tolled ten times and commotion erupted from the house. He clambered up the bench and saw Father Zafra flailing his hands, his movements rough and angry. The priest shoved a chair away and abruptly left the men. Soon, the front gate flung open and the priest rushed out into the wet night. The gate slammed. Using a cane, Father Zafra crossed the road toward the park, toward Jose; and Jose quickly hid behind the oleander bush. He wondered if he should step out where there was light so the priest could see him, but he remained still and quiet.

Father Zafra swung his cane at the bushes and tree trunks as he walked. Something had made the priest furious, and Jose knew it was not the right time to confront him, but the desire to talk to him had grown too large, he felt as if he were suffocating. He simply could not control himself—a few questions—that was all.

At some point, the priest yelled at the three young men who had earlier been playing basketball but who were now in the gazebo. "Are you boys drinking? Drinking and fornicating, that's all you boys think of."

"We've done nothing to you, mind your own business, Father!" someone yelled back, and the three broke out in laughter.

The priest approached them; he was waving his cane in the air. "I have heard it all in confession—lust, sins of the flesh, self-indulgence—you boys need to confess and repent." The priest swung his cane, hitting the shoulder of a young man. There was a sharp cry of pain as the young man sprung toward the priest to push him away. The priest shoved back and a scuffle erupted. The other two struggled to pull them apart. "Go home, Father! Have a good night's sleep," someone shouted as he pushed the priest away. They waited to see what Father Zafra would do, and when he left, they continued their chatter and laughter.

Jose slunk in the deep shadows, still mulling over what he should ask the priest. He wanted to be able to piece in his mind his son's last moments, see in his imagination exactly what the boy did, where he was, and how the child fell into the sea. He could not find the right words to phrase his questions, and time was running out.

When Father Zafra headed toward his orchid garden, Jose managed to call, "Father ... Father Zafra, it's me, Jose Vargas."

The priest turned, and still in his excited state, began waving his cane around. "Who? Who are you?" He was standing under the eucalyptus trees, where the starlings were quietly roosting. The priest's voice echoed loud and strong. "Stay away, leave me alone! I've told you I cannot agree to it. The land will be compromised." The priest moved away, toward the creek.

"Don't be afraid. It's me. The father of Danilo. The boy, who fell off the seawall. The boy who drowned." He moved toward the priest.

The priest paused then mumbled, "Sons are the heritage from the Lord, children a reward from him." Then in a louder voice: "What is it? What do you want from me? I did nothing to your son." He held his cane with both hands as if ready to strike.

"I only want to ask a few questions. The boy, surely you remember him. My wife … you remember her, do you not? Fernanda. She did the bookkeeping." He took a few more steps toward the priest.

"Why are you bothering me now? Yes I remember her—the priest's bastard. What do you want?"

Fernanda had never been spoken of in such a manner. Never. Jose stepped out, in full view now.

"Stay back. Don't come near me. Go away, leave me alone," the priest said, and he lifted his cane higher above his head.

Jose grabbed his arms and wrestled the cane from him.

Father Zafra fell and started shouting, "Help me! Help me!"

A dog started howling, a long mournful cry, drowning out the priest's cries. Overhead a few starlings flapped their wings in annoyance.

The priest scrambled up and rushed at Jose. Father Zafra managed to hit Jose in the stomach, but even though the priest stood tall and proud, his punch was weak, and Jose didn't even skip a breath. The priest grew more frantic and continued shouting. The starlings started twittering and would not stop. It was the noise—Jose had to stop it. He had to silence the priest before the servants and friars woke up. Jose grabbed him to cover his mouth. The priest struggled to pull the cane from Jose's hands, and finally there was no choice—the cane fell over the priest's head, and Jose heard the awful sound of bone cracking. He hit him over and over again until there was complete silence.

The struggle wore him out and Jose stood there breathing hard, the cane still in both his hands. He felt sticky fluid on the cane, his hands, and face. A weak moon shone on

Father Zafra who was sprawled on the muddy earth, his black robes sopping up the rain on the ground and the awful blood flowing from his head. The terror of what he, Jose, had done flooded his mind and he dropped down on his knees to help the priest up, to get him on his way, send him to the rectory, to his bed, so he could sleep and forget this nightmare. There was blood everywhere and the priest's body was limp. Jose bent down and shook him, but there was no movement at all. A cold chill traveled through Jose's body until he started shivering.

He stared not knowing whether he should flee or hide the body. He was a lawyer; he knew he should report the matter to the authorities, but he was certain no one would believe that he had meant no harm to the priest. His throat tightened when he remembered that murderers could get the death penalty, now by firing squad, no longer by garroting.

It was the sound of a dog barking that made him move. He had to do something. With the priest's cane in his hand, he fled into the darkness.

PART III

CHAPTER 14

THE TRAIN RIDE

It was Melisande who told Ines how Juan Dela Cruz was released from jail. "It was simple. Esteban wrote a notarized statement that he had been with Juan on the night the priest disappeared," she said.

"How do you know that?" Ines asked.

"While we were dancing, I asked Esteban, and he told me."

"I see," Ines said. "Juan did not tell me that."

"My dear Juan is brilliant, but very excitable, Ines. His mind flits here and there. If you get a notarized statement from Pilar that she was with Andres, that should help get him out," Melisande said.

The thought of dealing with Pilar Echeveria made Ines's head throb, but Holy Week was coming up, offices would be closed, her son was stuck in jail, and she had to do something.

Melisande continued, "I will go with you to Carcar. I have to talk to her mother about her gown, anyway. I also have to ask Pilar and her father if she can be a carnival princess."

Without wasting time, on Saturday morning, Ines and Melisande were on the train to Carcar.

As they were getting settled in their car, Melisande said, "Do you remember the inauguration? It seems like it was just yesterday." Her silk dress rustled softy as she put her things away. "I was here with Juan and Esteban. We had a wonderful time."

Melisande was talking about the train's inauguration in 1907, an event that Ines did indeed recall vividly. She and Pablo had taken the exhilarating steam engine ride from Ubec to Carcar and back, in a first-class car, finished in rich teak wood. Before then, one had to take a horse-drawn carriage to get from Ubec City to Carcar. Pablo had explained that it was the American mania for efficient transportation that got the Philippine Railway Company created.

Ines had felt as if she and Pablo were on some pinnacle as they hobnobbed with dignitaries. Pablo was a highly respected educator, newspaper publisher, a contender to be a candidate to the Philippine Assembly. Ines had no idea then that in less than a year, he would be dead.

"Pablo and I were here," Ines said, with some sadness.

When the train blew its whistle and started chugging, Melisande cocked her head to one side. "Listen," she said, "it sounds just like the train I took when I left Lyon. My mother had just died and I was moving to Paris to be with my aunt. I was afraid and excited at the same time." She wrapped her arms across her chest and lifted her shoulders. "I was leaving the only home I knew. Paris was a big city, very important you understand. I was scared."

Melisande told Ines about how she worked for her Tante Juliette in her aunt's dress shop on Avenue Bouquet, and how one April day, after delivering some clothes near the Notre Dame, her aunt fell from a carriage and broke her leg. Tante Juliette had to be brought to the Hopital Dieu de Paris where they waited along with people with broken arms, wrists, clavicles, hips, and legs.

Melisande became animated when she said, "It was terrible, Ines, and the waiting room smelled of antiseptic. It didn't have a single plant, not a bit of color, all gray and so very sad. And I kept thinking: how am I going to bring Tante back home when it had taken four men to move her to a gurney? How long would the leg take to heal? And would it heal properly? The father of Etienne, a boy I knew, fell from the barn and became a cripple. I heard of amputations of limbs that did not heal properly."

They were there for hours and in the meantime Juliette complained about her leg hurting more. When Melisande peeled back her aunt's coat, she saw that Juliette's leg had swelled. Melisande went to the nurse to ask where the doctor was. The nurse had been curt—no, she had been rude—and she told Melisande the surgeon was taking care of a man with a broken spine: "He would be along, please be patient Mademoiselle, sit down and wait."

It was mid-afternoon when a brash doctor burst into that purgatory-of-a-room. He was very animated, with a broad smile, and a faint five o'clock shadow which looked charming, not unkempt. "Madame," he told Melisande's aunt, "do not worry, you are in good hands. I am the best surgeon in Paris."

Ines laughed. "Did he really say that?"

Melisande's eyes sparkled with amusement. She lifted one finger up in the air. "Ah, but he corrected himself, 'Well, no, I am not the best surgeon, but I'm one of the best in all of Paris.' Can you just imagine his arrogance, Ines? He proceeded to chat with us, calling us beautiful ladies, mesmerizing us, and meantime he held my aunt's leg in both his hands—his hands were huge, his fingers long, like those of an artist—and suddenly, with a quick movement, he pulled apart the bones and snapped them back in place. Straightaway, my aunt fainted. I thought I would get sick."

"And that was Samir," Ines said.

"Doctor Samir Martine. He took excellent care of my aunt and even checked on her when she returned home. The first time he visited, he scolded me because my aunt had defied me and had climbed the stairs to her room! It was completely her fault, Ines. I had prepared a room for her downstairs but she flat-out refused to stay there. What a bullheaded woman! And Samir blamed me despite everything I did—and I tried hard, Ines, I did. It was not easy to keep up with the dress orders and run back and forth to the hospital, and later when she was home, to climb up and down the stairs to make sure she was all right. Oh, how angry I was at him, Ines! Samir made me angry … He made me happy … Samir made me … crazy. How can I explain?" Melisande heaved a deep sigh.

"You fell in love with him," Ines said, in a serious tone.

Melisande nodded and became quiet. For quite some time, they gazed out at scenes of nipa huts and farmlands, and carabaos soaking in muddy pools. Melisande had a dreamy expression when she resumed talking, "One Saturday afternoon, I decided to use the floor instead of the cutting-table to cut a bias-skirt. I was down on my knees, with my skirt hiked up, when I heard knocking on the door. It had been a warm day and I had left the door ajar. When I looked up, there he was staring at me, asking if I needed help." Melisande widened her eyes—"Ines, I was on all fours! My hair was in disarray. Some curls were falling in front of my eyes." She dissolved into laughter.

"And what did you do?"

"What could I do? I clambered up, brushed the lint off my skirt, and pretended nothing was wrong. That was the time he happened to see my sketches and realized that I could draw well. He had been giving my aunt some of his drawings, work that my aunt treasured but which were not very good. Once he showed off his charcoal drawing of the Eiffel Tower and asked for my candid thoughts. I told him it was well-rendered, that it was a faithful copy of the Eiffel. He probably sensed that I did not really like it, and he told me to stop censoring myself and to go ahead and tell him the truth about his work."

"Did you tell him the truth?"

"Oh, Ines, I told him that his drawing lacked something. I explained that when I look at someone's creation, I want to feel something—my soul must be touched, my soul must quiver, memories must be unlocked or formed…"

"In other words, you made him understand his work was lifeless," Ines said.

"How bluntly you put it, Ines. I did not mean to hurt his feelings. He was very kind to my aunt and to me. He was devastated."

"Obviously he did not disappear from your life."

Melisande shook her head slowly. "No, Samir was there. And Samir is still here." She placed her right hand over her bosom. "Because of him, I fled Paris, taking the train to Marseilles, then a steamship all the way to Ubec."

"You are very brave," Ines said.

"Oh, I'm not brave at all," Melisande said. "It was just something I had to do."

Ines reached over to touch Melisande's arm. "Thank you for coming with me."

Melisande flicked her hair away from her face. "Oh, it is nothing, Ines."

"Mama will be happy to see you. She will want to hear the details about the carnival." Ines remembered Pilar and Santiago and sighed. "I am not looking forward to seeing the Echeverias."

"We will go together. I will talk to Pilar and her father, and afterwards when they are in a good mood, you can ask for the document," Melisande said. "Things will be all right." The Frenchwoman smiled before arranging her skirt and sinking deeper into her seat.

"I am not so sure," Ines said. "Pilar may refuse to give the statement."

"Pilar will help Andres," Melisande said.

"I wish I could be as optimistic as you, Melisande, but I have learned that Life never takes a straight road. It meanders along with bumps along the way," Ines said, thinking of her widowhood, her dealing with Pablo's newspaper, and now her son in jail.

"Things will be fine, don't worry," Melisande said.

The train was well along its way to Carcar when a young man entered their car. "I was in the wrong seat," he announced, as he sat down across them. "The conductor told me to come here. I'm John Parker."

He was an American, young, with light brown hair and freckles on his cheeks.

"I'm on my way to Carcar," he said. "I'll be teaching high school in McKinley."

"You're a Thomasite then," Melisande said.

John Parker looked puzzled.

"There are many American teachers in Ubec now. They're called 'Thomasites'. You see, the first group of teachers arrived on the USS Thomas. There were five hundred of them. That was back in 1901."

The American laughed. "It sounds like a religious order. Does that mean I'm now a Thomasite as well?"

"Yes," Melisande said, smiling.

"My parents in Ohio will be amused," he said.

"Ohio—that sounds very far away—" And Melisande proceeded to give advice to the young man, telling him to watch out for cholera. "You have to be careful not to catch this. It's not ordinary diarrhea; cholera can kill you. Be careful and drink only boiled water. Don't eat uncooked vegetables, and never eat the peeling of fruit. A doctor I once knew said cholera comes from a little bacteria shaped like a comma. It can come from feces in the water or in vegetables and fruit."

"To tell you the truth, Ma'am, I've come here for the wilderness. I was hoping to see some headhunters, but I hear they're up North. The tribes still go on hunting raids."

Melisande made a face. "That's too gruesome," she said. "I like Ubec, small and peaceful, no headhunters, although we had a murder not too long ago."

"Is that so, Ma'am?"

"A priest. His remains were found early this week; he had been missing since January." She lifted her shoulders and shivered.

"I've just come from Manila and I heard a priest was attacked by tenant farmers," John Parker said.

"It's probably over Friar Lands," Ines said, as she pointed at the huge expanse of sugar cane fields that they passed by.

The young man blinked, not understanding.

"Church land," Ines explained. "The Americans bought the land from the church and have parceled it for new owners. Some people are not happy with the change."

Melisande leaned forward. "I heard that President Taft's brother is a lawyer and is able to get his clients Friar Lands and business contracts here," she said, then addressing Ines, she added, "It was Mr. Fitz who told me, Ines. He said Henry Taft's clients get huge parcels of sugar lands."

"Friar Lands are supposed to be parceled at sixteen hectares and smaller, but the Havemeyer were able to buy 55,000 acres," Ines said.

"I suppose it pays to be the president's brother," John Parker said. "It's this kind of greed I'd like to avoid. I hope Carcar is far from cities." And glancing out the window, he said, "Is that Carcar?"

They looked out at the twin towers of a church and the faint beginnings of a town.

"Yes, it is," Ines replied, and the three of them waited for a better view of the quaint houses and clean streets with plants and flowers.

Ines knew this town well. Her father's family had roots in this place. Even though she had a home in the city, she had always returned to Carcar to visit her family's hacienda. She knew all the landmarks of Carcar: the mansions of the hacienderos made of stone and wood and decorated with intricate lace woodwork; the town's plaza with an elaborate grandstand and forgotten generals on horses; the elite all-girls school, Santa Catalina. She had seen the American military army post, Fort McKinley, spring up almost overnight. There the post was, with sparkling white buildings and officer's cottages. It even had a baseball field and an enormous swimming pool—a veritable country club. The Americans had also renovated the marketplace, which now had corrugated roofing and neat rows of uniform wooden stalls for the vendors.

Melisande pointed out a cluster of white-washed buildings near the hills. "Catch a carriage and tell the driver to take you there," she told the American teacher.

When they arrived, Melisande said, "Take care of yourself, and stop by my shop when you're in Ubec. Printemps, everyone knows where it is." Then she surprised the young man by giving him a peck on each cheek.

The American gave a gallant bow before leaving, and Melisande watched him vanish into the crowd. "He is so handsome, Ines. Do you think he'll come by the shop?" she said.

Ines shook her head. "He's ten years younger than you," she said with a tone of reprimand.

Melisande started laughing. "Tante Juliette said young men have a lot of stamina."

"That is what makes people get ideas about you," Ines said.

"Oh, Ines, don't be so strict," Melisande said.

"But it's true, Melisande. You are French, first of all, so right there people get ideas about you, then you say these things."

Melisande flicked her right hand in the air. "Oh, let them talk. It means nothing to me what they say. Besides the women will still come to have dresses made."

Linking arms, the women found a carriage and told the driver to take them to Villa Fatima.

CHAPTER 15

INES AND SANTIAGO

A re we here, Ines?" Melisande asked when their carriage approached a sugar cane hacienda with an enormous house.

"No, that belongs to the Echeverias," Ines replied in a clipped tone.

"Oh, Pilar and Santiago's. The house is as big as the Oriente Hotel in Manila."

"Yes, it is huge."

"Oh look, there's a small church and store outside the walls. And look, nipa huts, I wonder who lives in them," Melisande said.

"They're for the workers and their families." She shifted her weight and looked away.

Melisande said, "Your family hacienda is near here, you are neighbors then?"

"Yes."

"Ah ... so you have known Santiago for a long time?"

"Our mothers were ... are friends, and Santiago and I were friends when we were children."

"I see," Melisande said. "I would never have thought that because you dislike him very much."

"It's a long story, Melisande. Santiago attacked Pablo and created that newspaper of his just to compete with my husband." Ines sighed. It was always a thorn in her side to see the Echeveria hacienda.

Indeed many people had forgotten that Ines and Santiago had spent their infancy in their Carcar haciendas that sat side by side, and that the two had grown up together almost like siblings. Ines and Santiago had been born days apart, and their mothers used to visit one another. As children, Ines and Santiago had eaten, slept, peed, and pooped together. The Echeverias, whose hacienda was twice as large as that of the Noels, had an assortment of toys: tricycles, wagons, swings, teeter-totters, and a playhouse made of bamboo and nipa leaves, which had been Ines's favorite. The miniature nipa hut sat under the shade of a huge flame tree where the breeze hummed constantly. Hanging from the windowsill were wind chimes that tinkled unnamed melodies whenever the breeze blew. Their mothers used to lay the children side by side on a woven mat for their naps while they lay in hammocks to chitchat or cat-nap.

Fearing the children would become provincial in the haciendas, the mothers made their city homes their primary residences when the children turned five. The children spent the school months in Ubec and their holidays and many weekends in Carcar. Santiago and Ines had enjoyed many childhood games together. Market-market was a favorite, where they used pebbles for pretend-money and leaves and rocks for pretend-vegetables, fish, and other food products. Tag games like hide-and-seek and the moon game were other favorites. Ines and Santiago joined the numerous religious processions, swam in the sea, attended fiesta celebrations, ate merienda together, climbed fruit trees for tambis or lanzones—Ines had a lot of memories of Santiago, all of which she thought she had expunged, but which now sifted upward in her consciousness.

One summer day, Ines and Santiago had been playing in the third floor of the Echeveria house near the secret stairs leading to the attic. The attic was a mysterious place; some people said it was haunted by enchanted beings, while others said geckos as large as baby monitor lizards lived there. Townsfolk talked of wood beams in the attic "as old as Mampur," meaning the wood beams were very, very old (the etymology of the phrase had now been forgotten and no one remembered who Mampur was).

The children were strictly forbidden to go the attic which only made the place an irresistible magnet. With no more than a glance at each other, the two agreed to defy the grownups and snuck into the library. One bookcase, the second from the right, hid the secret staircase that led up to the attic. Santiago knew where the levers were and he pulled the bookcase, which swung open like a door. The children silently crept up the narrow staircase and slipped into the attic. The place was terribly dark, musty, and filled with sticky cobwebs that clung to their faces. Ines was ready to turn back, but Santiago sounded confident as he whispered, "Put your hands out." He showed Ines how to push away the cobwebs as they went deeper into the attic. Ines hung on to his shirt, feeling both fear and excitement as she trailed behind him.

Some light filtered in through cracks and Ines could make out a small doorway at the far end of the attic. She expected Santiago to go there, but he stopped next to a wooden chest. "Lock, supplies," he said, as he opened the chest. "This is if Papa has to escape. He can grab these, then head to that door over there, and run."

Santiago's father, Policarpio Echeveria, was a revolutionary against Spanish rule, and fearful that the Spanish military would arrest him, had built these secret rooms, compartments, and exits in his house.

Santiago bent over the box and pulled out packages. "See this? Maps, dried fish, rice, and take a look at this..." He pulled out a long sword from its scabbard the sight of which made Ines suck in her breath. She had seen machetes, but this was the first time she'd seen a fighting sword. The blade caught a bit of light and glinted. Frightened, Ines said, "Put that away, you'll get hurt." Santiago laughed. It was not the first time that

Santiago tried to frighten Ines. He would, for instance, suddenly spring from behind doors to scare her. He was also wont to torment her, by pulling her pigtails and teasing her even when she begged him to stop. Now, he started shaking the sword in his right hand. Ines took a few steps back. He took a few steps toward her. Ines stamped her feet defiantly. "Put that down, right now!"

"Papa said he's killed several men with this sword. It's his favorite. He cut off their heads and he stuck the sword into their stomachs and sliced upward to make sure their intestines were cut."

Santiago made the sound like a chicken being gutted. Ines, who hated to see animals being slaughtered, placed her hands to her ears. "Stop it! I don't want to hear about it!" The image of the beheaded chicken made her cry. Sobbing, she turned and ran away from him. She heard the sound of the sword being slid back into its scabbard and clunked back into the box. Santiago raced after her. "I've put it away. Don't be angry with me," he said, in a voice filled with hurt.

Ines was near the doorway when she stopped and turned to face him. "You must not do that. It's mean." Her tears were rolling down her cheeks. Suddenly, Santiago reached out to touch her face. He ran his fingers over her tears, and then he placed his fingers to his mouth and licked her tears. "Your tears are salty, like Chinese plums," he said, his eyes large in surprise.

For a brief moment, Ines was stunned: her face froze, her sobbing ceased—salty tears? How could Santiago have likened her tears to salted plums? She wept louder.

Santiago shifted his weight before pulling out a handkerchief, which he handed to her. "Stop crying. Please. It makes me sad."

Ines took some deep breaths and wiped her face dry. They left the attic and went to the playhouse where they pricked their pointer fingers and squeezed out blood. They pressed their fingers together and swore never to tell anyone they had entered the attic.

It was a secret; a bond that kept them separate from the rest of the world. But surprisingly when they started high school in Ubec, they drifted apart. Santiago went to the all-boys San Joaquin School, while Ines attended the all-girls Inmaculada Concepcion. Ines had her girl friends, he had his boy friends. Now and then, Ines would catch Santiago and his friends ogling girls. The boys' favorite pastime was hiding under stairwells so they could catch a glimpse of the ankles of girls climbing the steps. Later, she heard stories of Santiago courting some girls. She didn't know what to make of this attention he was showing other girls because he had always been part of her life. She felt a-kilter for a while but she eventually saw how silly Santiago and his friends were. Santiago started to turn into some vague childhood memory. Then as Fate would have it, when Ines was a student at the university, she cut her hand on a broken glass. Her friends brought her to the most approachable and beloved professor, Pablo Maceda, thirty, dashing, and elegant. Pablo had efficiently cleaned Ines's hand and bandaged it. Straightaway Ines fell in love with Pablo, and Pablo was also quite enchanted with her. Not too long after, they got engaged.

One evening, after the wedding date was set and Ines's gown was being stitched, along came Santiago, startling the Noel family by his loud pounding on their front door. Looking haggard and depressed, he begged to speak with Ines in private. Ines led him to the garden where they sat on a bench under an arbor with jasmine creeping up the sides. Out of nowhere he talked about his love for her, and said that he had, in fact, loved her all these years, and that he was planning to marry her. So why, he asked, was Ines engaged to Pablo? He demanded that she break off her engagement.

Shocked, Ines reminded him that there was nothing between them. Why on earth could he have thought there was something between them? She gave him a little push. "Go home, Santiago, don't make a fool of yourself," she had said. And she had run back to the house.

Blanca consoled Santiago who refused to attend the wedding of Ines and Pablo.

Later on Ines learned that Santiago had declared Pablo his enemy, and his animosity remained even after he married Aphrodite.

CHAPTER 16

BLANCA NOEL

W hen Ines and Melisande arrived at Villa Fatima, there was an explosion of activity, with servants running here and there, picking up their bags, getting their rooms ready, opening windows to air the house, and so on. Blanca hurried down to greet them and she soon led them to the patio for lunch.

Despite her dread of having to discuss with her mother what had happened to Andres, Ines was happy to be in Villa Fatima. She found comfort in this place where time seemed to have stood still. The rooms—the private chapel with antique statues, the library with mildewing books, the music room with piano and harp—never changed. Even her mother Blanca seemed not to age. In Villa Fatima, Ines felt she could retreat into a cocoon of safety.

While a servant girl served lunch and another shooed away the flies, the obligatory chitchat took place. Melisande praised Blanca for her youthful appearance. The older woman elaborated on her nightly ritual of slathering coconut oil on her skin, and once a week a young servant girl rubbed hot coconut oil onto her scalp and hair. The two went on to discuss gowns and plans for the carnival.

After the small talk, Ines had no choice but to confess, "Mama, Andres was picked up by the police for questioning."

"Andres was what?" Blanca said, her fork frozen in

midair. A deep furrow appeared in her forehead. "What happened to my grandson?"

"It is all a mistake. He's in a holding cell, but he'll be released soon."

"A holding cell ... a cell ... oh, Ines, it sounds like a pig pen. You mean my grandson is in jail!"

"Just until the matter is straightened out."

Blanca put her fork down and shoved her plate away.

"The situation is not hopeless, Maman. There is a solution," Melisande said, brightly.

"What happened, Ines? Tell me everything," Blanca said, in an irate tone.

Ines told her about the discovery of Father Zafra's remains and how Andres and his friends had been picked up by Tonying Borja. It was all a mistake; they were innocent, she repeated.

"Now why would Tonying make such wild accusations? Murder? That is the most insane thing I've heard. Andres is an angel. My poor, dearest grandson, in a cell." Tears formed in her eyes, and soon, she was crying.

"Mama, please don't cry." Ines handed her another napkin. "The problem, Mama, was that the boys weren't together the whole night. The three of them left the plaza to serenade a girl, but later Mario and Jesus left Andres," Ines said.

Melisande spoke up, "In other words, Maman, the two have an alibi, but Andres doesn't. But once we have the statement, everything will be solved."

"What statement?" Blanca asked.

"We are here, Mama, to get a notarized statement from the girl he was with."

"A girl? What girl?" Blanca blinked several times.

Ines cleared her throat. A fly buzzed around the table, and for a few seconds the three of them watched it weave about before the nearby maid swatted it. Melisande finally spoke up, "Pilar Echeveria, Maman. Andres was with Pilar the night the priest was murdered."

"Pilar? Pilar Echeveria?" Blanca said.

"We need to talk to Pilar," Ines said. "Melisande has a reason to see her."

"Pilar is one of the carnival princesses. I will talk to her and her father about this. This is our excuse to be there," Melisande said.

"So Pilar and Andres spent the night together." Blanca stared at her plate thoughtfully.

"Mama, they did not spend the night together. Three boys serenaded Pilar; two left, leaving Andres with Pilar."

"That is what I mean. The two were together ... by themselves." Blanca said.

Melisande spoke up, brightly, "That is a good thing, Maman, because Andres has an alibi. We just have to convince Pilar to write a statement."

"I see," Blanca said. "Well then, we better see them this afternoon, after siesta time," she said. "Both of you should rest after that journey. I have some things to do, but I'll be ready by three o'clock to go to the Echeverias."

CHAPTER 17

PILAR ECHEVERIA

The wedding of Santiago and Aphrodite had been talked about, written about, and attended by luminaries from as far away as Madrid, Paris, and London. Ines and Pablo had been pointedly not invited, but since the wedding was held in Manila and only a fraction of the invited Ubecans could attend, their absence wasn't too obvious. Even if they had received an invitation to this so-called wedding of the year, Ines and Pablo wouldn't have attended; Ines had already heard ripples of Santiago's virulent anti-Pablo sentiments. After the wedding, and as if rubbing salt into an open wound, Blanca described to Ines in minute detail the grand ceremony at the Cathedral and the opulent reception at the Manila Hotel. She made sure her daughter realized what she had missed by not marrying Santiago: Arabian horses pulling the bride's carriage to church, the diamond tiara perched on Aphrodite's head, bigwigs from Europe and America, decorative flowers and ribbons made of pure silver thread, giveaways made of gold charms depicting the bride and groom, French champagne, English scotch, Spanish wine, Russian caviar, French foie gras, Argentine beef, Australian lamb, Belgian chocolates, et cetera.

In fact, the mindboggling extravagance was paid for by Aphrodite's father who had silver mines in Northern Luzon. If money could buy it, Aphrodite's father got it for his only daughter; he even paid off judges so Aphrodite would have the coveted title of Intramuros's Fiesta Queen. He had hoped to marry her off to a Spanish noble but before he could put her on the ship bound for Sevilla, Aphrodite and Santiago had a highly indiscrete whirlwind romance, leaving no choice but for her to marry Santiago. It was one of those cases where the couple had spent the weekend together in what they thought was a secret hideaway. There were no secrets in Manila (nor in Ubec for that matter) and to make the weekend scandal recede in the minds of people, her father made a big to-do about giving Aphrodite a Cartier diamond and platinum jewelry set— a faithful replica of a set worn by Empress Eugenie, wife of Napoleon III, and reportedly worth the price of a ship. The newspapers and public lapped it up, and indeed the scandalous weekend that had resulted in the rushed wedding faded in the background.

After the spectacular wedding and month-long honeymoon in Spain, Santiago brought Aphrodite to the Echeveria hacienda in Carcar. Suddenly the excitement of Madrid, Barcelona, Toledo, and Sevilla evaporated; the busy Manila society vanished. Gone were the nightly dinners and parties, the promenades at the Luneta, the visits by Aphrodite's multitude of girlfriends. All Aphrodite had were vague fragmented memories and great confusion as she tried to figure out the huge house with false walls and secret doors and hidden staircases and compartments. Twice, she locked herself in a room and couldn't find her way out; she had to shout for help. She couldn't understand the conversations (nor did she care) about hacienda matters; the servants only spoke Ubecan; and out there was sugar cane from one end of the world to the other, a relentless sea of green that rippled when the warm breeze blew, making her seasick, making her weep.

Some people suggested that Aphrodite died because she had no will to live. Her daughter Pilar, born prematurely and whom Aphrodite had never known, displayed more spirit and survived. Pilar was reportedly the spitting image of her mother, with an irresistible smile and large eyes fringed with long eyelashes.

Ines had seen pictures of Aphrodite and she had seen Pilar now and then in Ubec, and Ines never saw the similarity between the two. Aphrodite had a glitzy presence with her European gowns, heavy makeup, and elaborate hairdos; Pilar was a thin ghostlike creature wearing simple school uniforms or dresses—quite plain.

It was the same observation that came to Ines that Friday afternoon when their carriage rolled into the Echeveria hacienda. There, near the end of the dirt road stood Pilar with a group of children under a sprawling acacia tree. She was a toothpick of a girl wearing a pink cotton dress, her long brown hair tied in the back with a matching pink ribbon. Seated on benches eight children listened attentively to her. Pilar widened her eyes (indeed, she had large eyes with long eyelashes) and clapped her hands. "All right, class, catechism next week, at the same time. You can have your juice, but be careful not to break the glasses," she said, pointing to a nearby table with two pitchers and hand painted glasses.

The glasses were exactly like the glassware used by the kindly spinsters of Ines's youth! Something happened to Ines as she watched the children guzzling their juice and running their fingers on the painted images of wild animals—she was whisked back to the May days of her childhood when she and other children drank tamarind juice from the same type of glasses. Oh, how tender the memory was of those beloved glasses with painted zebra, lion, giraffe, and the unforgettable tiger!

Ines, who had been predisposed to disliking Pilar, now felt an unexpected warm feeling toward the skinny girl. Ines watched the children swarm around her as they said their goodbyes. Pilar hugged and kissed them before sending them on their way. Pilar then turned her attention to the three women who were getting out of their carriage. She kissed them on the cheeks, and she addressed them cordially as well— "Lola" to Blanca, and "Tiya" to Ines and Melisande. Linking arms with Blanca whom she knew well, Pilar led them to the house. The girl explained that she was preparing the children of the hacienda workers for their First Confession and First Holy Communion. She spoke in a clear voice, direct and devoid of artifice.

Ines and Melisande exchanged glances—the girl seemed very amiable.

Upstairs in the huge living room, Pilar helped Blanca settle down in a settee. Pointing at nearby chairs, she asked Ines and Melisande to please feel at home.

Ines had known this house from her childhood days but things had changed. The living room seemed more cluttered with elaborate furniture. A side table had a bronze statue that was also new to her. The figure was that of Atlas carrying the world on his shoulders, the sight of which made Ines heave a deep sigh and think of her own burdens.

"I'll call Papa," Pilar said in her crystal-clear voice.

"And your grandmother," said Blanca.

Pilar gave a little curtsey before leaving.

It didn't take long for the three Echeverias to appear—Santiago, Maria Christina, and Pilar. Blanca and Maria Christina embraced each other. These two women had known each other for over forty years. They were not true Ubecans; they came from wealthy merchant families of the Tondo district in Manila, traders of finely embroidered Manton shawls, enormous Sulu pearls, and other goods. As Fate would have it, they married land-rich Ubecans who could trace their genealogy to Spanish roots. The merchant-class Blanca and Maria Christina had initially lacked the polish and confidence of the Old Rich hacienderos. Yanked away from their island of Luzon and transplanted in the isolated haciendas of provincial and what some would call backward Carcar, the two women had clung to each other with pathetic desperation. Huddled together on the settee, they looked like sisters in their muted gray clothes and understated jewelry (daughters of Chinese merchants always thought twice about flaunting their wealth).

A servant girl appeared with drinks and some tortas, and Pilar made sure the tea cart was within reach of the guests.

Afterwards, Pilar sat near her father. The circle of s_x carried on an obligatory chit-chat, even though everyone knew something serious was looming. That was how Ubecans did things. The niceties had to be exchanged. One had to complement the other about their looks, their dress, the house, the curtains, any pleasantry at all. The tête–à–tête had to come to pass. No one ever simply "got to the point."

While the exchange went on, Ines tried to focus on securing the statement first and foremost, but before she had to chance to speak, Santiago said, "Ines, it's good to see you here. It's been a long time since you've visited our home. I never told you, but I'm sorry about Pablo's passing. I apologize I couldn't go to the funeral, I was in Manila."

Ines said nothing; that was water under the bridge; there were now more important matters to deal with.

Santiago sipped his juice before continuing. "I'm glad you've come to your senses, Ines. To tell you the truth I don't need the Miehl, but for old times' sake, I'm willing to get it off your hands. I knew it would be a matter of time before you'd come around and give up the newspaper business. It's not for a woman, certainly. Let me assure you that I will pay you the best price I can—"

It took Ines a few heartbeats before she found her words, "Santiago, you misunderstand. I am not selling the Miehl, not to you nor to anyone else. I am now in charge of *The Ubec Daily*. It will continue."

Santiago looked befuddled. "I see. May I ask why you are here then?"

Quite unexpectedly, Blanca stepped into the conversation. "It's very complicated, Santiago, it has to do with Pilar and Andres. They were together. Just the two of them. Alone."

Maria Christina placed her right hand over her heart. "Blanca here just told me what happened, Santiago. Isn't Carmen supposed to chaperone her at all times? That is why we sent her to Ubec, to watch over Pilar," she said.

Blanca reached out to touch her friend's arm. "Maria

Christina, don't worry; we are here to right this wrong——"

Ines stared at the women. She knew that for Ubecans it was improper for a young couple to be alone unchaperoned. It was considered scandalous. When that happened, the woman's name was as good as dirt, and the family of the "ruined" young women could seek restitution by insisting the couple marry. There was an Ubecan word "pikot" that specifically referred to the entrapment of a man to marry a woman for the purpose of salvaging the young woman's marred reputation. But Ines had always found this custom backward and unsophisticated, and certainly, now, while Andres was in jail, the chief concern should be to get him out. This simply was not the time to be quibbling over social mores.

"Mama, please stop," Ines said. "We are here to get Andres out of jail."

Stunned, Blanca sat back and placed her hand over her mouth, while Maria Christina placed her arm around Blanca in sympathy.

The room was momentarily quiet, until Melisande said, "There is something important that happened. It has to do with the dead priest. *The Light* wrote about it."

Santiago's eyes lit up. "Father Zafra, of course. We ran that issue with Tonying Borja's picture in the front page."

"Your friend Tonying Borja arrested my son and his friends."

"Andres? Now, why would Tonying do that? He told me he wouldn't be surprised if an American or a tenant farmer did it. I asked him if Bishop Logan could have been involved. These Americans and Spaniards are still sniping at each other."

"Bishop Logan?" Ines asked.

"Priests, even bishops, are not all saints, Ines. Just last night, we were talking about the murder of the Rector Provincial in San Pablo Church in Manila. He was stabbed to death in a chapel in the second floor."

"I never heard about this, Santiago. Did this happen last month?" Ines asked.

"No. Back in 1617."

"That was almost three hundred years ago," Ines said, exasperated.

Santiago kept on talking. "Some friars thought of a way to catch the murderer whom they believed was still in the monastery. They laid out the dead Provincial's corpse in the small chapel where they had found the body. They arranged his arm and hand so he was pointing at the door. These friars sat by the doorway and observed the other friars who were obliged to pay their respects to the dead Rector. One friar panicked at the sight of the dead man's accusing finger and ran out of the chapel. He was caught and hanged in the church courtyard."

"What is your point, Santiago?" Ines asked.

"My point is that the religious are not immune to committing murders." He sat back, pleased with himself, wearing an expression that the young Santiago used to have.

Everyone in the room watched them, especially the two mothers, Blanca and Maria Christina. From the time they had been young brides in Carcar, they had been cooking up ways to consolidate their friendship. They had wanted, with great desperation, for Ines and Santiago to get married, and when that did not come to pass, had been bitterly disappointed. Now, the two women felt hope: even though they had failed in marrying off Ines and Santiago, they could marry off Pilar and Andres.

Ines, who had been reminded of her youth and the countless days she had spent with the Echeverias, spoke in a softer voice, "Santiago, I am a widow as you know, and my son is all I have. We can get Andres out quickly if we have a statement. I have traveled from Ubec for this."

"A statement." Santiago sat forward. "From me?"

"No, not from you..." Then taking a deep breath she blurted out, "From your daughter." Ines threw a glance at Pilar who sat quietly with her hands folded on her lap. Blanca and Maria Christina started whispering to each other.

"Pilar? What does she have to do with this?" Santiago asked.

"Andres was with Pilar," Ines said.

"Pilar was with your son? When?" Then—"Is that true hija?" He turned to Pilar who sat still, mute and silent. "Hija, my Pan de Sal, answer me, this is a serious matter." (Pilar's nickname "Pan de Sal" came about because she was the size of a loaf of bread when she was born, and her mother's untimely death caused a lot of salty tears.)

"Santiago, I know it's upsetting," Ines said, "I, too, was upset—"

Blanca interrupted, "I have been trying to say all along that we are here to correct this wrong. To clear Pilar's name, it is necessary for her and Andres to get married—"

Melisande, who had appeared puzzled at the older women's intrusion, smiled. "Marriage sounds too drastic, Maman."

"Mama, everyone, please. The night the priest was murdered, three boys serenaded Pilar in Ubec; two left, and Andres and Pilar were by themselves. We need a statement from Pilar so Andres can prove he did not run off and harm the priest."

All of them turned and stared at Pilar who maintained her quiet composure.

Santiago said, "Hija, my Pan de Sal, is this true? If your mother were alive, she would be very upset."

This time Maria Christina spoke up, "Santiago, I'm having palpitations. My granddaughter's name is ruined. The Echeveria name is ruined. Blanca is right, there is no choice but for the two to get married."

And here the slight seventeen-year-old girl stood up and said, "Papa, Lola, this whole thing sounds like a comedy. First of all, Tiya Ines, I will give you the notarized statement that you need; and second of all, I have something to say to you, Papa and Lola."

Santiago and Maria Christina exchanged glances.

Santiago stammered, "Well ... ah ... Pan de Sal ... go ahead..."

Pilar looked straight into her father's eyes. "Have I ever lied to you?"

Santiago shook his head. "Never, my Pan de Sal, but…"

"And I've never given you any headaches at all, Papa, have I? Ever since I was small, I never wanted to add to your burden of Mama's early death. I've stayed out of your way; I've done my best in everything. Have I done well in school, Papa? Have the nuns ever complained to you?"

Santiago shook and nodded his head, in response to Pilar's questions. The crux of it was that he agreed that Pilar had never given him any problems.

Now Pilar addressed her grandmother, "Lola, I've loved you and obeyed you. I bathed, ate, slept, did chores as you told me to, Lola."

Maria Christina nodded her head.

"Papa, Lola, I love both of you very much, but it's no longer the 1800s, it's now 1909. It's no longer the 'Spanish times'; it's now the 'American times.' Things are different now. We have to move with the times. We can't get stuck with how things were twenty years ago. Now, a girl and boy can be by themselves to talk. That is all we did. Carmen was in the house, Lola. Don't be angry with her, but she was asleep. Andres came over with Mario and Jesus. Jesus played the guitar and they sang a few silly songs. Afterwards, we had something to eat and drink, after which Mario and Jesus left. By this time, the rain had stopped, and Andres and I wanted to see if the stars were out, so we went out to the verandah and looked at the sky. And we talked. And that was all that happened."

"But my Pan de Sal, propriety is a necessity of civilization," Santiago said.

"Papa, what is propriety?" She narrowed her eyes and stared at first, Santiago, then, second, Ines. "You two have been so busy fighting each other, and everyone in Ubec knows about this feud. Andres and I have had to sneak around so you two won't know we're seeing each other. Yes, Papa, I've been seeing Andres for six months now, ever since his class and my class went on a field trip to the leprosarium. We were there to give the lepers clothes and food."

It was so quiet that everyone heard the tinkling of the overhead chandeliers when a breeze blew into the living room.

"Papa, you have done everything you can to hurt the parents of Andres. And Tiya Ines, forgive me, but you have been hostile to my father and me for as long as I can remember. You always look so strict, I've been terrified to greet you."

Ines lowered her head. She felt irritated that this young girl would talk to her in this way, but at the same time she felt shame. Deep in her heart, she had to agree with the girl.

Pilar's voice grew louder as she continued, "You have no idea, either of you that Andres wants to be a lawyer so he can work for real changes in our country. And I, Papa—" she gave her chest a little thump, "I want to be a doctor so I can help our people. I want to help the lepers; I want to help pregnant women and little children. Are you aware, Papa, that half the children of our workers die?"

Then Pilar sat down, looking exhausted. Shaking her head, she said, "No, no, you do not. You don't even know their names. All Andres and I want is to make life better for our people. Can't you see how poor people are compared to us? Have you looked at our workers? At their children? Have you asked yourselves why they are poor and we are not? No, you haven't because you're all too selfish. I don't even know why I have to explain to anyone what Andres and I did that night. You will never understand." And then tears started falling down her cheeks. Her little body quivered as she wept silently for a long time.

No one moved or said a word. Some sparrows that roosted under the eaves of the windows started twittering, and the sound must have brought Pilar back to the room and she took several deep breaths. Using her lace-trimmed tea napkin, she wiped away her tears. Even as she struggled to control herself, she addressed Ines in an honest voice, "Tiya, I will get the document needed on Monday. And Tiya Melisande, I will help you with the carnival. I'm sorry I have to go now, but the nurse at the clinic is expecting me."

And with more grace than an adult woman could muster, the seventeen-year-old girl left the room, leaving everyone mortified.

CHAPTER 18

EN VINO VERITAS

Ubecans were masters at sidestepping anything unpleasant. An agreeable demeanor was always maintained even during the worst of times. Fate was blamed for negative events in one's life; and "mañana" was always said for matters that caused discomfiture.

Everyone knew Ines was peeved at her mother; everyone knew that Blanca was contrite. Still, dinner at the Noel house blithely went on as if nothing eventful had happened. Blanca, Ines, and Melisande politely chatted about how hot the weather was, how crowded the City of Ubec was becoming, and there was the carnival to discuss, who the princesses would be, who might be chosen among them to be carnival queen, et cetera.

But when dessert was served, Ines could not stop herself. "Mama, you shouldn't have—" she began in a stern voice.

Blanca interrupted her. "Maria Christina and I had wanted our families to be one. From the time you and Santiago were infants, we had dreamed ... oh, how we wanted you two to get married—" she broke down crying.

Ines knew about broken dreams; she and Pablo had many dreams that ended with his death. She understood about the dreams that her mother and Maria Christina had, two displaced human beings who had yearned to meld their families

131

together. What fantasies they must have spun when Ines and Santiago were playmates; how frustrated they must have felt when she and Santiago parted ways. And there, hope sprung again with the talk of Andres and Pilar being together, only to have Ines throw cold water at the spontaneous wedding plans that Blanca and Maria Christina had concocted for the young couple. Ines went to her mother and wrapped her arms around her. "It's all right, Mama. Everything will be all right," Ines said.

Later when Blanca had calmed down, and as a token of her contriteness, she offered to accompany Ines and Melisande to the Santa Catalina Church the next day. And as another tangible sign of her contriteness, she handed a bottle of wine to Melisande, saying, "The French consul gave this to me. I prefer Spanish wines. You are French; enjoy it." She kissed Melisande and Ines on the cheeks and slowly trudged upstairs, her footsteps echoing throughout Villa Fatima.

Tired from their journey and the tense afternoon at the Echeveria's house, the two women thanked the servants and retired to their rooms as well.

Later that night however, after the church bells had rung ten o'clock, Melisande knocked on Ines's door. "I can't sleep," she said, "let's try the wine Maman gave me." She held up the opened bottle and two wine glasses.

Ines's exposure to drinking alcohol was limited to tasting fermented coconut sap, rum, and Philippine beer, and she excused herself. "I don't drink."

Melisande insisted, "Come sit with me, and bring a candelabra."

And so in their pin-tucked cotton nightgowns, the two trailed out to the upstairs verandah and sat on two plantation chairs close to a table. Earlier that afternoon, the gardeners had built a bonfire of twigs and leaves so the pungent smoke would drive away mosquitoes. Chinese porcelain pots with flowering plants decorated the verandah. A waxing gibbous moon overhead cast enough moonlight to make the flowers shimmer like bits of gold.

Melisande set the wine and glasses on the table and poured a glass for Ines. "Drink a little bit. It will make you feel better. You will get the statement on Monday and—voila!—problem solved."

"Pilar could still change her mind. I'm still reeling from the tongue-lashing that girl gave us," Ines said, before eyeing her glass suspiciously. The white wine sparkled golden from the moonlight.

"Little sips, that is all. Wine is good for the body and soul." Melisande held the bottle next to the candelabra. "Chateau Hau-Brion 1899—from the Bordeaux region. The French were planting grape vines since the time of the Romans 2,500 years ago." She turned to Ines and said, "Such a long time, Ines. Imagine, the French have been drinking wine for over two thousand years. In France, wine is served with all the meals. Even when I was a little girl, I could tell good from bad wine."

Melisande poured a glass for herself, then she tilted it and studied its contents from different angles. She swirled it and with her finger traced the streaks of wine as they rolled down the side of the glass. "This one is magnificent." She held the glass in front of her face and sniffed. "Hmmm," she said, before taking a sip. "Excellent!" Later she closed her eyes, and in a dreamy voice said, "When this wine was bottled, I was seeing Samir. The wine has aged beautifully. I, on the other hand, simply aged." She giggled at her joke.

A breeze wafted in the faint sweet smell of molasses from the distant Sugar Central. They sighed and settled comfortably into their chairs. From where they sat, they could look out at the sprawling garden with an arbor, trees, and shrubs. It was Melisande who saw it first—"Look, Ines! I've never seen anything like that before. The tree is glowing." She pointed at the ylang-ylang tree that was dotted with flickering fireflies.

"Oh, they still come here!" Ines said, feeling her spirit lift. "The fireflies have always liked that tree. They're beetles, you know. The females hover in the tree and they blink their lights to call the males."

"How magical," Melisande said, in a dreamy voice. "It's like a woman wearing a red dress to attract a man. That is what I do, I make blinking lights for my clients."

Ines sniffed her glass of wine and scrunched her nose. "It smells like vinegar."

"Oh no, this is not vinegar. This is a work of art. Swirl it, then place it under your nose this way. Now inhale and watch out for the fruity bouquet."

Ines did as Melisande told her but she finally shook her head and sipped her wine. "You think of Samir still," Ines said.

Melisande heaved a deep sigh. "The truth is I think of Samir all the time. Even when I am working, even when I have my own life here, I think of him. He is like a ghost beside me— forever beside me. Even though I've come to this end of the earth to escape him, he is still with me." She paused before confessing, "I did not tell you, but before we left for Carcar, I received a letter from my aunt."

"Ah, so that was why you talked about her in the train. What did she say?"

"It was a very long letter; Tante Juliette can go on and on. She wrote about Samir. I had asked her never to mention his name to me again, but she did. I should be angry with her, but instead I'm filled with longing for her, for France, and yes, for Samir."

"It's normal to be lonely."

Both women sighed together, and when they did that, they looked at each other and smiled.

"I will tell you of the first time Samir did a charcoal drawing of me," Melisande said.

"In the train, you said his drawings lacked something."

"Feeling. But he practiced, Ines, and when he thought he was better he asked if he could draw me. I hesitated, but Tante Juliette reminded me of how kind he was to us and to go. She liked him, you know, but then my Tante flirted with all men." Melisande rolled her eyes upward. "In any case, one Sunday I went to his flat. I was nervous, you understand, because he was this important surgeon, and I was a simple dress maker. And I was young, twenty-two years old, a Lyonnais and the Parisians looked down on us."

"Did they? French people are all the same to me."

"Parisians liked to say that people from Lyon were only good at making silk and sausages."

"Some snobbery, then."

"Oh, yes, Parisians are snobs."

"You went to his flat, and what happened?"

"I was very proper. I brought cakes with me, fresh from the patisserie. His flat was up four flights of stairs, narrow, winding, and dark, and I remembered my heart thumping away—up and up I climbed and when I reached the top suddenly light burst through the darkness. It was like magic. I looked up and saw a huge skylight that glowed like the moon. It was beautiful and I was staring at it, when suddenly his apartment door flung open and there he was, holding a metal whisk. He pointed it upward and said he had put the skylight up himself and what did I think of it. I said it was nice."

"'Nice' doesn't sound enthusiastic, Melisande."

Melisande poured more wine into her glass and took a sip. "Samir made a face and said in a withering voice, 'Nice? It's fantastic. Come in and watch how, aside from being one of the best surgeons in Paris, I am also one of the best cooks.'"

Both women laughed.

"Did he really say that?" Ines asked. "Could he cook?"

"Yes and yes. He made omelets, soft and fluffy and warm, and before we sat down to eat, he placed a pat of butter on top of each one. He had warm bread, cheese, raspberries, and delicious strong coffee, which he said came from a Brazilian patient of his. 'Broken wrist,' he said, 'but I also fixed it perfectly.'"

"—Because he's the best surgeon in Paris," Ines said, chuckling.

"*One* of the best. He was more humble about his art. He said he considered the matter of feeling in art. He wanted to see if he could draw me, the Eiffel, and have feeling in his work all at the same time."

"And did he succeed?"

Melisande grew pensive and in a more serious voice continued, "Yes he did. He made a charcoal of me with the Eiffel Tower and paulownia trees heavy with flowers. It was well done, although when I first saw it, I felt embarrassed. He had captured the long hair, the face catching the sun's rays, the expression that seemed lazy and happy, the mouth in a half-smile, but it was that look of longing in the eyes that surprised me. He had drawn a sensuous woman, and I did not know how to feel exactly."

"You were unhappy with his drawing," Ines said.

"Those were his words exactly. He asked what was wrong with it. I started to tell him that it was rendered well, and he became annoyed saying I had said the same thing about his drawing of the Eiffel, and did I mean to say that this picture of me lacked feeling as well. He went on and on."

"He probably did his best, Melisande, and you hurt his feelings a second time."

Melisande winced. "I did not mean to, Ines. I struggled to find the words to make him understand that this time his work was good, that it was excellent in fact, and that it had feeling."

"And he understood that he had succeeded."

"Yes, Samir did," Melisande said. "We had a lovely afternoon together."

"You are still very much in love with him, Melisande," she said, sounding like a doctor delivering bad news.

Melisande studied her glass of wine for a long time. It wasn't until a dog barked when she snapped out of her reverie and said, "Tante Juliette wrote that Samir is now divorced. He married someone else, you know, someone his mother wanted him to marry. But now, it's over."

Ines waited to hear more, but since Melisande remained quiet, Ines said, "So there is divorce in France? There is no such thing here. When you marry, you are married until death do you part. That was why I hated the idea of forcing

Andres and Pilar into marriage."

"Pilar has common sense. I like her courage."

"I thought she was good to the children, but she was somewhat brazen in the way she talked to her elders. I would never have talked to my parents in that way."

Melisande did not reply; she looked up at the moon and said, "Look at that. It'll be full next week. My father used to keep track of how large the moon was for his farming. He planted when the moon was waxing. He said the plantings would grow big with the moon that way."

Crickets were chirping and from somewhere came the occasional cawing of a bird.

Ines, still remembering what Pilar had said that afternoon, asked, "Am I really strict?"

Melisande smiled at Ines. "Are you thinking of what Pilar said? You are what you are. Don't worry about what she said. Her grandmothers were setting her up for a marriage she didn't want. She was trying to save herself."

Ines paused before saying, "I was surprised to hear Pilar say she's afraid of me. Of me? She made it sound like I'm a cruel person. I try to be a decent person. Now it's true that Santiago and I dislike each other, but I didn't like hearing it said like that, especially from that girl."

"Aha!" Melisande said, and like a fortuneteller gazing into a crystal ball, she stared into her glass of wine and said, "You told me that Samir loves me, and it's my turn to let you know that Santiago loves you."

Ines almost dropped her glass. "What a ridiculous thing to say!"

"People say love and hate are two sides of the same coin. This is true. The opposite of love is not hate; it is indifference."

"There was nothing between us, nothing at all. We grew up together—yes, but he was always spoiled—the only son of an only son. We were friends when we were young. That was all, just friends."

"Did you like him? Even a little bit?"

Ines paused before saying, "He was always just Santiago to me, but some of my friends thought he was good-looking. This was a long time ago, before he put on weight. I will admit that he could be personable and charming. He was always good to his parents. But he was very social, far more than I am."

"All right, this is the last time: I think Santiago loved you then, and he loves you still. And I suspect you loved him at some point and may care for him even now. That is all I have to say." Melisande replenished their glasses.

Ines was starting to enjoy the wine. It made her feel dislocated from her body, as if she were looking down at her own self. "Melisande, how can you say that? I loved Pablo, and only him." Her voice softened, "Pablo focused on a few things: his family, his work, and Truth. He believed in Truth and always tried to present the Truth to the world. He said there are no gray areas between Falsehood and Truth, between right and wrong, nor between Good and Evil. 'It is man who creates the gray areas,' he used to say. To Pablo, Truth was as sacred as God. This was something I admired greatly in him."

"I will always remember his kindness to me," Melisande said.

Ines felt her tongue loosen up. "I never understood fully the things Pablo wrote about, but now and then I would find in his writings kernels of truth—crystal clear, like pure raindrops, majestic and simple. When Santiago started attacking Pablo in his paper, I despised him. His spiteful editorials had hurt an honorable man. If you put together all of Santiago's goodness, it would fit a thimble, while Pablo's would have filled a lake."

"It is possible to love more than one person. I believe that," Melisande said. "There was a boy Etienne whom I loved when I was very young, and then there was Samir. The capacity to love is infinite."

By this time, Ines was experiencing a nice warm feeling, a sense of freedom that was new to her. "Tell me more about your aunt's letter. When she wrote that Samir is divorced, does she mean he is free to marry you now?"

"Yes, I'm afraid that's what she was really saying. She says he loves me still."

"You have just said you cannot forget him. What will you do?"

Melisande shook her head. "I don't know, Ines. I've made a life in Ubec; I'm happy here. What if I give up this life for him and he hurt me again as he did?" She turned to Ines. "What would you do, if you were me?"

Ines said, "Well, as you know, I am very strict, so I would hang on to the hurt he gave me and leave him to suffer in his hell." She maintained a serious expression even as she downed her drink.

Melisande had to look at Ines carefully before she said. "Ines, you're drunk!"

"Is this what being drunk is? I can think very clearly now. No wonder people drink." Ines refilled her glass.

They both laughed.

Later Melisande said, "Tante Juliette said he has suffered a lot."

"He probably deserves to suffer, Melisande."

"If you were in my place would you write to him?"

Ines shook her head. "Never! When it's over, it should be over."

"I tried, but it's not over."

"He should write you at least."

"He doesn't know where I am exactly."

"You can tell your aunt to let him know."

"I could do that, but I'm not sure I want to see him nor hear from him again."

"Are you afraid?"

"Yes, I am. It's difficult to love someone too much. After Samir, I learned not to surrender my heart completely. It's much easier this way."

They were silent again as they listened to the church bells ringing midnight.

When the bells stopped, Ines said, "Melisande?"

"Yes?"

She hesitated before blurting out, as if in confession. "I will tell you a secret. One summer night when I was fifteen, we were playing hide and seek here. It happened that Santiago and I hid behind the clump of coconut trees." Ines stopped, unable to continue.

"Did something happen?" asked Melisande.

Ines nodded. "Yes. I hugged the trunk of the coconut tree so I would not be seen. He was behind me. We were very close together, then something happened—and suddenly we were no longer like brother and sister. I turned and whispered, 'Santiago,'—but he kissed me on the lips. I am ashamed to say this—his lips were soft and moist, and I enjoyed the kiss. I couldn't sleep all night and I wondered how things would be between us the next day. But when morning came, Santiago acted as if nothing had happened. He made me very angry."

"Ines, I like what I do because I draw the design, I make the pattern, I cut the cloth, and it is all quite simple. Matters of the heart are very complicated."

"I was furious! The kiss was important to me, but it wasn't to him."

"Two sides of the same coin," Melisande said, smiling.

"Maybe I liked Santiago a little bit when I was very young. But I loved Pablo when I was a woman. I love him still."

The two women became quiet again until Ines broke the silence. "Melisande, I've changed my mind. I think you should go to Samir."

"I don't know what to do."

"Life is short, Melisande. Look at Pablo—he was with us, and now he's gone," Ines said.

"My aunt said the same thing. She said that in the end we are all going to end up in a cemetery somewhere."

"Will you write to Samir?"

"I'm afraid, Ines."

"I never thought you'd be afraid. You left your home; you made a new life here. You are very brave. I could never have done what you did," Ines said.

"You would, if you had to save yourself."

"Melisande, I know what it's like to be afraid. When I lost my babies, I was afraid. When Pablo died and even now, I'm afraid."

"I know."

"Melisande, the world is spinning."

"It's the wine. Stop drinking and let's go to bed. When your head is clear, I'll show you my Tante Juliette's letter."

CHAPTER 19

JULIETTE'S LETTER

March 19, 1909

My dear Melisande,

I didn't tell you but after you left, I felt a longing to return to Lyon. It was a peculiar restlessness that grew in me, a melancholia for what had been, a yearning for answers to questions still unformed in my head, and I wanted to see your parents' graves. So last August, I closed the shop and took the train to Dardilly.

I stayed in our old farm house—you remember it of course. Your uncle and his wife put me up in the same room I had shared with your mother when we were children and fought over who got what side of the bed. It was good to be back, to walk through the familiar rooms, to run my hand on the hundred-year-old wood panels on the walls, and to feel the warmth of the morning fire from the stone fireplace. I shed my "Parisian" ways and dressed in simple farm clothing. I slept late, took walks, and visited the school, the butcher shop, the bakery, the flower shop—the haunts of my youth. At night my siblings and their spouses brought me to bouchons to drink wine and eat andouillette, duck pate, liver, tripe, all that rich food that we grew up on.

Once, we visited a quiet tributary of the Rhone where

we used to go as children, and now as grownups we waded in the river to catch frogs, slipping and falling as we did so. What joy to be an innocent again! We also went to the Vieux Lyon to visit some friends of our parents; they remembered us still. And we listened enraptured to their stories about them and us when we were babies and children. It was wonderful!

My brother, who had once considered becoming a priest, brought me to Ars to visit the shrine of the blessed priest, Jean-Marie Vianney, whose incorrupt body was kept in a glass-covered tomb on top of the altar. It was a new experience to be in a church again. I stared in awe at the stained glass windows that glistened like jewels—emerald green, ruby red, topaz yellow, primary colors muted by the dust of ages— and I felt as if I were in the center of a kaleidoscope. I felt engulfed by the rainbow itself.

Some of the pilgrims there were cripples with canes, and I remembered that April day when I broke my leg, and how that accident set you on another course of your life. How strange, is it not, that one incident like that can alter one's life drastically? If we had not delivered the dresses that day, and the horse had not reared, and I had not fallen and broken my leg, would our lives have been different? Would your life be different, my dearest niece?

My brother urged me to pray, and to my surprise, halfway through the chaplet, I found myself weeping. My mind filled with memories of my life in Dardilly as a simple farm girl, as a girl in love with your father, as a broken-hearted young woman who fled to Paris. Like you, I had to leave, so I would not destroy myself, so I could continue surviving. I understand you completely, Melisande, I know why you had to take that ship and travel as far away as you could.

I cried for a long time in that church, there beside my brother where I was completely safe. It had been so long since I'd been home. I had exiled myself because your father had chosen your mother, and even after they died, I continued my self-exile, away from the comforting arms of relatives who loved me no matter what.

I did not have the courage to visit your parents' graves until shortly before my return to Paris. Soon after the roosters finished their morning crowing, with flowers in my hands, I set out to the cemetery. It had been decades since I'd been there and I was surprised at how vast it actually was. I walked past the towering angel that marked the common gravesite of the plague victims to your father's family burial plot, and there I saw their names side by side—the two who had forged me into the person I am today—there they were, reduced to bone and dust, silent at last.

I lay the flowers in front of their markers and I ran my hand over their engraved names, and the sadness of the cemetery seeped into my bones, until I felt as if I were one of the dead myself. For decades I had been stuck back in time, when the small triangle of your father, mother, and I had danced our minuet of laughter and loving, of feuding and hating. There in that forlorn cemetery I finally cursed them, I blessed them, I begged for their forgiveness, and I also showered them with my forgiveness.

Something else happened to me there in that lonely cemetery in Dardilly—I saw how very small each one of us is in relation to the world—our love affairs, problems and all of life's drama that consume our energies, no more than an imperceptible drop in this vast universe and eternity. That cemetery made me feel infinitesimal, but also free.

How can I make you understand, dearest Melisande, that the drama you shared with Samir is a miniscule dot and so you must not be so consumed nor tormented by it? Not anymore, dearest niece. It is over. He made his mistake and paid dearly for it.

But you need to know that after you left, he continued to stop by the shop, once a month like clockwork, and for the longest time I was angry at him for what he did to you. He knew that, but he would come by anyway to ask about you. Sometimes we would sit together in silence in the rocking chairs by the window, while Paris blinked and blared outside. It was as if words would only fail us. And indeed words could never heal the hurt that smoldered within.

All these years, Melisande, and he never stopped visiting regularly to ask about you.

My anger towards him diminished when I saw how broken he was without you. It was not an act. His face became drawn and tight, and his blunderbuss waned. He stopped being funny; he was no longer so cocky. It was this cockiness that had endeared him to me, you know—a young, cocky, handsome man is very amusing. He slowly turned into a somber, quiet, brooding man, which gave him an aura of mystery, and in a way made him more interesting. But the quality of his being had changed—the lightness had left him, and a heaviness had taken its place.

But despite his disintegration, I could not offer him any sympathy. I agree with you completely that it was all his fault. He had created the hell that you and he found yourselves in, a hell that I too experienced because of my love for both of you. He did not have to obey his mother—he should not have. Marriage is not a game. It is binding and the entanglements are complicated. Whatever possessed him to think he could have a wife and you, at the same time?

I saw his mother over a year ago at the patisserie on Bouquet. Yasmin is still beautiful— hair dark and luxuriant, skin clear, figure still nice, although she was starting to get thick around the middle. Samir was there with his little boy, Didier, a spitting image of Samir, very charming. When Samir greeted me, Yasmin stood back, with what I first took as a haughty expression, but when I greeted her, I detected fear in her eyes.

I did not ask about Samir's wife, but a few weeks later, Samir stopped by and told me that she had left them. She disliked France and the French; she wasn't fond of his mother even though Yasmin was Algerian like herself; and she wanted to return to her parents' home in Algeria. She did not even want custody of her son at all.

What an irresponsible and heartless woman.

Yasmin has learned a bitter lesson and no longer involves herself with Samir's personal life. She has Didier to occupy her time.

I know you had begged me never to mention Samir's name to you, and I have honored this request for years, but I thought you should know all this, ma cherie.

He stopped by the other night. It was late; he had just come from the hospital. He brought a bag of roasted chestnuts, steaming hot, comforting for that chilly night. I opened a bottle of bernache and we sat down and ate and drank. He informed me that the divorce between him and his wife has been granted. He heaved a sigh of relief. We toasted his new freedom. And as always he asked in a voice filled with longing: "Tell me, what news about Melisande?"

I don't know what you will want to do upon hearing this, but remember that in the end, after all of our life's drama, we only have the implacably lonely cemetery like the one in Dardilly waiting for us. It is good to enjoy life to the fullest, while one is alive.

Love always,

Tante Juliette

CHAPTER 20

THE BABAYLANES

I only have a vague recollection of Father Zafra in Carcar," Blanca said, in response to Ines's question about him. "I don't keep up with what's going on at Santa Catalina, but you can ask some people at the church about him."

The three women found Santa Catalina Church dark and cool and smelling of incense. Just a bit of sunlight filtered through the glass stained windows, which were covered with centuries of smoke and grime. Like the other churches built by the Augustinians, Santa Catalina was made of stone and was massive. It was early in the morning of Good Friday, and no one else was present.

"Lent is a good time to pray to our Lady of Dolours," Blanca said as they walked down the aisle. Blanca pointed out the statues of saints and said a few words about them: San Antonio, who will find lost items; Santa Clara, who will help one find a husband or wife; San Jose who will help sell property, and so on until she arrived at the statue of Mother Mary who was clad in purple, her heart pierced with seven swords. Mary's shoulders drooped; tears glistened on her cheeks.

"Imagine the pain." Blanca swept her fingers over Mary's heart.

"Maman," Melisande whispered, "why are those swords sticking into her heart?"

147

Ines knew what her mother would say next. Every Lenten season, Blanca had brought her to visit this statue.

"Each one has a story," Blanca began, "the first sword pierced Mary's heart when Simeon predicted that one day her Son Jesus would die. The second happened when King Herod ordered all male infants under the age of two killed. And that one, the third, when Jesus disappeared in the temple."

"It is very sad," Melisande said. "We have the same statue of the Virgin in France, but I didn't understand what the swords meant. I sometimes went to church with my Grandmere."

"You should have gone to church more often, Melisande."

"My own Maman didn't go regularly. In France, the church and state are separate. The priests there do not control the people as the priests here do."

"How so, Melisande?" Blanca said.

"The church had become too rich, and the revolutionaries of 1789 closed the churches and took away all church property from the priests."

"The Americans have also taken away the Friar Lands from the religious orders."

"Our revolutionaries were more severe, Maman. There was actual fighting between the church and state; many priests were imprisoned or executed. Napoleon later negotiated with the Pope and officials and the church was allowed to function under the state's authority."

"The priests here are very powerful," Blanca said.

"In France, they do not interfere too much with our lives. It is different, Maman. And what about this sword?"

"That's the fourth one," Blanca said, "It pierced Mary's heart when she and the other women of Jerusalem met Jesus on the Via Dolorosa as He was carrying His Cross." She paused and sighed. "Melisande, every mother has experienced swords like these in her heart."

Ines closed her eyes. She could feel the sharp pricking of the swords in her own heart. There was the one when Pablo died; there were the two swords for the babies she lost, and the newest sword was when her son was arrested. She prayed that Andres was fine.

"Now, let us kneel," Blanca said as she got down on her knees. "Melisande, we kneel out of respect because the fifth sword pierced Mary's heart when her son was crucified on Golgotha. Her only Son whom she loved was mocked as the King of the Jews; His own heart was pierced and blood and water gushed out of His wound."

Blanca went on to talk about the sixth sorrow representing the taking down of Jesus from the Cross in the presence of John the Beloved and the Tres Marias (Mary the Mother of Jesus, Mary Magdalene, and Mary of Bethany).

"The last sorrow was Christ's burial in a borrowed tomb," Blanca said. "Very few of His friends remained to bury Him before sunset and the beginning of Sabbath." She nudged Ines. "Are you listening? Let us ask our Mother Mary to take care of Andres."

"Yes, Mama," Ines said softly. She was glad the church was dim so no one could see the tears welling in her eyes. Her mind was filled with worries: that Andres was not eating properly, that he did not have a comfortable cot to sleep on, that Pilar Echeveria would change her mind about providing the notarized statement, that Andres's legal case could drag on for years, and worst of all, that he could be charged guilty of murder.

The shadowy figure of a man near the altar interrupted her thoughts. She rose quietly and approached him. "Let me finish this and I'll help you," he said as he lit the candles on the candelabra. He was old and bent with sunken cheeks and an expression of one who has known poverty all his life. He was chewing on betel nut and his mouth and few remaining teeth were stained red. When he gave Ines his attention, she asked, "I need information about a Spanish priest who had worked in this church. Do you remember Father Nicolas Zafra?"

Vicente was his name and he said, "I've worked here for almost forty years, but it will be better if you look at the list of priests." He led Ines to a hallway with a huge framed document on the wall with names done in elaborate calligraphy. "These were the pastors of Santa Catalina," he said.

By this time, Blanca and Melisande had joined Ines and the three of them studied the list. "There he is," Melisande said, pointing at Father Nicolas Zafra's name. Beside his name were the years he had served in Santa Catalina: 1893-1896.

"He was here for just three years, Ines, no wonder I hardly remembered him here," Blanca said.

Ines looked thoughtful when she said, "Bishop Logan said Father Zafra was in Ubec in 1902, so the priest must have been in Iloilo between his assignments in Carcar and Ubec. But where was he before Carcar?"

"Spain, of course. He was Spanish," Blanca said.

"No, Mama, according to the bishop he finished working in Sevilla in 1884. So there are some years between 1884 and 1893 that are unaccounted for?" Ines replied.

"I don't understand you, Ines. This love you have for numbers makes me crazy," Blanca said.

Melisande said, "You know, Ines, one of my clients mentioned that Father Zafra was in Mexico. Her husband had assets in a silver mine there ... let me see if I remember the city ... Guanajuato, I believe."

"You didn't tell me that before," Ines said.

"I didn't think it was important."

Ines turned to Vicente who had stood behind them quietly chewing his beetle nut. "Please tell me what you know about Father Zafra."

Vicente shifted his weight. "The church will be filling up, Ma'am. I have work to do." He started to walk away.

Ines reached out and touched his arm. "No, wait, it's very important. My son is in trouble."

"Your son?" he said, as he fixed his eyes on Ines. "How old is your boy?"

"Nineteen. It's a long story, but I need to know the truth about Father Zafra," Ines said.

"The truth ... who knows what the truth really is?

Some say Father Zafra was good, some say he was evil … who knows, except God," Vicente muttered, but he proceeded to tell the story of Father Zafra, young at the time and looking more like an actor than a priest, with his fair looks and eyes that changed from green to yellowish with the time of day, just like the cat's eyes. Father Zafra arrived to replace the parish priest in Carcar who had died in his sleep, a no-good priest who had stolen and sold the church's gold monstrance. Father Zafra had ministered not only the people of Carcar but others who lived in the surrounding areas, mountaineers who walked three hours just to hear Mass.

Things had started out fine. Father Zafra had performed his priestly duties and he had even asked a doctor to visit weekly to work in the clinic. The place was crowded with people with eye infection, those with goiter, sick babies, pregnant women, cripples—they all came. It looked like a scene from the bible when the sick would go after Jesus. Later, Father Zafra started a feeding program, and by this time people started to look at him as if he were Christ himself.

"In the beginning I also thought he was a saint," Vicente said, "But saints can be found only in heaven." Vicente continued his account about Father Zafra hiring a laundrywoman named Celestina, a mother with two children. Celestina used to pick up the dirty laundry in the rectory, walking softly from room to room, with a huge basket on her head. She spent all day at the creek, soaking, washing, paddling the clothes, hanging them to dry, and in the afternoon and even at night, she ironed the clothes.

"But then things became strange. Celestina skulked about with her head bowed, not talking to anyone. The children who used to run around the church grounds became quiet, invisible. Something happened … something happened…" Vicente said.

"Is Celestina still around? Where can I find her?" Ines said.

"She's dead, but her daughter is around. Kidlat lives at the foot of the mountains."

"The healer?" Blanca said.

Vicente said yes and Blanca addressed Ines, "I know where Kidlat lives. We can go there."

Outside the church, their carriage driver resisted going to Kidlat's place, saying it was haunted and occupied by witches. "Don't be foolish," Blanca said. "They're just women. They live there to be safe from soft-minded superstitious people."

Turning her attention to Melisande, Blanca continued, "Kidlat is a babaylan, a priestess. They say she can transform into a dog or bird, and that she can fly, even become invisible. People say she can cause deaths and create potions to steal a man or woman's hearts. This is all nonsense. I see her for my headaches, and she uses herbs, oils, sometimes rocks to massage me, to make me feel better."

"Her name is unusual, Maman."

"Kidlat means 'lightning,' Melisande. It is a good name for a strong woman like her."

Ines explained further, "During the time of the Spanish, the babaylanes were the healers and leaders. The Spaniards went after them, accusing them of being witches, and the women had to hide. There aren't too many babaylanes left, but they're still around."

"It's interesting because this happened in Europe as well," Melisande said. "One of the tests to determine if the woman was a witch or not was to tie her hands and ankles, then throw her in the water. If she floated, she did so with the help of the devil and she had to be killed. If she sank, she was not a witch. There was no way of winning, Maman, no way at all. In either case, the accused died."

Blanca said, "Ubecans believe in many supernatural creatures that live right here alongside people. Our witch stalks pregnant women, and it has a long tongue that can suck out fetuses from their mothers' bellies. There is the agta, who takes the shape of a black giant and who lives in ancient trees. The manananggal is another strange creature that can detach its head and entrails and float about in the night sky."

"They sound scary, Maman, but also fascinating."

"Kidlat is not a witch so don't be afraid. You will enjoy her place. She has a lot of birds."

They continued chatting until the sugar cane fields vanished and in its place stood tall trees and thick bushes. The air turned cooler and not too long after, they heard the raucous sounds of birds singing and cawing.

"Are those her birds, Maman?" Melisande asked, turning her head here and there to locate where the racket came from. "There are many of them."

"The mountaineers give her the birds. You see, when the American loggers and plantation owners clear the land, the animals become displaced. They have nowhere to go: their food supply has been disrupted, some of them are hurt, the young are abandoned by their mothers."

"It is such a shame, Maman. It is sad to think of the animals driven away from their homes. They would feel just like us, lost and afraid."

The bird sounds grew louder as they approached Kidlat's house. And when the women alighted from the carriage, there beyond the dirt road was the source of that cacophony of twittering and singing—a huge aviary filled with birds of all colors and sizes. Ines and Melisande stood transfixed at the sight of the riotous birds.

A woman spoke: "The white one is a heron, and that one back there is an egret, and the black one near you is a mynah." Her voice was soft and melodious. "That trogon had a broken wing, and I set it with bamboo splints. It can now fly, but it will not leave this place."

It was Kidlat, with a child straddled on one hip. She was unlike any other woman Ines had seen. She had pure white hair like strands of light. Her eyebrows were also light in color as to give the impression that she had none. Her skin was translucent and unlined. She wore a wraparound sarong with her breasts exposed. She looked ethereal.

Kidlat greeted the women and pointed out the door to

the aviary that was gaping open. "They are free to go, but they like it here. I close it at night to protect them from the monitor lizards. There are too many birds, and if you want some, I'll send some home with you."

The healer asked Blanca to proceed to her house, while she led Ines and Melisande to a shady clearing with some bamboo chairs under some mango trees. In the distance, a thick hedge of heliconias heavy with their bird-like flowers kept the forest at bay. Some turtles toddled about on the ground, and up above, a monkey rested on a branch and watched them.

"He will not hurt you, but be careful, he is naughty and can steal your things. Rest here while I take care of Señora Blanca. It has been a long time since I've seen her. We'll have lunch afterwards." And looking at Ines directly, she added, "Do not worry."

When Kidlat left, Melisande said, "She knew you have been worried, Ines." Her eyes glinting with excitement. Ines had settled into a chair while Melisande guarded her things from the monkey that was now making cooing sounds.

"It was not magic, Melisande. One just has to look at my face." Ines ran her fingers over her forehead.

"It is true, you worry too much. And when you are worried you are either very quiet or very busy." She laughed, then pointing at the house, added, "Oh, look there are other women in the kitchen."

Ines caught sight of four young women talking and laughing as they worked. "They don't look like witches," Ines said.

"No, they don't," Melisande said. "They are lovely. There are no men?"

"I don't see any."

"But they have children. They are like Amazonian women," Melisande said.

When the monkey swung to a lower branch, Melisande moved away, toward the aviary, where she resumed playing with the birds. "Ines, these birds are wonderful. Samir liked birds. He had a birdfeeder for wild birds. He hung it right at the edge of his balcony. In the middle of Paris, can you imagine?"

"Are there birds like these in Paris?"

"We have sparrows, starlings too, blackbirds and a lot of pigeons. But I've never seen some of these birds before, like this black one with a bit of yellow on his collar. He is very handsome. His black feathers have undertones of peacock green—such an elegant bird."

Then to their surprise, the bird said, "Hello."

"Ines, did you hear that? It talks! Like a parrot!" Melisande poked her fingers through the aviary. "Hello, say hello again."

Not only did the bird talk once again, but it allowed Melisande to touch him.

"Oh Ines, I want him. The healer said she will give us birds," Melisande said. "What do you think? He'll remind me of Samir."

"I thought you wanted to forget Samir."

Melisande gave a little pout. "Oh, Ines, you simply don't understand matters of the heart. I'll put him near the doorway so he can greet the clients, and at night I'll bring him to my bedroom."

"You don't need a bird to greet your clients, Melisande."

"I know that, Ines, but I want him. I get lonely at the end of the day."

***

After lunch, when the other babaylanes rolled out mats so the children could take their siesta, Kidlat led her guests out to the sun-dappled benches under the mango trees. "Ines, your mother says you need help. What can I do for you?" she said.

"I am looking for information about a priest, Father Zafra."

"Father Zafra … I knew him fifteen, sixteen years ago.

He must be in his mid-fifties now," Kidlat said.

"He is dead. His body was just found in a creek in Ubec."

Kidlat lowered her head and was still for a long time. When she spoke, her voice was strained. "I have tried to forget but now and again the memories come back." She swept her hands at her house and nearby forest. "I surround myself with beauty and life, hoping to get rid of this thing inside me that is the opposite of all this, but the healer cannot heal herself. I will tell you what I know about Father Zafra."

Kidlat spoke of her grandmother, a famous babaylan, who was arrested one day by the soldiers for being a "witch." Kidlat, her younger brother, and mother were left on their own. Her mother, who was not as resourceful as the grandmother, had a difficult time making ends meet. They went hungry; they eventually lost their home, and they were grateful when someone from Santa Catalina church offered her mother work as the laundry woman.

Kidlat's family moved into the servants' quarters of Santa Catalina, and for a while life was good. They now had food; they had a place to live in; the children could play in the church grounds; and the employer Father Zafra would even give them sweets and little toys.

It didn't take long for their bit of paradise to change. "My brother and I started having nightmares," Kidlat said. "We had the same dream about being chased by a scary creature. We fled from this monster, but it ran faster than us. In my dreams, just as the creature was about to catch me, I would suddenly fly. My brother, however, did not fly in his dream. He woke up screaming just as the creature caught up with him. I never saw the face of this creature, but my brother saw Father Zafra in his dream."

When Kidlat's mother learned about the nightmares, she kept Kidlat away from the church and rectory. The girl was kept a virtual prisoner in their room.

"What I remember most of all was being in that small,

dark, and airless space," Kidlat said. "The only light came from wooden slats that covered the windows. One afternoon, my brother disappeared and my mother told me he had ran away. Not too long after, my mother took me away from that room, away from that church, and we went to some babaylanes who helped us."

When Kidlat finished her story, the women had become somber. "I am sorry for upsetting you," she said. "Come, let us cleanse our spirits."

The women followed her as if in a daze. The babaylan took them on a walk through the forest where she pointed out the plants that she used—ginger, moringa, hibiscus, charantia; they all had healing properties. After their walk, Kidlat took care of the birds. "It is a hot day, I have to make sure the birds have water," she said.

Near the aviary, Melisande brought up the matter of the mynah that she liked. "Your birds are all magnificent. I love them so ... they bring back happy memories ... but there is one that is special. He is black, with a yellow collar; he is very beautiful."

"Do you want it?" Kidlat asked.

Blanca said, "She wants the bird, Kidlat."

Melisande beamed. "Oh, yes, I like him very much."

Kidlat studied Melisande carefully before saying, "He will be happy with you. You can have this one, and I will find a mate for him so he won't be lonely. It'll be a good-looking one."

"Two birds, Ines!" Melisande said, sounding like a happy child. "I can have a big cage made for them, a nice wrought iron one with scrolls all over. Maybe they'll have babies. I'll have a family of mynah birds."

Kidlat added, "He eats fruits and insects. He needs water of course. Another important thing is that you mustn't leave him alone or else he'll die from loneliness."

"He'll die from loneliness"—Ines had heard those words before. "My lawyer said almost exactly the same thing about his bird. It talks, but all it says is 'I remember.'"

"Was it missing a foot?" Kidlat asked.

Ines stared at her, incredulous.

"That bird came from me. A man from the city got him. He had a sad story about his son wanting a mynah but he had refused because the boy was too young. His son died and the man regretted he hadn't gotten him what he wanted."

"Do you remember his name?" Ines asked.

"There are many people who come here and I don't remember all their names. But I remember that he said his wife worked for the parish priest in Ubec."

The somber scene of Attorney Vargas and the black bird in his office was in the mind of Ines when they said their goodbyes to Kidlat and the other babaylanes.

***

In the carriage, Ines said, "Now I understand."

Melisande cast a questioning glance at her.

"Did you hear what Kidlat said? She said Father Zafra came from Manila."

Melisande thought for a moment then said, "Yes, she did. I heard her say that before she talked about what happened to them. I was worried about the children. I wonder what happened to her brother."

Ines continued, "Melisande, you said your client saw him in Mexico. Father Zafra served in six parishes. Six: Sevilla, the silver town in Mexico, Manila, Carcar, Iloilo, and finally Ubec."

"Guanajuato is the city in Mexico, Ines. Yes, six. In France, if a priest is moved around like that, it meant he has been doing something bad," Melisande said.

Blanca spoke up, "It's clear to me that Father Zafra was doing something wrong. Three years in Carcar ... these priests usually spend their entire lifetime in one place. It's no wonder Kidlat's brother ran away."

"It's a terrible thought, Maman, but in other words, it's

possible that Father Zafra abused the boys. After he was discovered, his superiors transferred him to another place. That is what 'six parishes' means." Melisande's voice rose in anger.

"There's another thing that bothers me," Ines said. "Attorney Vargas got his strange bird from Kidlat. I wonder if he had come here to get more information about Father Zafra."

"If he did, then he knows," Melisande said.

Ines said, "Oh, Mama, I have to get back to Ubec right away!"

PART IV

CHAPTER 21

JOSE VARGAS AND THE CANE

He had told her, "Trust me, Mrs. Maceda, when I tell you that I will do everything I can to free your son." His words echoed in his mind as weariness washed over him. It was a lie; he would do everything in his power to keep Andres Maceda in jail.

In the darkness of his office, he waited until he heard the front door close behind Ines. He had grown accustomed to this womb-like gloom; he could lie or sit still for hours, his mind flipping back and forth to the past and what could have been until his brain was in such chaos and his head felt like bursting. When he was certain she was gone, he went to his cabinet and opened the bottom drawer. He rifled through documents, then sucked in his breath as he reached underneath. His fingers fanned out, groping, until—there, tucked away was the cane that he had used to strike Father Zafra. Jose had intended to get rid of it, but something prevented him from doing so. Even during that moment of panic and horror, his lawyer's mind had realized the cane might be useful and he had washed off the blood and hid it. A shakiness gripped his bones and he took several deep breaths to steady himself. He had killed a man and according to the law deserved to die.

He pulled out the cane and carefully brought it to his desk. He laid it down onsome folders. As he moved, the meager light from the window shone on the ivory handle and he paused to study it. It was carved in the shape of a duck's head. The shaft was made of dark ebony wood inlaid with mother of pearl on the upper part, near the thick silver collar. He wondered where the priest had gotten the cane and how long he had owned it. Jose ran his forefinger over the mother of pearl that gleamed bone-white against the dark wood. The cane was handsome. Those priests lived well, he thought, and his mind wandered to the huge tracts of Friar Lands which were wrangled over in courts.

The tolling of the church bells made the bird squawk and Jose stirred. "Five o'clock," he said. "She'll be on the train to Carcar, and there, who knows?—She may learn the truth." He cocked his ear and listened to the stacking of papers, closing of drawers and windows. When he heard footsteps approaching his office, his heart beat faster and he reached for the cane. His hand wrapped tightly around the shaft. He knew who it was, but he kept still until the sounds stopped—the person on the other side was listening too. "Good night, Attorney," a woman said in a throaty voice. It was his secretary, Miriam.

One afternoon, after Fernanda had left him, Miriam had surprised him by entering his office without knocking. There was uninvited familiarity in the way she started tidying up his office. She had, in fact, been building up this intimacy. She started by bringing him a thermos of hot chocolate in the mornings and later, she handled the payment of personal bills, not just office ones. She even took care of his laundry and gave instructions to his maid to hang them in his armoire. He had noticed, but his life was in such turbulence that it was a relief to have someone handle these mundane matters.

That afternoon a lifetime ago, he had watched Miriam pick up a rotten banana from the bird cage. When she had proceeded to move some files which were stacked up on the floor, he had said, "I'll take care of that." His tone had not been unkind.

"There are too many files scattered about, let me help you." She paused. "Jose—" she said, "you look tired." The soft rustling of her skirt and the scent of her perfume reminded him of Fernanda. Miriam was a large woman with ample breasts, unlike his wife, but Miriam was not unattractive. She had an earthy quality, like the models in European paintings, huge women with generous buttocks.

"You haven't been eating. If you like, I can cook supper for you. You should rest and not worry too much." Her voice had dropped to a sonorous whisper. He was mesmerized. He felt as if he were rocked by waves in the sea. Her hand brushed his arm tentatively. He did not pull away and soon both her hands were on his shoulders. "You're very tight," she had said, as she proceeded to massage him.

The kneading of his tight muscles was relaxing, and he gave an involuntary sigh. He rolled his head slightly. She continued pressing his flesh. He was gone, for a spell, until she whispered, "I could stay, if you want me to."

Someone had told him that a needy woman was good in bed. He had been tempted—what man wouldn't have been? But he knew that would have been wrong. He reached up to touch both of her hands, stopping her. "Miriam, it will not work," he said. And when he saw the pain on her face, he added, "It's because of me, not you."

He had thought she might quit, but she didn't. But never again did she enter his office without knocking.

Now, as he stared at the cane, he called out, "Good night, Miriam. See you on Monday." His voice seemed too loud and he wondered if she sensed something was wrong.

She had been the fat neighbor child who smelled of malt beer, and who used to play with him. He had suffered many whippings from her tattling. But it was his mother who had told him that Miriam needed a job. He hired her and to his relief, Miriam was a good worker. Her childish malice had turned into a moroseness that fortunately didn't affect her work performance. He didn't mind; he had learned about the brokenness of people. He and Fernanda had shattered like glass with Danilo's death. Fragmented into infinitesimal pieces. Barely human.

Miriam's heavy footsteps faded toward the front door. The door opened and slammed shut.

He was alone.

Alone with the priest's cane.

The "incident" bubbled up in his mind again—the rain, the noisy starlings, the dog howling, the priest threatening him with the cane; his grabbing the cane from him—and he had struck him, not once but several times. That had not been his intention, but the deed was done.

Now, he had no choice.

He picked up the cane—how cool it felt. A chill swept up his spine. From the corner of his office, the mynah bird flapped his wings and started talking, "I remember ... I remember."

"Yes, Yuyoy," he said, rising from his chair, "you and I both remember. You are not alone, now be quiet."

It seemed to him that he and the bird were becoming more alike—dark, somber, and ... he couldn't quite find the word—stuck? The bird was obsessed with its two words, while he was consumed by what had happened: the death of Danilo, Fernanda leaving him, and then the matter of the priest. Could he not escape this hell?

As if understanding him, the mynah ruffled its feathers and became still and silent, like a statue.

But he had to move; he had to act. He could not sit in his office waiting for Police Inspector Borja to put two and two together and arrest him for killing Father Zafra. Once, he had seen a postcard of a man in Bilibid prison being garroted. Five officials surrounded the shirtless man who was seated and who was slowly being choked to death. The postcard had been published by the American company, Philco. Americans amused him at times. They printed postcards of what they considered an exotic death execution, but at the same time, they banned garroting and used a firing squad instead. There were no postcards of deaths by firing squad. Garroting to him seemed to have more poetry than the rude shots fired at a condemned man—perhaps the slow dying allowed one to find the boundary between life and death. Perhaps it allowed one to review one's life before dying. But either way ended up with a dead man. And he did not want to be that man. He could not.

Holding the cane in his left hand, he paused at the open doorway. His breathing grew rapid. He peered down the hall before walking towards Andres's office. In his heart, he still believed Fernanda would return and they could try to be happy again. Perhaps they could move far away, where no one knew them, and start over. They could have another child. A boy, perhaps. Although a girl would do. They could be joyful still, he was certain of it. Even though their son was dead and he had done the unthinkable to her, they could still find a way. As long as there was life, there had to be hope.

He used the cane to push open the door and was impressed once again at how small his apprentice's office was. Before he hired Andres, it had been a supply room. Jose had it cleared and painted, and he filled it with a desk, a filing cabinet, and a table with his old Underwood typewriter. It wasn't such a bad office for an apprentice. Generally, apprentices shared space with secretaries and clerks; but he had seen that Andres Maceda had potential. He was smart, amiable, and even though soft-spoken had a presence that would do well in the courtroom. He had liked the young man; he liked him still. His decision to plant the murder weapon in Andres' office had nothing to do with his liking or disliking him. It had to do with basic survival.

With a few strides, he was near the small table with the Underwood typewriter. He took out his handkerchief from his pocket and carefully wiped the cane. With his handkerchief wrapped around the handle, he leaned the cane in the corner, next to the window. Very carefully, he arranged the drapes to partially cover it. It must be discovered; when someone searched this office, the person must find the cane. He studied the office, noted how tidy it was, and he stared once more at the partially-hidden cane. Satisfied, he turned to leave when he caught sight of Andres's nameplate on the desk. Nearby was his cup with the lace handkerchief shaped like a flower. Jose reached over and touched the tip of the handkerchief. A faint gardenia scent wafted upward, and instantly he was transported back to that day at the Culyo Leper Colony when he first met Andres Maceda and Pilar Echeveria.

The nuns who worked at the colony had a singing program by some of their patients, lepers who did not have lesions and presumed non-contagious. Jose was there because the resident physician, Dr. Gerald McAllister, was his client. Some students were also present, among them a young man and woman sitting together, laughing and talking in a most animated way. The latter was slight and pallid, with a firm jaw, reminding him of Fernanda when he first met her at the St. Joseph's Orphanage, just a girl, with buckteeth, unearthly white skin, and thick braided hair hanging down her back, and with such an air of determination. How captivated he had been with Fernanda. He had loved her the first time he saw her; he loved her still. Despite everything, he loved her still. He wondered if she had returned to the Sisters of Charity in Intramuros after she left him.

The lepers were there, singing their jaunty folksongs about farmers and carabaos, nothing sad, but looking at them was painful. Most had lost their fingers and tips of their noses; many were blind; all had awful lumpy bumps on their faces and bodies. They were deformed; they were broken; and these were the lucky ones. But even though they were "negative," they could not return to their families and villages. Their deformities drove people away. Once a leper, always a leper.

Horrified, many of the students sat in the back of the room. To close the program, Dr. Gerald McAllister, the Director of Health, gave an update on the research being done at Culyo Leper Colony. They were sharing information with the Leper Home in Carville, Louisiana, he said, and he spoke of how in the near future, there would be a cure for leprosy. He was in his early fifties, with thick white hair. "Are there any questions?" he asked.

It was the pallid young girl, thin as a twig, who bounced up. "Doctor McAllster, in your opinion, how is leprosy transmitted?"

Jose knew that usually students didn't even ask questions, that they could hardly wait to get out of here and back to their flirtations and foolishness. The doctor lit up. "That is an interesting question. The assumption has always been via physical contact, however—" he slowed down and enunciated carefully, "only one per cent of the spouses of those with Hansen's disease have contracted leprosy. One percent." He paused for effect, but only the young girl was impressed.

"Further," the doctor continued, "among those of us who live and work among the lepers, only one—one— contracted it after working here for five years. This person had a family member with the disease, so it's hard to tell if he got the disease from his family or from Culyo. I myself live and work here. Before working in Ubec, I had worked at Carville, in Louisiana. I was a resident physician there as well."

"In other words, Doctor, there is no reason to fear lepers?" The girl threw a castigating glance at students who were cowering in the back.

"As of now, there is no definitive answer to your question. Research continues. For instance, we are checking to see if air and dust, if food, or if secondary parasites play a part in the transmission of the bacillus of leprosy."

"Secondary parasites?" the girl asked excitedly, "such as flies, or lice?" She was deeply engrossed in her conversation with the doctor. "That is a fascinating idea, Doctor."

The other students started squirming in their seats. The young woman, sensing they were tired, said, "I have one last question: How effective is Chaulmoogra oil in curing leprosy?"

The doctor removed his eyeglasses and peered at her. "And what is your name, young lady?"

"Pilar Echeveria, Doctor."

"And how do you know all these things?"

"I read about them, Doctor. I would like to be a doctor one day."

"I see, well, talk to me after the program," the doctor said.

Jose was beside the doctor when Pilar Echeveria grilled him some more: "Doctor, is it true that one can catch leprosy from the armadillo? And what exactly does an armadillo look like, Doctor, we don't have this animal. And does Chaulmoogra oil really work? What about the side effects?"

The girl had amused Jose. She had courage; she had a good mind; and she was pretty if you really studied her. She displayed a single-mindedness that he now realized could be a good or a bad trait. In Fernanda's case, her pointed focus on material things had brought about their undoing. He was swimming in regrets and pain about Fernanda when he caught sight of a flutter of white. It was Pilar's handkerchief, slipping out of her pocket and falling down. Before it hit the floor, Andres, who sat beside her, caught it and he tucked it into his own pocket. He was a tall young man who had followed Pilar around with dogged devotion, listening to everything she said, nodding in agreement to the words she uttered. Jose had caught snippets of their conversation, which had to do with the ills in the Philippines and how they wanted to fix them. An idealistic young man and young woman, in love with each other.

It was this episode that had prompted him to offer the apprenticeship at his law firm to Andres Maceda, not his grades nor referrals.

As Friday evening set in, Jose could hear the sounds of horse carriages and people rushing home. His own blood seemed to pound in his head. He pressed the veins on his temples. What was happening to him? How could he plant the murder weapon in the office of Andres? How could he destroy the young man's life? True, he had lost his child and his wife, but would he also sacrifice his decency? Could he not find a way of out his conundrum?

He turned to consider the cane once more. He could take it away, hide it once again in his office; he could even throw it into the sea. But the thing was, it was a miracle that Borja thought Andres had killed the priest. The murder weapon in Andres's office would round out that story. And unless something else came up, he, Jose, would not even be considered a suspect.

Jose straightened the nameplate and cup before leaving the small office of Andres Maceda.

From his office, he went to his parents' home for supper, and late in the evening, he returned to his residence above his office. He had kept it exactly as Fernanda left it, with her expensive furniture and other "riff-raff" as he usually called her purchases. This evening he felt less hostile to her beloved items. He even paused to admire the delicate painted flowers on the Austrian china in the cupboard. But when he saw their four-poster matrimonial bed, he felt a terrible foreboding, an unraveling of the strands that he'd been trying to hold together. He went over to Fernanda's side of the bed, pulled out her pillow and buried his face in it. After she had left, he had done this now and then to catch her scent, but now he only caught a musty odor. She was gone for good.

He had an impossible time falling into sleep and when he finally did, he dreamt that Pilar's handkerchief covered his face, smothering him and he had to struggle to remove it. When he did, he realized his nose was missing, and he had lesions throughout his body. In his dream, he had turned into a leper.

Lepers terrified him. When he was a child, he had seen lepers begging at churches, their hands fingerless, their legs mere stumps, the skin on their faces doughy lumps; the tips of their noses missing, eaten by the disease. He used to cling to his mother's skirt, but his mother would chide him and force him to drop coins in their begging cans.

He was in bed, curled up on his side, as he mulled over

his dream. Now, in many ways, he was a leper. He was not whole; his soul, his spirit was riddled with sores, huge portions of himself were missing. Like the lepers who were separated from their families, he too was alone. He was a cast away, someone who deserved to be reviled, to live in caves; someone who should shout out "Unclean."

He remembered a woman he had seen at the leper colony's marketplace. The lepers whose disease was inactive were allowed to sell their produce and goods to non-lepers. Jose had been on his way to Dr. McAllister's house when the woman called out, "Good morning, Sir, some orchids?" She was smiling as she presented young orchid plants nestled in coconut husks. Each plant had a spray or two of lilac and white flowers. They were beautiful and quite a novelty. He considered buying two plants for his mother, but he hesitated. The vendors were presumed healed, but who knew for certain if they really were no longer contagious. Even Doctor McAllister acknowledged that there was no cure for leprosy.

Jose wanted to run away, away from this leper, but he forced himself to stop. He turned toward her and shook his head apologetically. She was in her early thirties, comely, with her long hair anchored into a bun by a tortoise shell comb. Some strands of her dark hair fell charmingly down the sides of her face—and then he saw it, the dark sore on the side of her right nostril. The leprosy bacillus had infected the cartilage of her nose.

She selected two healthy plants and placed them on the edge of the table. "You can have these for the price of one," she said amiably.

He did not answer. He was focused only on her infected nose. He froze, not wanting to touch the plants, not wanting to be near this woman, feeling a tremendous weight.

Her eyes turned glassy and she quickly walked away to rearrange the plants on her stall.

In Jose's dream, he had hurried away as fast as he could.

CHAPTER 22

THE ISLAND OF THE LIVING DEAD

Soon after the Americans acquired the Philippines, they learned that almost 4,000 people had leprosy. The figure was staggering; Carville Leper Home in Louisiana had 325 patients. Authorities were also shocked to discover that some of their veterans of the Spanish American War had contracted the disease.

Quarantine was the American answer to leprosy. Putting all lepers in one place would end contagion; as the lepers died-off, the disease would be eradicated. Using Carville as their model, the Americans turned Culyo, a speck of an island near Ubec, into the Philippines's leper colony. But while Carville was built on a rundown Southern plantation, the Americans had the luxury of starting from scratch in Culyo.

They split Culyo into two parts, one for the lepers, the other for non-lepers, with a guarded gate in between. A second gate near the pier separated the colony from the rest of the world. They built a hospital, research laboratory, over four hundred houses, theater, town hall, school, and church. The colony had piped-in water, reservoirs and a sanitary sewer system. It had its own municipal government, with representation from the various ethnic groups. It even had its own monetary system. It was like a small independent country, in many ways better than the rest of the Philippines, except of course for the lepers.

The simple fact, however, was that even though the Americans had built a spic and span, modern colony, Culyo was a place of tears. It was a virtual penal colony. Most patients were forced to leave their homes to move to Culyo. Some had to be shackled. These lepers, even the inactive ones, would never return to the home that they grew up in, never worship in the churches where they had received the sacraments, never see the schools, the roadways, the creeks, the world that they had known and loved. That life was dead to them.

This was why Culyo was known as the Island of the Living Dead.

***

Attorney Vargas was in the boat on the way to Culyo. It was a warm day and beads of perspiration sprouted on Jose's forehead. He reached into his pocket for his handkerchief and he wiped his brow. Jose felt an optimism, not a wide expansive feeling, but a guarded one. He looked out at the sparkling sea and blue sky and noted the brilliance of the day. Jose had been wallowing in darkness and he welcomed the sliver of hope that he now felt. It was like seeing the faint flush of dawn after a black night. He would find the leper woman, buy orchids from her, make amends, reverse the pain he had inflicted on her.

Jose Vargas had been visiting Culyo ever since Dr. Gerald McAllister hired him to prepare agreements about sharing research data with other institutions. The first time he had traveled to Culyo, he was worried that the leprosy bacillus was on the handrails and seats; and his stomach had turned at the sight of the basins with disinfectant, his mind going on about the thousands of hands and feet dunked into those bowls. Holding his breath, he had rushed to the safety of Dr. McAllister's office. The lingering smell of muriatic acid inside had given him some comfort and allowed him to breathe a little easier. Back home, he had hurriedly removed his clothes and asked the maid to wash them in boiling water. He had taken a long bath, scrubbing every part of his body, removing every trace of the leper colony.

He relaxed with the successive visits, and this Saturday, instead of cowering in the back of the boat, he sat near the boat's captain, a short round man, who had his pet monkey beside him. "His name is Momoy," the captain said, "he's five years old. My wife doesn't want him at home because he almost started a fire." He gave the monkey a papaya, then started talking about the German doctors who were just in Culyo. "Three of them. Young, but with white hair," he said, then straightening up in pride, he continued, "Culyo is the largest leper colony in the world, that's why important people come. Why, just last week, the Police Inspector was here."

Jose sucked in his breath—had he heard right? Police Inspector? "Antonio Borja?" he asked.

"Yes, soon after the priest's body was found."

Jose felt faint; his earlier optimism faded. He took a deep breath to clear his mind. Why was Borja in Culyo? Borja's visit had to be related to his investigation. It was as simple as that. But what information would Borja get in a leper colony? Was there any possibility that he, Jose, would be implicated? To encourage the captain to talk, he asked, "Was Borja with the doctors?"

But the captain did not hear him. He was now watching some children who had surrounded the monkey that was sitting on a wooden crate, at eye-level with the children. "Not too close," he warned, stretching a protective hand over his pet. It was a futile act, like trying to hold back the tide, because the children were enthralled and wouldn't leave the animal alone. Finally, one boy breached the imaginary boundary and reached out to try and pet him. The animal made an ugly face and snarled. The captain pulled the leash and scolded his pet. To the children, he said, "Don't worry boys and girls, he has no teeth."

Another boy spoke up, "The last time I was here, you said he killed a giant rat." He stared at the monkey's canines intently. "What are those?"

"They're not real," the captain lied, to silence them, but

the children asked more questions: How exactly did the monkey kill a rat that was bigger than him? And did the captain get money for the rat's tail?

Jose turned away and became somber as he wondered why Borja had been in Culyo. His tentative feeling of joy had vanished; he felt as if he were one of Ubec's despised rats, hunted by people so they could get bounty for their tails. He considered catching the noon boat to Ubec once they docked, but if he did that, he would call attention to himself. This same talkative captain would tell everyone about him. Jose wondered if the captain knew his name at all. He didn't think so, but the guards at the gate knew him from his past visits to Dr. McAllister.

He stared at the sea, which had turned choppy. He couldn't afford to attract scrutiny and he decided to proceed with his plan of seeing the leper woman. When they docked, he hurried off the boat without bothering to hold his breath. That had been a useless exercise in any case; even he knew that. The palms of his hands became damp when he spotted the armed guards at the gate. Would they arrest him? He tried to act like the other people, giddy in their anticipation of seeing their loved ones, compliant with the strict rules imposed by the Americans. He smiled amiably as he explained he was there to see Dr. McAllister. He did not wince during his ablutions in the detested disinfectant. The guards waved him through, and he heaved a sigh as he entered Culyo.

The noonday sun glared overhead. The market was only partially covered and the heat made the smells of fish, meat, and overripe fruit swirl around him. He pushed through the crowd to the stall where he had last seen the leper woman. She wasn't there. He looked around but couldn't find her. Perhaps she had gone home for lunch, he thought. He had wanted to see her. The next boat for Ubec wouldn't leave until late in the afternoon. He had hours to kill. He was standing there, with his hands thrust into his pockets, when he heard a man's voice: "Joe, what are you doing here?"

It was Dr. Gerald McAllister, wearing a dark suit with

a hat on his head. Flustered, Jose stammered, "I ... I ... need to discuss something with you about..."

Dr. McAllister held up his hand in protest. "Joe, I've just come from a funeral Mass. Let's not talk about legal matters today. I promise I'll visit your office after Holy Week. Let's go home and have lunch," he said.

"Doctor, I..." he said, trying to beg off.

"No excuses, Joe. Agustina will tan my hide if you don't eat with us. Your boat's not leaving until four in any case."

He had no choice; the doctor and his wife would be offended if he didn't join them.

As they climbed up the hill to the cluster of houses for the medical staff, it came to Jose that Dr. McAllister would have heard of Borja's visit. Jose would ask him about it.

The doctor's house was a two-story clapboard house, white and airy with a spacious front porch. There were young trees and shrubs around it, and to one side was a vegetable garden where a woman and two girls laughed as they weeded. When they saw the men, they abandoned their work and hurried toward them. The girls, eleven and four, jumped into the doctor's arms for a kiss. The woman was smiling broadly, her long hair streaming around her. She too kissed the doctor before turning to Jose. "Attorney Vargas, I'm glad you're here. I made a very nice fish relleno and the cook has tinola soup." Her voice was sweet and clear. Her movements, her smile, the way she carried her head, evoked confidence, which only heightened Jose's embarrassment for showing up unexpected, invited only a few minutes ago.

"Mrs. McAllister, I ... I ..." he stammered.

She waved a hand to stop him. "My husband tells me you're a big help to him. He loves his patients and he can peer into microscopes forever, but he detests legal documents. We are both very grateful to you." And with eyes twinkling, she added, "Please do not worry, I am not as strange as people say I am."

She and the doctor laughed.

Fantastic stories about Agustina had been circulating in Ubec. Her father, people said, was an enchanted being, and Agustina had horns on her head. Like all Ubecans, Jose was intrigued by her.

The two girls tugged at the doctor. "Papa, come take a look at our garden," they said, giggling and straining as they pulled him.

"Come along, Joe, the girls will appreciate a larger audience," the doctor said.

"The girls are learning a lot about what the earth has to give, from the garden," Agustina explained, as she pointed out the neat rows of green onions, and tomato plants filled with bright red tomatoes. There were vines of squash and bitter melons on stakes, and a patch of strawberries.

"My squash is taller than me," the younger one said, as she stood ramrod-straight beside the staked vine.

"I see that," said the doctor.

"Will you garden with us?" the older one said.

"When it's not so hot," the doctor replied.

The girls giggled happily.

The doctor put his arm around Agustina as they led the way to the house. It was a tidy place, not cluttered at all like Jose's that was filled with Fernanda's things. Instead of heavy European style furniture, the doctor had wood furniture with simple lines and little ornamentation—Mission style, the doctor explained, after he had changed and washed up.

Agustina and the girls were charming; the doctor's home was picture-perfect. Jose felt a pain in his gut. He knew the doctor had helped many people in Ubec; Dr. McAllister had even acted as the advocate for Filipinos to the Philippine Commission. Jose was not jealous of Dr. McAllister, but the children's chatter reminded him of the time he and Danilo had made Christmas lanterns. How happy they had been; how miserable he was now. It was clear to Jose that Fate had dealt him a bad hand. Why him, of all people? He thought of leaving, but couldn't, not now, not without upsetting the McAllisters.

Jose stumbled through lunch, barely tasting the food that Agustina pressed on him. He tried to keep up with the chitchat but his mind was unfocused.

After lunch, Agustina and the children left to prepare palm fronds for church. Jose considered excusing himself but the doctor insisted on showing his gazebo, a magical place, he said, where he watched the sunset one evening and suddenly, just like that, he found the exact proportions of Chaulmoogra oil to be administered to minimize nausea among the patients.

The gazebo sat, perched on top of a hill, overlooking Culyo and a pristine seashore and blue sea. The wooden structure was painted a dazzling white, with red tile roof, a handsome edifice with a wrought iron table and chairs inside, and a young bougainvillea vine starting to creep on one side.

The doctor pointed out the leper part of Culyo with its hospital and small houses scattered on rolling hills studded with coconut and flame trees. "It is not so sad; the land is beautiful; they receive a stipend and are free to do what they want."

While the doctor was talking, Jose saw on a distant hill a line of people snaking along a dirt road toward a cemetery. It was a funeral procession; he could make out the dark coffin being carried. Flowering frangipanis and pink-flowered vines rimmed the boundary of the graveyard but did little to quell the melancholy sight.

The doctor followed Jose's gaze. "It's Father Francisco," he said in a low voice. "He chose to live with the lepers although he wasn't one. Before he died, he asked permission from his superior to be buried here. He said if lepers live and die here, he wanted to do the same."

"Did he work closely with the patients?"

"He blessed them, gave them their sacraments; he was not afraid."

"But did he catch the disease?" Jose said.

"No. Only five percent of people exposed to it get it. It's easier to catch a cold."

"As you know, Doctor, I'm terrified of it," Jose said.

"If it's not highly contagious, why did the Americans start the segregation program?"

"I was assigned to create the program, Joe; and I did a good job. But to be honest I have mixed feelings about the matter. It disturbs me to force lepers away from their homes to come here, but on the other hand, there is no cure for Hansen's disease. Not now, in any case, although I believe there will be a cure one day soon. There is a great deal of research going on in Carville and here. Doctors from all over the world come here to learn more about Hansen's disease."

Jose took a deep breath—now was the time to ask about Borja's visit to Culyo. "The boat's captain mentioned that some German doctors and Captain Borja were here," Jose said in a voice so calm, even he was surprised.

"Oh, yes the German doctors with their schnapps. Every night they drank the stuff. I have no idea how they could function in the daytime."

"Why do you think our Police Inspector came here, Doctor?"

"I asked the same thing when I learned he was here. Sister Margarita at the hospital said he wanted to talk to Father Francisco. The priest was very ill and Sister Margarita told him 'no,' but Captain Borja insisted on talking to him. The nun was certain his visit had something to do with the discovery of the body of Father Zafra. Zafra used to confess to Father Francisco."

Jose felt a lurch in his chest.

"Borja may have wanted information, perhaps about the people Zafra associated with, people he may have angered," the doctor said.

"A priest never discloses what is told to him during confession."

"I'm a Methodist, Joe, so I know nothing about that. Sister Margarita was livid that Captain Borja had bullied his way to the room of Father Francisco. I must say I've heard that adjective used of Captain Borja many times before." The doctor laughed and Jose joined in, but the sound of his laughter was tinny.

The doctor removed his eyeglasses and cleaned them with his handkerchief. "Joe," he said, after slipping his eyeglasses back on, "you have not been yourself. You seem distracted—no, it's more than that. There's something going on. We've known each other for a few years now, and I feel I know you well enough to ask—is something wrong?"

And there it was, that proverbial American frankness thrown at his face. Jose squirmed in his chair. He studied the nearby bougainvillea. He felt as if he were back in school with a teacher interrogating him. He wondered if his guilt was written all over him. He shouldn't have asked about Borja.

"You don't have to talk about it. We could chat about the rat epidemic or the priest's body that was found, but as you know, I've been a doctor for a long time and I can sense when a person is suffering."

"I'm sorry. It's true that I've been distracted ... my son ... I still think of him." Jose rubbed his temples. He could bring up his dead son since everyone in Ubec had heard about it. He wasn't sure if the doctor knew that his wife had left him. Even though his son's death was more painful, it was something that could be discussed without shame. Fernanda's disappearance opened up too many questions.

"Yes, of course, I know about your son. And Joe, I also know about your wife. Ubec is a damned small place, everyone knows other people's affairs. To lose a son, and then a wife, must be living hell."

Jose said nothing. He wondered what people said about Fernanda and him.

"You may not know this, but I was married once before."

"I've heard of it." People had talked of how unhappy the doctor had been, how heartless he had become because of his grief for his first wife. He had been in this state when he had met Agustina, a widow herself; and she had changed his life. Most of the stories told by Ubecans about the doctor revolved around his love story, not his life in America.

"I was a young doctor then, and my first wife was also young. We were the Golden Couple and thought we had everything until she got sick. To make the story short, she died ... of consumption." He paused to compose himself. "My life ended. I was breathing, you understand. I was moving. I would wake up, go to work, go to sleep, but for all practical purposes, I was dead. One day I thought I'd make it official: I'd kill myself." He stopped and smiled. "This sounds very melodramatic now, but at the time it wasn't."

Jose nodded. He understood what the doctor was talking about.

"When you really think about it, you have a lot of choices. There's poison, or hanging; you could shoot yourself, or jump off a building or bridge. My mind was going through all these, when suddenly, I heard, not with my ears but with my heart the word—Leave." He stood up and stared at the sea. "And so I left."

"I met you back in 1903," Jose said.

"Soon after I arrived. I was full of bile until I found Agustina. And here I am. I am not sure what prompted me to tell you my story. Perhaps it's to let you know that no matter how bad things are, there is hope."

Jose wished to confess to the doctor; the weight in his chest was heavy and it would have felt good to unburden himself. He could trust this good man. But Jose didn't even know where to begin. Would he start with his son's death? Or should he explain about Fernanda's need for material things, which was why Danilo had been neglected? Would he reveal that he had raped his wife in his anger? Would he confess of how he had killed the priest by accident, because it *was* an accident? What words would describe his universe of despair? In the end, all he could mutter was a weak, "Thank you."

The distant laughter of the two girls brought them back from that desperate world of dead priests and wives and sons. Rising from their chairs, they turned their faces toward the mirthful sounds. "They'll be wanting me to garden with them," Dr. McAllister said.

They left the gazebo and headed back to the house. The girls met them half way and greeted them with a song about planting rice not being fun. Inside the house, Agustina had prepared a pitcher of lemoncito juice and some rice cakes. The girls were giddy with excitement that their father would spend time with them soon. After taking his merienda, Jose said his goodbyes to the family that symbolized what he had lost. But regardless, the doctor had given Jose something to consider, a sliver of—did he dare call it hope?—to hang on to, and Jose hurried down the hill toward the dock. Jose had a lot of things to do back home.

PART V

CHAPTER 23

THE TROPICANA

Ines and Melisande found Juan Dela Cruz perched on top of a table, pale and terrified as he tried to shoo away three rats that were poised to climb up. "The rats! The rats! They are attacking me!" he cried out.

Melisande grabbed an umbrella and used it to swat the rats. Ines stamped her feet. When the rats ran off, the women helped Juan down the table.

Wild-eyed, Juan rambled, "I was mapping out the choreography and while inspecting the auditorium to study its layout, I flung open the curtains and found three rats feasting on a bloody carcass. I couldn't tell what it was ... a cat ... or a puppy. The rats were colossal! My screams attracted the rats. They moved toward me. I managed to save myself by clambering up the table. I've been fighting them off for almost an hour."

The women checked the auditorium to make sure the rats were gone, after which the three of them ran to the manager's office.

"Mr. Fitz," Juan said to the English manager of the hotel, "There are rats here! You must do something about them. What are they doing in the International Hotel? What will your guests think? These foreigners will say we are primitive and dirty."

Juan continued ranting while Melisande greeted Mr. Fitz with a kiss on the check. Ines nodded her greeting. "How are you, my dears?" he said, smiling amiably at the women. "Melisande, my dear, how is your business doing?"

Melisande smiled back. "Printemps is doing very well, Mr. Fitz."

"Very good, my dear." He turned to Ines and said, "And you, my dear, how are you? I had wonderful conversations with your husband about politics and world events, and I sorely miss him."

Ines remembered the times Mr. Fitz visited their home. The house had been very lively then, with Pablo's students and friends in the Smoking Room, their cigars and cognac in their hands. The thought made her chest tighten and she had to hold back her tears. "Those were happy times, Mr. Fitz," she said.

Mr. Fitz reached over and patted her arm, "There will be happy times again, Mrs. Maceda. And please be assured that the hotel will be buying a full page advertisement from your newspaper. I have already discussed it with your young assistant."

Melisande beamed at Ines, but Juan was still fuming. "The rats, Mr. Fitz, I'm talking about the Goliath rats!"

Mr. Fitz calmly pulled out stationery and started writing a letter. "Please accept my sincerest apologies, Mr. Dela Cruz," he said, "I do my part to exterminate them. We have rat poison in every nook and cranny of the hotel, short of the kitchen. As you know there is a rat epidemic, and I can only do so much." He handed the letter along with some restaurant vouchers to Juan. "We are sorry, Mr. Dela Cruz, and wish to make amends. We hope you will enjoy dinner and drinks at the Tropicana. It just opened last week."

Juan glanced at the letter and vouchers. "Oh, the Tropicana? Esteban and I have been talking of dining there. I hear the decoration is fabulous." He tucked the letter and vouchers in his bag.

"By all means, Mr. Dela Cruz, do so, with our compliments. And please take these brave ladies, your saviors, for drinks and hors d'oeuvres."

Subdued, Juan said, "Thank you, Mr. Fitz." He turned and smiled broadly at Ines and Melisande. "Shall we?" He threw his hands up in the air, bowed, and made a large sweeping movement with his arm before leading the women down the hall toward the restaurant.

"The Tropicana's supposed to be as good as the restaurant at the Oriente Hotel," Juan said.

"I've stayed at the Oriente," Melisande said, "It's fabulous and the restaurant has excellent French food."

"Huervas, the Spanish architect, designed the Oriente to the tune of $100,000. My father knew Huervas and the owner, Don Marqueti. Papa used to take us there for special occasions," Juan said.

The Tropicana had huge Bohemian crystal chandeliers, crystal coconut trees with fronds, and waiters in crisp white uniforms. The maître d' led them to a table by a window overlooking the swimming pool where bathers lounged around, an image from an American magazine.

Juan and Melisande huddled over the menu.

"Look at this, Ox Tail a la Angalise, and Roast Mutton, my favorite," Juan said.

"Goose Liver Patties au Champignons is my favorite—" Melisande rolled her eyes —"but ooh-la-la, it's nine dollars."

"Did you see the wine list? Moet & Chandon for seven dollars a bottle. That's the same price as the Oriente."

"This place is expensive, Juan." Melisande widened her eyes and sat back.

"Mi amor, we have vouchers," Juan said, waving the vouchers in front of Melisande.

They ordered and their drinks arrived along with a platter of hors d'oeuvres, including a block of foie gras with crackers, fresh mussels, and fried cheese.

Ines wanted to get to the point of their visit with Juan, which was to secure his lawyer's name, but he and Melisande started bantering about what they'd do if they were millionaires.

"What would you do, Melisande?" Juan asked. He was leaning back with his eyes half-closed, enjoying his drink.

"I'll get another sewing machine and hire another girl," she said.

"A million, Melisande. You can do more than that."

"In that case, I would arrange for my Tante Juliette to visit me here. I would like to see her again. I miss her."

"Why don't you go to Paris?" Juan said.

"I couldn't do that, Juan. She can come to Ubec."

"It's because of that man—what is his name, again?" Juan said.

Melisande sighed. "Don't bring him up, Juan. It breaks my heart." She cast a glance at Ines. "What would you do if you were a millionaire?" she asked.

As far as Ines was concerned, it was a silly conversation. She didn't have a million dollars and she never would. She failed to see the point in useless speculation and she remained silent.

"Ines?" Melisande prodded. "You pretend, Ines. We're just playing now, like children," Melisande said, in an amused tone.

"If I were that rich, I wouldn't have to work," she said, then paused to consider Santiago's newspaper, its mediocrity in particular—did she really want *The Light* to be the only one in Ubec? "But I think I would want to work anyway," she added.

"Oh, so now you want to continue the newspaper," Melisande said.

"Ubec needs more than *The Light*," Ines said. She had heard Pablo and Felix say this many times, but this time, she understood what they meant: It was important for Ubecans to have different perspectives from which they could draw their own conclusions.

"That is true, Mrs. Maceda," Juan said. "Me? I'd like to buy a place in Barcelona so Esteban and I can visit it regularly. He misses Spain sometimes. He's given up a lot to be with me here in Ubec."

"He loves you, Juan," Melisande said, as she contemplated the hors d'oeuvres platter. She selected the foie gras on a cracker this time.

Juan beamed. "That mysterious man whom you are running away from loves *you*, Melisande."

"Don't say that, Juan," Melisande said, but she giggled.

The waiter returned with another round of drinks, which Melisande and Juan welcomed, but which Ines refused. Ines stared at the poolside and saw a mother and two boys gathering their belongings, getting ready to leave. It was late in the afternoon, and finally Ines said, "Mr. Dela Cruz, we looked for you today to get your lawyer's name."

"My lawyer?" Juan looked startled. "Why would you need his name? I thought you had your own lawyer."

Melisande leaned forward and assumed a more serious expression. "It's a long story, Juan, but we no longer trust her lawyer. Ines has a notarized statement from Pilar Echeveria testifying she was with Andres the night Father Zafra disappeared. The girl is an angel, Juan. We were afraid she would refuse, you know, but she promised to get it, and true to her word, she showed up with the document. She even gave us woven cloth which I can use for the carnival."

"Who is your lawyer, Mrs. Maceda?" Juan asked.

"Attorney Vargas."

"Jose Vargas?" Juan said.

Without hesitating, Melisande said, "We think it's possible that he killed the priest."

Juan listened carefully as the two women related what they had learned in Carcar. "I see," he said when he had heard the whole story. "Since the Inquisitor had targeted me, I find this interesting. But between you and me, I can't imagine the mild mannered lawyer killing a cockroach."

"For revenge, he could, Juan," Melisande said. "Anyone could."

"Could you, mi amor? I can't imagine it. You have such a soft heart," Juan said, as he reached over and chucked her chin.

Melisande smiled at him and before the two resumed their nonsense, Ines quickly said, "Mr. Dela Cruz, refresh my memory—Father Zafra had dinner at your house, then you had a quarrel, after which the priest left—am I correct?"

"He had dinner with us practically every Sunday, Mrs. Maceda. The ingrate. The worm." He crossed his arms and scowled. "Father Zafra was a demon. He wanted to use me and Esteban. When we refused, he called us vile names. But Esteban and I knew what he really was." Juan's face had turned ugly.

"We learned he liked little boys," Melisande said.

"And who told you?" Juan said, with one eyebrow lifted, looking impressed.

"Someone from Carcar," Melisande said.

Juan paused before speaking, "Esteban and I knew about the priest's fondness for young boys. We even heard that two of his altar boys died mysteriously."

"What do you mean 'mysteriously'?" Melisande asked.

Juan looked at her and lifted an eyebrow. "The parents had no proof but they think the priest may have—"

Melisande and Ines gasped at the same time. "Murder? The demon priest actually killed children?" Melisande said.

Juan became pensive. "We have no proof of course. It is all hearsay. So, you think Vargas may have killed the priest for revenge?"

"Neither do we have proof, Mr. Dela Cruz," Ines said. "My son insists Attorney Vargas is a good man. I talked to him at length and he insists I should continue to retain him as our lawyer, but Melisande suggested we talk to you."

Melisande said in a firm voice, "Ines, you can't trust Vargas." She addressed Juan. "Is your lawyer in Ubec? Ines has a notarized document from Pilar Echeveria saying she was with her son on the night the priest disappeared. That should get him released, am I correct?"

Juan hesitated before answering, "Mi amor, Attorney Ceballos is the top lawyer in Manila. He is there where the money is. My mother sent him all the way to Ubec. He's the best, but unfortunately he's far away and it's Holy Week. Offices are closed." Juan resumed drinking his whiskey. "You can contact my lawyer after Easter."

"I have to get my son out as soon as possible," Ines said.

Juan leaned forward. "I have an idea Mrs. Maceda. If we can prove that Vargas is the murderer, Borja will have to release your son. Go to Vargas and pretend as if you know nothing. Melisande and I can go with you. Can't we, mi amor?" He pulled out his pocket watch. "It's too late now, but we can go tomorrow morning at ten. You'll be safe, and we can ask him some questions, trap him, you understand? Make him admit things that will incriminate him."

"It's a plan, Ines," Melisande said. "If we discover something, anything at all, we can go to Borja and convince him that it was Vargas who should be in jail, not Andres. Otherwise, we have to wait until after Holy Week."

"I will personally send the telegram to my lawyer to help you. There is, as the Americans say, 'no other game in town,'" Juan said.

Ines reluctantly agreed.

By the time they left the Tropicana, the waiters were rushing about getting ready for the dinner crowd. Several of them were setting a huge ice sculpture in the middle of a buffet table.

A few guests had started to arrive. The men wore white dinner jackets and the women long sequined gowns, some of which Melisande recognized, and she pointed them out, as they quietly left the Tropicana.

CHAPTER 24

THE CEMETERY

I t was half past six when Ines walked to the San Francisco cemetery or City of the Dead, as it was also called. She winced at the creaking of the rusty cemetery gate as she opened it. The sharp grating sounds made her teeth hurt, and she made a note to instruct the cemetery keeper to oil the gate. He was somewhat lazy, Ines thought, and even though she paid him extra, he didn't always keep Pablo's grave tidy.

She fussed with the red roses in her hands as she wound her way through the cemetery that was riddled with ornate vaults and mausoleums. Ubec was near sea level and burying people underground was impractical; the graves would get soggy and fill up with water. During rainy season when flooding occurred, coffins sometimes floated away, a most disconcerting sight.

Above ground burial was the answer.

And so Pablo's grave was in a mausoleum that shone chalky white this sunny morning. Ines had managed to get a bit of cemetery land for her family. She had not invested in Corinthian columns or generous slabs of Carrera marble as other families had, but she paid an artist to do a carving of a weeping woman on the slab that covered Pablo's tomb. The Grecian style piece was beautiful though forlorn.

She brushed off the dry leaves and broken branches on Pablo's grave and considered complaining to the cemetery keeper, but stopped herself. It was simpler to remove the dirt herself than hunt for the man who was always busy, sealing graves, fixing broken markers, whitewashing walls, polishing inscriptions on the markers. Sometimes, he had the dreary and thankless job of moving the bones from one crypt to another.

The deserted cemetery and graveyard silence made her realize the dead didn't care about such meticulousness. Only the living did, and most of them visited the cemetery only on All Soul's Day and All Saint's Day. She pulled out her handkerchief from her purse and continued brushing off the dirt. Afterwards, she arranged the flowers in front of Pablo's inscribed name.

"Here you are, Pablo, your favorite flowers," she said in a low voice, before settling down on a bench beside an overgrown hibiscus bush. "I'm sorry I haven't visited you but things have come up. You need to know that your son is in jail. I need your advice." She proceeded to report to her dead husband the events that had happened, and as usual, there was no sign from Pablo. She finally pulled out her rosary to pray. It was during her silent prayer when she heard the cemetery gate creak open.

She looked up to see Attorney Jose Vargas walking toward his son's grave. Ines had known his son was buried there but had not expected to see him. Vargas's shoulders were slumped forward, his face smeared with tears. Ines hid behind the hibiscus bush and watched him in silence. He carried a briefcase, which he placed beside him as he collapsed on a bench. Shoulders shaking as if he were weeping, he stretched out his right hand to touch the inscription of the marker.

Ines was uncertain about what to do. Ever since she realized he could have killed the priest, she felt some fear of him; and here she was unable to leave the cemetery without being seen by the lawyer. She huddled still, barely moving, barely breathing. She could hear his sobbing.

She felt contempt for his self-pity—it was her son who was in jail. She considered the lawyer who had known all along of her son's innocence and said nothing. He had sent her on a mission to Carcar in fact, to side track her, to get her out of his way. Her ire grew until finally she got up and made her way to where the lawyer was.

"Attorney Vargas," she called in a firm voice.

He turned. "It's you," he said, jumping up and wiping away his tears,

"I need to know…" she started.

"I didn't expect you here," he said, as he looked around them.

"I came to visit my husband," she said, pointing at her family mausoleum.

"And I, to visit my son."

"My son trusts you, but you said nothing," she said.

He paused, taking in what she said.

"You knew," Ines said. "You knew, but said nothing."

His words stumbled out of his mouth, "I am not sure—I don't know—what you mean."

She stood just a yard away from him. He was bigger and stronger than she was, and when he leaned forward, she became frightened. But she drew on some primal strength that came from deep within her, the courage of a mother protecting her son. "I have just returned from Carcar. I know everything." She stood defiantly before him.

Her words seemed to make him shrink, so he appeared like a frightened little man.

"I know, Attorney Vargas, what the priest did to your son and to other boys." She took a step toward him. "I know that you killed him in revenge."

He straightened his spine as he stared at her in surprise. "What do you mean—'what the priest did'?" His brows were furrowed, his face had turned pale.

Ines could see that the lawyer did not know what she meant. Was it possible that he had not known? "The priest, Attorney Vargas—do you not know?"

His eyes became wild and he turned toward her. "Tell me!" he pleaded.

"We visited the babaylan in Carcar where you got your bird."

He sucked in his breath and froze like a statue. "Danilo had wanted a mynah, but he died, and I had to get one. He was young, and he had suffered so much," he said, his voice cracking.

"I know everything, Attorney Vargas."

"I had suspected—" he continued, in a voice filled with rage and sorrow, "that was why I wanted to talk to him. I did not want to hurt him, but he started hitting me with his cane. Had I known what he had done to my son, I would have killed him. I would not have hesitated. My Danilo ... oh, my son...' His words turned into a soft wail.

"And my son, Andres is precious to me, Attorney Vargas. But you were willing to sacrifice my son. You never considered his innocence. You, of all people, should have thought of justice and fairness." Her voice had taking on an accusatory tone.

The lawyer slumped on the bench and wept. "Mrs. Maceda, I did not mean any harm. I only wanted to find out what happened to my son. Andres is a good young man. I have great respect for him. When the priest's body was not found, I almost convinced myself that what had happened had been a bad dream. But when his body was discovered, I was certain I would be arrested. I was in a panic. When Borja arrested Andres, I did not have the courage to tell the truth." He held his briefcase tighter against his chest, and in a pained voice said, "I was afraid, Mrs. Maceda, afraid that I would end up shot." He hesitated before saying, "I did things ... shameful things ... to save myself." He wore a defeated look on his face.

"You lied to me and to the world, Attorney Vargas," Ines said.

The sun was behind her; and the lawyer placed his right hand over his brow to shield his face from the brightness of the light. "Forgive me, Mrs. Maceda. I am sorry—I say this to you and your son with all sincerity. I was not thinking properly.

I had lost my son, everything. My son ... my Danilo..." he moaned.

"You were willing to sacrifice my son for your sin," Ines said. "He came from my flesh, just as your son came from yours."

He was on his feet and he flailed his arms wildly. "I have lost your trust. I do not deserve your trust, nor anyone's. I have lost not only my son and wife, but my name. I have lost everything, I am nothing." He had a wild expression as he continued weeping. With a quick movement, he suddenly reached for what seemed like a long stick wrapped in paper.

Ines took a step back, fearful that he would strike her.

"Don't be afraid," he said as he peeled back the wrapping to reveal a cane with an ivory handle. "It belonged to the priest."

"Is that the murder weapon, Attorney Vargas?"

"It is," he said simply. "I was planning to throw it into the sea." He turned his head toward the cemetery gate. "I thought I could go someplace far away, away from this nightmare. I thought if I find my wife, we can start a new life again. Even without Danilo, perhaps we can be happy again. It was a foolish dream."

The anger and fear that Ines had felt had dissipated and as she stared at Attorney Vargas, she saw not a successful lawyer, nor the murderer of the priest, but a parent weeping for his dead son, a man who had lost both his wife and son— a broken person. She had had her swords of pain: the miscarriages, Andres in jail, Pablo's death, but now she wondered if the agony that Attorney Vargas endured might surpass hers. If Fate had dealt her those cards, she would go mad, and yes, she would have been capable of murdering the person who hurt her son.

She took a deep breath and her voice was softer when she said, "We were planning to see you later this morning. I have a notarized statement from Pilar Echeveria vouching she was with my son on that night. I understand my son can be freed with the statement."

He wiped his eyes and tried to compose himself. "Of course, yes, a notarized statement." "Your son will be freed."

"You did not tell me about this, Attorney Vargas."

"Andres is innocent, Mrs. Maceda; he has a good alibi; he will be released. Police Inspector Borja has not yet filed charges. They cannot hold him forever. Your statement will prove he was someplace else that night. All you have to do is show him the statement. Borja has no case."

"Do you guarantee his freedom?"

He lifted his eyebrows and nodded, and Ines felt a great burden lifted from her shoulders.

The lawyer said, "I went to the Island of the Living Dead." He turned to gaze at a distant part of the cemetery. "I saw the doctor and his family. They were very happy. He talked about coming to Ubec, and how he found a new life here. I dared dream of starting a new life as he had done, but now, I see, I am unworthy."

"What will happen to you, Attorney Vargas?"

"I will be arrested, and I will end up in a place like Bilibid before being shot." He looked pensive. "It doesn't matter, any more, Mrs. Maceda. After my son's death, nothing matters."

His tone of defeat touched her—his son, that boy who had suffered much. "It is difficult being a parent, Attorney. I am a parent myself." She studied the sharp morning shadows in the forlorn cemetery. "Melisande Moreau and Mr. Dela Cruz and I had planned to be at your office by ten, Attorney Vargas," she said, "It is only seven. I will leave you now, but we will be at your office by ten."

"I understand," the lawyer said.

She straightened up, to leave the lawyer and cemetery. "Good bye, Attorney Vargas," Ines said.

"Good bye," he said, with a bow of his head.

CHAPTER 25

THE NEWS ARTICLE

FRONT PAGE ARTICLE OF *THE UBEC DAILY*

Friday, April 16, 1909

LAWYER DISAPPEARS IN UBEC
By Ines Maceda

Attorney Jose Vargas, a well-respected lawyer of Ubec who has practiced in the city since 1902, has disappeared. The parents of Attorney Vargas, Mr. and Mrs. Arturo Vargas, filed the missing person report at the police station on Monday, April 12, 1909.

Their report stated that they had dinner with their son on the night of Monday, April 5, and that his secretary, Miriam Santos, saw them the next afternoon to inform them that their son did not show up at work that day, Tuesday.

This reporter interviewed Miss Santos who stated, "When I said good night to him on Monday, he said 'See you tomorrow.' But he didn't show up in the morning as he usually does. I was worried but I thought it was possible that he had an appointment in another town and so I waited until the end of the day before I informed his parents."

Mr. and Mrs. Vargas also wondered if their son had left on a business trip and thought it prudent to wait until Monday before reporting the matter to Police Inspector Borja.

Mr. Jose Vargas was born and raised in San Nicolas. He was married to Fernanda Jimenez Vargas, from whom he was separated. The couple had lost their only son, Danilo Vargas, in a drowning accident on August 15, 1908.

This is the second mysterious disappearance in Ubec. Last January 4, 1909, the Augustinian priest, Father Zafra, had gone missing and his remains were discovered on March 29.

CHAPTER 26

MELISANDE WEEPS

Ines and Melisande were walking along, observing the frenzy that had possessed Ubec: tents and booths blossomed in the Plaza Independencia; workers hung banners and streamers to decorate the streets; the Fernandez boys, who had discovered Father Zafra's body, were plastering posters on walls; vendors were staking out places along the streets for their carts and tables; business people were checking into the hotels; people from barrios crowded into their relatives' homes; dancers, musicians, acrobats, circus people were congregating in Ubec for the two-week carnival that would start in a few days with coronation night.

At that moment, the foremost question in people's minds, including Ines's was: Who would be carnival queen in 1909? The carnival queen was chosen from among young ladies from the best families of Ubec. Since only one would be chosen, the queen came to symbolize the best of what Ubec had to offer by way of womanhood. Even the runners-up of the carnival queen had important status—their names along with the carnival queen merged with the hallowed names of the important people of Ubec, right there with the martyrs, heroes, and politicians.

Despite the fact that coronation night was looming, the carnival committee was in disarray. "Juan has been drinking," Melisande grumbled. "Esteban and I have been doing most of the work. Esteban will handle the announcement to the press but I have to inform Pilar that she's been selected."

"Is Pilar the carnival queen, then?" Ines asked, feeling some delight that she was privy to this important revelation. She had been feeling joyful ever since her son was released from jail. It had taken a simple visit to the carcel and a talk to Captain Borja to get the job done. Borja had not even asked for Pilar's notarized statement; he had acknowledged with a mild apology that Andres and his friends had been picked up by mistake. Someone else had killed the priest; someone who was at large.

"Three out of five voted for her. The two who voted against her complained that she's too plain." Melisande gave a wan smile.

"She does dress simply," Ines said, realizing that she herself was wearing black widow's clothes, but then she was what she was, while Pilar was a young girl, an heiress to boot, who had no reason to be wearing drab dresses.

Melisande waved her hand to poo-poo the matter. "I can turn her into a beauty queen. It is easy Ines: fix the hair, rouge the cheeks and lips, apply kohl on the eyelids. I can teach her how to walk like a queen—back straight with a scepter in her hand."

"Well, everyone says she's a nice girl," Ines said. She was thinking of her son who was clearly taken by this skinny girl. She had accepted the possibility that one day Pilar would end up her daughter-in-law and, given Ines had no choice about the matter, she was relieved that Pilar was cut from a different cloth from her high-society mother.

Melisande said, "Committee members talked about her love for the poor, for lepers, how she wants to be a doctor. Those voting for her said, 'She's a saint, and an heiress,' meaning her father will donate a lot to the carnival foundation. I had to remind them that it's not all about money, although the fact that these girls come from high society makes the event important."

"It makes people buy tickets to the events, you mean."

Ines did not intend the rebuke in her voice. In fact, she was interested in how money in this case could be made by giving importance to the daughters of the wealthy.

"Yes, it does Ines. People are always curious about rich people. It's just like in Paris, where people paid a lot of money to go see the actress Jeanne Aubert."

"Wasn't Pilar's mother also a fiesta queen?" Ines asked.

Melisande wrinkled her nose and made a face. "Everyone knows Aphrodite's father paid for that title. You can't imagine how much these parents want such titles for their daughters. Just last week, two parents approached some committee members to try and bribe them so they'd select their daughters."

By this time, they had arrived at the Echeveria house. Melisande patted her forehead with her lace handkerchief and tugged at her skirt before asking the maid for Pilar.

In no time, they heard footsteps clambering down and there appeared Pilar who greeted them with a kiss on their cheeks. She led them upstairs to the verandah with potted frangipani plants, and instructed the maid to bring them juice and Jacob's crackers with white cheese on the side. The three of them chatted about how busy the city was with carnival preparations. They had sips of their juice and a few bites of the crackers with cheese before Melisande got to the point of their visit.

The Frenchwoman spread her hands on her skirt and leaned forward. Voice lilting with excitement, she informed Pilar that the carnival committee had chosen her carnival queen. She sat back and waited for Pilar's reaction.

The young woman blinked several times before saying, "I thought I'd be one of several princesses."

"The committee selected a queen from those princesses, Pilar, and they chose you." Melisande flashed a smile.

Pilar took a deep breath and exhaled. "I see. I was hoping someone else would be chosen queen."

A scowl crossed Melisande's face. "It is an honor Pilar

for you to be selected. All princesses are fine young women from the best families of Ubec. The event is a fund raiser, Pilar, and the participation of these families is vital for success."

"I realize that, Tiya Melisande, and I don't want to sound ungrateful. The title would make my father and grandmother happy, I know that," Pilar said.

Melisande nodded. "The theme of coronation night is Egyptian. Pilar, you'll be dressed like Cleopatra. You'll have an elaborate headdress. Gold and turquoise are the colors I'll be working with. And for your entourage, you'll have the princesses, priests, and a retinue of slaves—"

Pilar froze. "Slaves?" she asked, her eyes turning glassy. "Slaves? Tiya Melisande, slavery is contrary to democracy. We should espouse freedom and equality. Abe Lincoln said, 'We think slavery a great moral wrong.' I can't have slaves in the entourage."

"Egyptian royalty *had* slaves," Melisande said, in an irritated tone. "Everyone knows that their slaves were buried with them to accompany them on their journey to the afterlife. You must have slaves." Melisande stared at Pilar before picking up a fan from the table to fan herself. "In any case, this whole thing is all just pretend," she added, with a wave of her hand.

"Tiya Melisande, I don't believe it's a good message to send to the people, and certainly America who speaks of equality ought to frown on the idea of people's inequality." Pilar said this calmly but her lower jaw jutted out in determination.

There was an impasse for a few seconds, with Melisande fanning herself and Pilar staring stoically down at the floor until finally, after an interminable time, Pilar lifted her head and said softly, "I will think about being carnival queen carefully, Tiya Melisande, and give you my answer in the next few days."

As they walked away, Melisande was furious. "Can you believe that, Ines? Any other girl would have been jumping up and down with joy. Everyone wants to be carnival queen. So what does this girl do? Make a big issue about the slaves. This is not politics; we are just having fun."

Ines paused to think, then said, "Can the committee make a donation to the leper colony? I think this will change her mind."

"I can talk to them, and I'm sure they'll agree," Melisande said.

"And perhaps you could rethink the slaves," Ines suggested. "The children from wealthy families don't want to play the part of slaves, Melisande. Perhaps you could have flower girls instead."

Melisande squinted her eyes as if in deep thought. "Egyptian flower girls ... hmmm."

"I'll explain the situation to Andres and ask him to talk to Pilar about being queen," Ines added.

They headed to the International Hotel to find Juan. "I should be finishing the gowns," Melisande said. "Juan was supposed to check on the decorator, but he wasn't even up when I stopped by this morning."

"Maybe he's overworked, and needs to rest," Ines offered.

"Juan has done very little work, Ines. He's just been impossible. He has been sulking, and when he does show up, is short-tempered. The other day, he screamed at the committee for what he called their incompetence. I had to work hard to smooth down their feathers." Melisande threw her hands up in the air and sighed.

They found the decorator wild-eyed, prancing about the auditorium of the International Hotel, befuddled about what to do. Melisande calmed him down before showing a sketch of what the stage and room should look like. She told him how to place the paper mache columns on either side of the stage, and how to center the throne and arrange the potted palms in clusters near the steps.

When the decorator asked more questions about where to put tables and chairs and what decorations to put on tables,

Melisande was at a loss. Her patience had run thin, and in a loud voice, she said, "Right now. I will talk to Juan, right now!"

She gathered her belongings then turned abruptly and headed toward the door. Ines ran to catch up with her. Melisande was scowling, something she never did because she said it encouraged wrinkles. Then near the hotel lobby, Melisande suddenly stopped. She crossed her arms and started sobbing. "I can't take any more of this!" she declared.

Ines stared at Melisande with surprise. The Frenchwoman was bent over, weeping like a child. When some people in the lobby turned their heads towards them, Ines pulled Melisande away from their watching eyes and led her to the outside patio where they sat under a huge acacia tree.

"Melisande—" Ines said, not knowing what else to say. It had always been Melisande who had comforted *her*, and now she didn't know how to help her friend.

Melisande babbled like a child. "Juan has been terrible, and I have so much work to finish, and there's Pilar balking about being carnival queen. Everything is falling apart, and on top of all that, I had a strange dream last night."

"A dream?" Ines said, "I too had a strange dream. It's similar to the one I had before, of rats swimming in water, but there were fewer rats this time. I was not as afraid of them."

Melisande sniffled and sat up. "I abhor rats," she said as she crossed her arms on her chest. "We found a nest in the back closet, in a basket. There were shredded bits of paper and cloth." She shivered. "We burned it."

"What was your dream about?" Ines asked.

Melisande tilted her head to look up the acacia tree. A shaft of light pierced the thick foliage, lighting up her face. "I dreamt the Eiffel Tower was right here in my room, now how it could have fit in my room, I don't know, but there it was, and my aunt and Samir were also there. It seemed that we were back in time when my aunt was still healing from her leg, and she was on the bed, with her crocheted cover barely hiding her legs—what a coquette Tante Juliette really was! You should have heard how she giggled and carried on whenever Samir checked her leg. In my dream they were talking about the Eiffel Tower."

"It was built in '87, was it not, by Gustave Eiffel?"

"Eiffel designed it, but it was Koechlin and Nouguier who constructed it. It was built in stages, platform by platform from '87 to '89."

"What did your aunt and Samir talk about in your dream?" Ines said.

"My aunt carried on about the Eiffel being useless, that it did not fit the other structures in Paris, it was too modern, it ruined the skyline of Paris. It was the same conversation they actually had when Samir visited us with his drawing of the Eiffel."

"The one you didn't like."

Melisande stuck out her lower lip and blew so that the tendril of hair above her brow quivered. "You do not have to keep repeating that, Ines. Samir had many drawings of the Eiffel. He found it charming, appealing, and beautiful. 'Consider' he said, 'that it's made of metal and yet it manages to be delicate and graceful. And throughout the day, as the sun moves, its appearance changes. The shadows it casts alters the landscape as well. It is like a woman that way, changeable and seductive.'"

"What else did they talk about in your dream?"

"In my dream my aunt told Samir that the Eiffel is called 'The Iron Lady'—we do call it that, Ines. Countering Samir's comments about the Eiffel being like a woman, my aunt continued to ask what was so feminine about a rigid structure thrusting up in the middle of Paris like a gigantic phallus?—her words exactly 'gigantic phallus.'" Melisande widened her eyes and they both laughed.

"It sounds like you like the Eiffel," Ines said

"I grew to like it. I used to pass by it several times a day. It had a presence that could not be ignored, Ines. I felt it the first time I saw it, looking gray and slick in the rain. When I was new in Paris, I used it as my beacon to guide me back to my aunt's shop. It was reliable, fixed."

"I wonder why you would dream of this now. In Ubec we believe dreams have meaning. Here you are, in a hurly-burly over the carnival, and then you have this dream about your aunt and Samir talking about the Eiffel Tower. It's very interesting," Ines said.

Melisande closed her eyes and thought hard before adding, "Ines, I think I understand the dream. I just said it, the Eiffel was a beacon, it is reliable and fixed. And the two people I love were here with me, in my room. I think the dream is saying I must bring the Eiffel back into my room, into my life. It's clear to me now. I can't go on living without Samir."

"It's true that you have been missing Samir."

"The truth is ever since I got my aunt's letter, I have not stopped thinking of him." Melisande stood up and straightened her back.

"Oh, yes, your Tante Juliette's letter. Thank you for letting me read it," Ines said.

"You never said anything about it," Melisande said as she fished out her handkerchief from her bag and blew her nose. Afterwards, she arranged the folds of her long skirt and continued, "In any case, Samir has been suffering, and it pains me too. It's as if I'm suffering like him."

"Your aunt's letter moved me. It's full of the wisdom of a woman who has lived more years than us. It's true that life is very short because I only have to look at my Pablo and our short time together. We still had many dreams, but they're gone. I now have to make my own dreams, my own goals. I can't tell you what to do, Melisande, but if you love him still, then you should bring him back into your life." Ines glanced at the lobby and noticed that the people who had watched them earlier were gone. There were, however, many visitors at the desk, all there for the carnival, Ines supposed.

"Of course I love him. The problem is—" and here Melisande paused before continuing, "that I don't want to get hurt again. Once was enough. I don't want to give him the chance to hurt me a second time. He married another woman; he had a child by that woman, and I was supposed to sit around waiting for him." She stamped her feet in anger. "I hated him! I hate him now when I think of this."

"He wronged you, Melisande. There's no doubt about that. For a brilliant surgeon, he displayed poor judgment. But now, here you are saying you love him still. Is there a solution to a situation like this?"

"I feel pushed and pulled at the same time." Melisande placed her hands to her forehead. "My head feels like it's splitting when I think of him, and unfortunately he's in my mind all the time."

Not knowing what to do, Ines reached out and patted Melisande's arm, as if comforting a child.

"My aunt suggests I forgive him." Melisande said this softly.

"Ah, forgiveness," Ines said, as if discovering a new word. "Of course, that is the Christian thing to do." Ines gave a short laugh.

"Why do you laugh?" Melisande asked.

"Because it's one of those things people say but rarely do.

"I received a letter from him, Ines." Melisande's voice was barely a whisper, a soft fluttery breeze.

Ines placed her hand over her heart. "A letter from Samir?" she whispered.

Melisande nodded. "My aunt—" she said, and waved her hand. "At first I was livid when I realized she had given him my address, but his letter made me so happy that I forgot. But Samir's letter also brought pain ... and a lot of confusion." Melisande sighed and looked up at the majestic acacia, a centenary tree whose sprawling branches extended over a large area. "You see, Ines, my love for Samir is big, bigger than this tree." She paused and in a soft voice continued, "My love for Samir is the greatest thing I have ever experienced."

Then, with her logical mind, Ines said, "Then you have no choice."

Melisande looked at her questioningly.

"You once said the capacity to love is infinite. Perhaps

the capacity to forgive is also infinite. You love him, therefore you have to forgive him, and get on with life."

"As simple as that?" Melisande gave a quick laugh.

"You can make it complicated, if you wish, Melisande. I'm just answering your question," Ines said.

Melisande brushed her skirt before getting up. "Come, let's go to Juan's house," she said with some lightness in her voice. "I know what you are saying, Ines, but I have to consider all this carefully."

CHAPTER 27

JUAN'S DRAMA

Ines had kept her conversation with Attorney Vargas in the cemetery a secret. She alone knew why Attorney Vargas had gone missing. Her son was back home and that was what was important to her. The matter of the murder of the priest was thrust back in her mind as if she no longer had anything to do with it; she was taken aback when this topic cropped up once more at Juan and Esteban's house.

It was early afternoon when Ines and Melisande found the composer and dancer in their upstairs verandah. This verandah which had been part of Ines's past always culled up a sense of well-being, but now that feeling was jarred by what confronted her. There in the far end, past the fountain, near the tambis tree whose branches shaded that part of the verandah, Esteban and Juan were shouting at each other. "Juan, don't!" Esteban said as he reached out to grasp Juan's arm.

Juan pulled his arm away. "I want to die! I want to die!" Juan repeated as he retreated toward the ledge of the verandah.

"Juan, please," Esteban pleaded. "I've left my family, my home, everything to be with you, you can't do this."

Juan clambered up the ledge and he turned to face the fruit orchard below him, swaying as he did so. Ines sucked in her breath and stretched out her right hand with her palm extended; she remembered past admonitions never, never to stand on the ledge lest she fall and break her neck. Esteban also froze in mid-step, his dancer's body a graceful form in the dappled terrace, his golden hair glinting under the sun. It was Melisande who, without any hesitation, strode toward Juan, reached up and grabbed his arm.

"Don't be foolish, Juan," Melisande said somewhat gruffly.

Juan spun around. "Melisande?" he said, looking surprised.

"Come down right now," Melisande said as she helped Juan off the ledge. She led him toward a settee near the fountain. "Now sit down and tell me what is wrong!" she asked in a reasonable voice.

Juan flung his arm over his forehead. "Why did you stop me? I'd made up my mind to kill myself."

"Why would you want to do that? We have work to finish before coronation night. Do you know that Pilar refused to be carnival queen?" Melisande's voice was soft and cajoling. "She does not want a retinue of slaves in her court."

"She did?" he asked, eyes widening, momentarily taken by Melisande's aside, but recovering, he said, "I don't have time for that, Melisande. I'm through with life."

Esteban strode toward them and said, "He's been drinking a lot. When he's drunk he gets crazy like this."

"You—" Juan pointed his finger at Esteban, "you are now telling other people our secrets?"

Esteban continued, "His drinking has gotten worse. First it was wine, now vodka. He used to blame his father, now it's Father Zafra."

Melisande held one hand up to silence Esteban. To Juan, she said, "I'm not 'other people' Juan. Tell me: what is wrong, mi amor?"

Juan threw Esteban an angry look. "Catalan traitor," he hissed under his breath.

Melisande patted Juan's arm. "Shush, shush, tell me what is going on," she said, sounding like a mother.

Right there, in front of everyone, Juan dissolved into

tears and started babbling, "It's been too much! I can't take any more. I've had nightmares. Terrible nightmares."

"It's just a dream, Juan. Why, just this morning, Ines told me about her dream of rats, and I also dreamt of a bedroom. We're just overworked from the carnival," Melisande said.

"I see him all over again. Right there on the muddy earth, with blood all over his face. It repulses me." Juan shivered with disgust. His words hung in the verandah.

While this drama had unfolded before her, Ines had remained near the doorway to the verandah. The excessive behavior that went on embarrassed but also intrigued her. She could never indulge in such dramatic behavior, and she wondered at the verve of people who could. If it were up to Ines, the world and mankind would spin along like clockwork, following all laws of nature and man, everything black and white, cut-and-dried, everything low-key. But curiosity overcame her, and she approached the composer. "Who do you see, Juan?" Ines asked. "Who's in your nightmare?"

Juan spun around. "That priest!" he spat out—"that despicable, hateful man-of-the-cloth." Leaning against Melisande, he said in a doleful voice, "Oh, Melisande, I did something terribly wrong."

Esteban stepped forward. "You're upset, Juan. You don't know what you're talking about." Addressing the women, he said, "Juan keeps talking about the last time Father Zafra had dinner with us. It was January and as usual, we served the priest's favorite dishes, but Father Zafra wasn't himself that night. He was in a foul mood. He kept talking about the fire that broke out in the rectory the night before. He was sure someone had done it on purpose."

Juan interrupted. "The priest was crazy that night. He argued with us; he screamed at the servants. Then he brought up his ridiculous business proposal again, and once again I told him we were not interested."

Esteban explained, "We said no, we would not do it. He stomped around and started calling us names until finally we drove him away from our house. From that time until morning, Juan was by my side."

Juan pointed his finger at Esteban and said, "You don't know everything, Esteban. You always act like you do with your Spanish superiority, but you don't. You were asleep when I left the house for a walk."

Esteban opened his mouth to say something but Juan said, "Stop. Let me tell my story." And to his astonished audience, Juan announced, "I killed Father Zafra."

Esteban shook his head.

Ines and Melisande stared at each other. Ines could not fathom Juan's words. What she had known—and from the proverbial horse's mouth itself—was that Attorney Vargas had killed Father Zafra.

Juan went on, "It was almost midnight. I couldn't sleep. He had been our friend, you understand, someone we trusted and welcomed into our home, and I was hurt and upset. I wanted to clear my head so I took a walk in the plaza." He waved his hand to indicate the direction of the Plaza Independencia. "It had rained earlier and the ground was wet, but the air felt cool and damp. There was a loud murmuring sound, like crickets, but more raucous. It took me a while to realize that the sound was made by starlings; I used to see them when I was a boy, hundreds of them in tall trees where they roosted. I followed the sound..." Juan's voice trailed off and he closed his eyes as if imagining that night all over again. "I was crossing the plaza toward the San Agustin grounds, when a dog started howling. The sound made my hair stand on end. I should have turned and returned home but I didn't. I could make out the tall eucalyptus trees and knew the starlings would be roosting there. I heard moaning and movement coming from the bushes near the creek. Could it be an animal? I wondered and I approached the tormented sounds."

Esteban interrupted, "Juan, say nothing more. You are drunk." He looked at the women with pleading eyes. "Please, ladies, perhaps you should go—"

Juan interrupted: "I want to finish my story." He got

up and started walking around in agitation. "I saw Father Zafra on the ground," he said. "There was enough moonlight to see him. He was sprawled on his back, on the muddy ground, his head and face covered with blood, moaning, asking for help. He must have fallen earlier, after he left our house, and there he was in very bad shape, struggling to sit up. I bent down to help him. He opened his eyes and his eyes flashed with hatred when he saw me. 'You!' he said. 'You abomination, get away from me!' On and on he shouted. And then it happened—" Juan stopped, as if overwhelmed with emotion.

"Tell us what happened, Juan?" prodded Ines in a calm voice.

Juan said, "I was trying to keep him upright, but he kept pushing me away. I let go, and he fell backward, hitting his head against a rock. And then there was no movement. I didn't know what to do. I panicked. I dragged his body and pushed it over into the creek. Then I turned and ran all the way home."

There was momentary silence. Ines, who knew about the confrontation between Father Zafra and Attorney Vargas earlier that January night, was uncertain about what she should say or do. Finally, seeing Juan in such agony, she spoke up, "It was an accident, Juan. You did not kill him. Someone else had been with Father Zafra, which was why he was bloody when you found him."

"Someone?" Esteban asked, his eyes flashing. "Was it Attorney Vargas?"

Ines said, "I'm not sure. There was a stranger lurking around the rectory at that time. It's possible that person did it."

"But I'm guilty. I left him there, and I didn't tell anyone, until now," Juan insisted.

Melisande had gotten up and linked arms with Juan. "Mi amor, you did try to help him Put it out of your mind. The priest was not a good man. He was assigned to many parishes, first Spain, then Mexico before serving in the Philippines, which can only mean one thing, you understand."

Ines took a deep breath and sighed. "We think that

when the church received complaints, they transferred him," she said.

The four of them were quiet for a spell. By now, the glaring afternoon sun had subsided and the drama that had unfolded in the verandah had died down. Later, Melisande said, "Mi amor, I have many gowns to finish ... all this work to do. We must go."

Ines and Melisande said their goodbyes, and Juan whispered, "I promise I won't do anything foolish. I'll rest and later tonight, I'll take Esteban to the Tropicana. I promised him I would." He turned and smiled at Esteban who beamed back at him.

"Promise me, Juan, that you'll take care of yourself," Melisande said as she planted kisses on his cheeks. And turning to Esteban, she said, "Let me know if there's a problem."

Esteban was calm and had returned to his debonair self.

"I'll be fine, dear Melisande, and I'll be back at work tomorrow," Juan said.

Long after Ines and Melisande left Juan and Esteban, the mind of Ines whirled with the new information she just learned about Father Zafra's death.

CHAPTER 28

INES'S GOWN

Whave to finish all these before coronation night," Melisande said, sweeping her hands to show gowns in different stages of completion. "We are working overtime, Ines." Her voice rose above the clatter and activity in Printemps. The sun was setting outside, but two seamstresses were still furiously kicking their sewing machines, while three embroiderers did their delicate stitchery.

Ines studied the gowns, all decorated with embroidery, beads, sequins, rhinestones, even genuine pearls. She had not given any thought to what she'd wear at coronation night. Now the glimmering silk, chiffon, moire, velvet, lace, brocades, and other rich fabric made her uneasy; she had a solitary black gown hanging sadly in her armoire, stark and simple, and which she had already worn to several functions during this time of her mourning.

"Look at this, Ines," Melisande said, with pride in her voice. She held up a red beaded gown with a train. "This is for the mayor's wife. It has a streamlined silhouette with a low décolletage to show off her breasts. It's the latest in Paris. Tante Juliette says clothes are now fitted with higher-waists and narrow skirts. The bustle is finished; the corset is dead." She said this with finality as to suggest that the rest of the world had burned their corsets and had dispensed of the pigeon-look.

She selected two more gowns. "This Belgian lace is for

Mrs. Bustamente of the shipping lines. The turquoise brocade is for Agustina McAllister. She's one of the Damas and those dresses over there are for her two daughters. They are flower girls, part of the retinue of the carnival queen." Melisande lifted her eyebrows and added, "Note that I followed your advice and got rid of the slaves."

"That's a good decision, Melisande. I'll make sure Andres informs Pilar," Ines said, remembering Pilar's bullheaded stance earlier.

"Having flower girls really isn't correct, Ines. Egyptians did not have flower girls." Melisande shook her head. "But since Pilar will not have make-believe slaves, well, there is no choice. Hopefully this accommodation will convince her to be queen. It's too late in the game for us to be hunting for another one," she said.

"Don't forget the donation to the Leper Colony," Ines added.

"That too. In any case, this allows us to include young girls, like the McAllister sisters, which guarantees their parents' presence at the event." Melisande opened her arms out and said, "Everyone is part of the program. That is how we get people to attend." She laughed as she went to another rack with evening gowns.

The sight of the extravagant gowns gave Ines a sinking sadness. She felt left out, as if she were not part of this sorority of women, these lucky owners of haute couture designed by Melisande, whose name had become a legend in the world of women. Anything with Melisande's brand conjured a sense of the Parisian, implying a blend of culture, art, sensuality, and beauty.

Ines sighed, knowing her plain black gown would set her aside from the rest of the women who would show off their "Melisande" gowns. These women would flaunt their heirloom jewelry as well so they would glitter perhaps more than the crystal chandeliers of the Grand Hall.

Melisande returned with more gowns in her arms, which she set on a table. "This is mine," she said, spreading out an apricot silk chiffon evening dress with crossover front bodice and a tiered skirt. "And this one is your mother's." This was blue silk satin chiffon trimmed with black passementerie with gold metallic and ecru lace. It was showy, but beautiful, and Ines felt a twinge imagining her mother in the elaborate blue gown and of herself in the stark black gown—not that she competed with her mother on trivial matters like this, but she could almost hear her mother nagging her again to dress better and fix herself, and so on.

"Did Maman say when she'll be in Ubec?" Melisande asked.

"She's arriving tonight," Ines replied.

"Remind her to come in to fit her gown," Melisande said, as she reached for another gown. This one was made in the traditional Filipina style with a top with full sleeves and a long skirt. The blouse was made of ecru pineapple fiber with intricate black embroidery, the skirt of silk with black and off-white stripes. "This is yours, Ines," Melisande said. "Try it on."

Ines placed her hand over her heart. She had not ordered a dress; she had been so caught up with events and had no time to think of such triviality. Besides she was still in mourning. "But—" Ines started, when she was quickly interrupted by Melisande.

"No buts," Melisande said. "Your son will be on stage; you must look exquisite."

"I can't, Melisande. It's not completely black ... It has not been a year; our custom dictates—"

"—Pooh on custom," Melisande said as she scrunched her nose and flicked her right hand dismissively. "This is almost all black, Ines." She held up the dress and shook it so that it shimmered.

Both women stared at the gown, which now seemed to have picked up a luminescent quality: the black embroidery contrasted handsomely against the lighter background, the silk skirt had an indescribable unearthly shimmer. "It's a beautiful gown, Ines," Melisande continued.

"You must wear it. It's my gift to you." And because

Ines remained silent, Melisande prodded, "Andres will like it. Everyone will be dressed to the hilt. You've seen what the women will be wearing, all fabulous. You, the mother of the prince consort, must not be outshined. Try it on to make sure it fits." Melisande gave her a little push into the dressing room.

The room was nothing more than a small cubicle with a three-way mirror, and standing in that confined space, Ines weighed the rightness and wrongness of not dressing completely in black while in mourning versus the desire to look nice on the night her son would be one of Ubec's luminaries, a night when everyone would be dressed in their finest—and how painful it suddenly felt to consider being clothed in something nondescript on such a special night. In the end, she removed her widow's dress and slipped on the black and white gown. As she smoothed the skirt down, she remembered the diamond set that Pablo had bought for her from the Star of Siam Jewelers and she knew the jewelry would complement the evening dress.

Melisande clapped her hands in delight when Ines presented herself. "It fits, perfectly," Melisande gushed, as she led Ines to a full-length mirror. Melisande fussed with Ines's hair, pulling out a few strands on the sides so curly strands appeared near her cheekbones. "Don't pull the bun too tightly," Melisande said. "Keep it loose, with some curls to soften the face."

Ines stared at her image with astonishment. Since Pablo died and she had been wearing black, her skin had turned sallow, as if the dark color had seeped into her and leeched the life out of her. But now the ecru-colored gauzy fabric brightened her face, made her look younger, happier somehow. She fingered the silk skirt which had a softness and sensuality that seemed alien to her. For months, she had felt like a soldier in a battlefield, taking on the world, figuring out finances, worrying over Pablo's business; then there was the harrowing scare regarding her son—clad in the armor of black, swimming in her widow's sorrows and fears, she had become stiff and unyielding. She barely recognized the woman in the mirror. She did not mean to, but tears formed in her eyes. Embarrassed, she lowered her head so Melisande would not see her face, but the Frenchwoman did, and she rushed to Ines and embraced her saying, "You are beautiful! Wait and see, coronation night will be perfect."

Tears fell down her cheeks, even as Ines smiled.

***

It was almost suppertime when Ines found her mother getting off a carriage in front of her house.

"The train was crowded," Blanca complained. "Everyone's here for the carnival. Come, help me with my bags," she said.

Before Ines could do so, Andres and Felix popped out of the newspaper office, and they kissed Blanca on the cheeks to greet her.

"Andres, how are you hijo?" she said, and without waiting for a reply, turned to Felix, "And how is your grandmother, Felix? When I was here last, she sent some fried crablets, which were delicious."

The young men picked up Blanca's bags and led the way to the house.

"She's discovered crab roe," Felix said.

"Crab roe? I love crab roe. Where does she get it? It's hard to find," Blanca said.

"Lola has her sources," Felix said, continuing the banter.

They made their way past loud crickets into the house where Valentina rushed about to add another place setting at the dining table. "Make that two, Valentina," Ines said. "Felix, eat with us before continuing your work," she added.

The young man shuffled his feet, then said, "I have to set the type, Ma'am."

"I'll help you," Andres said. "Eat with us. Valentina made fish rellenos. I saw her pounding the fish this morning."

Felix brightened. "Fish rellenos? Ah, all right then," he said.

When they were enjoying the food that Valentina had prepared—fish rellenos, grilled pork ribs, ampalaya vegetable, rice, and fried plantains, Ines described the gowns she had seen at Printemps, and she reminded her mother to try her gown soon because Melisande had only two weeks to finish the clothes. Ines related how Pilar had balked at being carnival queen and she asked Andres to let Pilar know there would be flower girls instead of slaves, and that the carnival foundation would make a donation to the Culyo Leper Colony.

Andres thought that was a reasonable compromise and said he would discuss it with Pilar.

They were having their dessert when Blanca said, "Felix, do you remember the fire at the San Agustin rectory?"

Felix nodded. "I wrote about it. It happened right after New Year's day," he said.

"Did the police ever find the person who started it?" Blanca asked.

Felix shook his head. "Some people had seen a stranger in church before the fire broke out, an albino, people said, but he disappeared after the fire."

Blanca said, "I found out something from Kidlat and I think it has to do with the missing arsonist."

Felix placed his fork down and listened. "I've been wondering who was responsible for the fire, Ma'am. I've suspected the fire had something to do with Father Zafra's death, although I don't believe our Police Inspector saw a connection. What did you find out, Mrs. Noel?" Felix asked.

"Before coming here, I visited Kidlat in Carcar. I saw a man there whom I'd never seen before. Kidlat did not introduce him to me. But he was exceptionally fair like Kidlat," Blanca said.

"The people who saw the suspected arsonist described him as an albino," Felix said.

Ines, who had been following the conversation said, "In other words, it's possible that Kidlat's brother who ran away as a boy may have returned." She paused before adding, "He could have started the fire in the San Agustin rectory for revenge."

"Did the brother of Kidlat want Father Zafra dead?" Felix asked.

Blanca said, "If you really consider the matter, Felix, many people probably hated Father Zafra. The question of who killed Father Zafra has become very muddled, with Tonying Borja picking up anyone and everyone including..." Blanca paused and nodded toward Andres—"but to me the point is that Father Zafra was an evil man, may God forgive me for saying this, but it's absolutely true. He ruined many lives, and frankly Ubec and the world are so much better off without him." Blanca picked up her napkin and dabbed her lips with a note of finality.

Dismissing the matter, Blanca turned to Ines and said, "Wake me up tomorrow at seven so we can go to Printemps. I have to try on my gown."

CHAPTER 29

CORONATION NIGHT

When Ines and her family walked into the Grand Hall of the International Hotel, Melisande was checking the gowns of the women and flower girls, tugging at skirts and sleeves, and adjusting headdresses on the princesses. Melisande beamed when she saw them, and shimmering in her apricot gown with tiered skirt, she whisked Andres and Pilar to the dressing rooms. When they later remerged, Ines and Blanca were surprised to find the young woman transformed into a carbon copy of her glamorous mother, Aphrodite. Blanca stared at her in disbelief, but Ines shrugged her shoulders and muttered, "Melisande," as an explanation for the young woman's transformation. Pilar wore her Cleopatra costume with dignified resignation, while Andres looked amused at his Egyptian costume. Melisande had put kohl around his eyes, which made him look older and mysterious. Andres had always been a good-looking young man, but now he had an exotic quality that made even grown women glance at him with a restlessness in their eyes.

Ines felt her chest expand with pride as Andres escorted Pilar around the Grand Hall and down the red-carpeted aisle toward the stage and queen's chair. Several times Ines caught Pilar and Andres whisper to each other and laugh at what exactly, Ines wasn't sure, but the young couple looked animated and joyful. *Pablo,* Ines thought, *look at our son. How happy he is, how handsome.*

Ever since Pablo died, Ines had waited for some sign or manifestation from him. Like other Ubecans, she believed that the dead could visit their loved ones in the unlikely form of butterflies, birds, lights, sounds, dreams, or even scents— yes, the floral perfume that would inexplicably fill the air surrounding mourners signaled the presence of the deceased.

Those who learned that Pablo had not even appeared in her dreams (considered the least impressive of these supernatural apparitions) consoled her by saying he had certainly gone to heaven and could no longer be bothered with earthly matters. But Ines's longing to have contact with Pablo remained and more so on coronation night. "Pablo!" she had called out to him earlier, as she got ready for the big event— "Pablo, where are you?"—but he had not answered.

Despite the fits of desperation that Melisande had gone through, despite the doubts that the other members of the carnival committee felt, coronation night unfolded flawlessly. The committee had worked hard and had considered everything, including donating three dozen eggs to the nuns of Santa Clara so the saintly sisters would pray for good weather, not that there was any danger of rain that summer night, but the committee dotted their i's and crossed their t's, and indeed Ubec evoked postcard perfection, with a clear starry night, swaying coconut trees, and a gentle sea breeze that cooled the city. Ines herself was impressed at how Ubec was transformed into a seaside paradise. People crowded the festive carnival booths and rides in the Plaza Independencia, and the Grand Hall of the International Hotel glowed with the presence of Ubec's best families, decked out in mind-boggling finery, many of them present to see their sons and daughters who were in the program as flower girls, princesses, consorts, singers, dancers, flag bearers—a cast of three hundred recruited by the carnival committee precisely to lure Ubec's high society to the affair.

Everything was perfect except for the fact that Pablo

was not present. Ines was brooding over this, when suddenly, she caught the whiff of Pablo's cigar. Could it be—? She paused and turned here and there to try and locate where the scent came from. A feeling of yearning swept over her. It was La Corona, a Cuban cigar, no doubt about it; she recognized the rich, pungent smell, a scent slightly different from Philippine cigars—a distinction she had learned from Pablo's soirees at their home.

Ines was seated in a table with her mother and Dr. and Mrs. McAllister, and she quietly excused herself. Lifting her head, she sniffed about like a mouse and allowed her nose to lead her way. She found herself in the verandah where some men were smoking, plumes of white smoke lifting up into the balmy night air. With half-closed eyes like a sleepwalker, she continued searching for the source of the La Corona smell. There at the end of the dimly lit verandah, she could make out the figure of a man holding a glowing cigar. The man was as tall as Pablo, and even though Ines knew the person could not have been Pablo, she briefly entertained the idea that at last her husband had finally come to visit her—not as a dream, nor as a silly butterfly or bird, but as a flesh-and-blood human being.

Her throat caught at this idea: to touch him again, to hear his voice again!

She felt dizzy at the thought. She hadn't felt such emotion in a long time. She would tell him she loved him; she would let him know that Andres would be going to law school soon. She would inform Pablo about Pilar who could very well end up their daughter-in-law. She would relate the story of how his newspaper business turned from being in the red to now being in the black. There was so much to say, but most of all, she ached to lead Pablo to the Grand Hall so he could see Andres, their child, in his glory as one of Ubec's darling sons.

Ines hurried toward the glowing cigar, a cool wind laden with the beloved cigar smell whipping around her—it was madness, a part of her knew that, but still, she forged on. "Pablo," she called out, when she was near.

"Mrs. Maceda?" the figure said, turning so that a bit of

light shone on his face.

Ines stopped, completely flustered. It was Police Inspector Antonio Borja.

"It's you, Tonying," she said, with great disappointment.

"What are you doing out here?" he asked, as he nodded his greeting.

Ines watched a ribbon of white smoke float upward from his cigar, and she felt like plucking the cigar from Borja's fingers and flinging it away.

"No hard feelings about your son, Mrs. Maceda," he said, in an amicable tone.

Ines sucked in her breath. No hard feelings? This man standing in front of her with Pablo's cigar had arrested her son, had subjected her to fear and humiliation like she'd never felt before. Of course she had hard feelings. She wanted to tell him what an abusive fool he was. Just because he had a bit of authority he had to push people around. He was cruel, it was as simple as that; he was notorious for inflicting water treatment on prisoners. He was no different from the tarsier-of-a-child, the abandoned orphan, with large eyes who plucked off the wings of coconut beetles for fun. "And no hard feelings, my son is free, Tonying," Ines replied.

"Mrs. Maceda, I was just doing my job. A man was murdered. Fortunately, your son found an alibi."

"My son did not have an 'alibi,' he had Truth," Ines said. She placed her hands akimbo and continued, "Tonying, if you ever do anything like this to my family again, I promise you I will do everything so you will never have a political future again."

Borja gave an embarrassed laugh and ran his hand over his hard. "Witnesses fingered the three young men, including your son. In any case, I hear he is going to law school, so I want to congratulate you and him."

She had said what she wanted to say and Ines decided to drop the matter. "So, who killed the priest, Tonying?"

Borja hesitated before speaking. "Since the case is

closed and for old times' sake, I'll let you know what I think. The problem with Father Zafra was that the more you looked at his life, the more enemies you discovered. I'll admit that I was surprised to learn what I did. Like everyone else, I thought he was a nice priest, caring and so on. I should have known better." He paused to take a puff from the La Corona. "I did my civic duty and interrogated the last people who had seen him including our flamboyant composer and your son and his friends, but then there was Attorney Vargas whom I later figured could have done it. You know, do you not, Mrs. Maceda, about his son?"

"What do you know, Tonying?" She was surprised at how civil Borja was sounding.

"His son drowned, everyone knows that, but I learned that his wife had worked for the priest. In fact I was about to go to his office to talk to him when he disappeared."

"So you think Attorney Vargas did it?"

"I'll be frank with you, Mrs. Maceda: If the priest did to his son what people said the priest was capable of doing to young boys, then yes, Vargas could have killed the priest. What man wouldn't want revenge?"

"But what happened to Attorney Vargas, Tonying? Could he have disappeared as Father Zafra disappeared? Will we find his body some day? Hidden in some rocks like the priest's?"

"I doubt it. I think he fled. I have alerted the police in Manila to watch for him," Borja said.

Ines took a deep breath before speaking up. "There's one person you failed to investigate."

"And who's that?" His tone had become defensive, and fiery flashes sparkled in his eyes.

"Did you not talk to Kidlat the babaylan?"

In an irate tone, he replied, "Of course I did. That's how I learned that Father Zafra had a penchant for boys."

"You knew, did you not, that Kidlat, her brother, and mother lived in the church rectory in Carcar, and that her mother worked for Father Zafra?"

Borja blew a smoke ring before answering, "Believe it or not, Mrs. Maceda, I've done my homework. Not only do I know that Kidlat's brother had been abused by the priest and he ran away, but I found out where Father Zafra had been assigned."

"And where was he assigned?"

"It's very interesting, Mrs. Maceda—Six years in Sevilla; five in Guanajuato; four in Manila; three in Carcar; six in Iloilo; and another six in Ubec. I ran out of breath reciting where that priest had been."

"Not bad, Tonying, but what about the fire in the church rectory the day before Father Zafra was murdered? Who was responsible? And was that connected to the priest's murder?"

Borja hesitated. "What are you trying to say? The fire was caused by candles."

"That's what the official report was. But did you know there was a stranger who visited Father Zafra before the fire?"

Borja said, "Are you suggesting this stranger started the fire?"

"The stranger had white skin and hair, an albino," Ines said.

"How do you know this?"

"I'm a newspaper woman, Tonying, I have my sources," Ines said.

"Hmmm, Kidlat's brother then? He was alive and returned for revenge?"

"You can draw your own conclusions, Tonying, but I should be going back in. My son is the prince for the night."

"Mrs. Maceda," he called out as Ines was walking away. "Do you remember the coin you gave me? I used it to buy sweet rolls. I never thanked you, and I'd like to thank you now."

Ines recalled that day, a long time ago, when she had handed a coin to a hungry orphan child, and she gave a slight nod before walking away.

PART VI

CHAPTER 30

THE SS PACIFICA

It was Samir's mother who had said, "Take Didier and go. I'll be all right."

The idea had germinated, taken root, and like a wild plant branched out and filled Samir's mind. With Melisande's letter in his hands, Samir had read to his son the part about the two talking mynahs in a huge cage beside the picture window with the mannequins.

Didier, who had been his biggest concern, lit up when he heard about the birds. "I can't wait to see them, Papa. Do you think they'll talk to us?"

The boy had not even turned to say goodbye to France when their steamship, the *SS Pacifica*, pulled away from the dock of Marseilles; he was busy studying the seagulls, gannets, and other seabirds. Later he drew pictures of the birds in his sketchbook—Didier also had a passion for drawing.

And so Samir and Didier sailed on the *SS Pacifica*, which traveled at twenty knots per hour, and slowly they left behind the cold European winter. The ship paused at Port Said for coaling, and father and son watched the glowing torches of the barges carrying the coal. They strained to see the shadowy figures hauling heavy baskets up steep planks to the steamship, the men singing in unison while they worked. It took eight hours to get the job done, and by then, the sun beat down on the statue of Ferdinand de Lesseps. Samir's chest expanded as he told Didier of the marvelous feat the Frenchman had done—ten arduous years it had taken de Lesseps to unite the waters of the Mediterranean and the Red Sea; ten years Samir had been separated from Melisande.

Slowly, the *Pacifica* inched through the narrow Suez Canal. At times, it seemed the ship would scrape the sides of the canal; and just a stone's throw away was Egypt, with its people, camels, donkeys, and ancient ruins. He bought from some men on feluccas a silk jalabiya for Melisande and a fez for Didier, which the boy kept on his head even while they dined with the ship's captain and surgeon. (They had peacock and camel's hump for dinner that night.)

Samir sketched the enormous sand dunes that reminded him of his painting of his mother in the Arabian dress, the same image that had upset Melisande, but which drew them close. He often thought of that Sunday, that afternoon of lovemaking—the memory helped sustain his spirit.

It had been with them, Desire, from the moment Melisande had stood outside his apartment door, through lunch, on to the drawing session on his balcony. He had seen a shadow cross her face when she finally saw his drawing of her. It was not from unhappiness, she later explained, but from the emotions that welled up, that indeed his work had feeling. He had pulled her close and touched her face, slowly as if he were a blind man committing it to memory—his fingers molding her cheeks, her forehead, her eyebrows, her lips, his fingers sliding down to her neck, to her shoulders. He had caught the scent of citrus from her hair. He had desired her, knew he could take her, but restrained himself. Later that afternoon, it was the portrait of his mother that drew tears from her eyes—she had mistaken the Arabian woman for his lover. How could he stop himself from saying, "Spend the afternoon with me. I want to give you pleasure." There was no protest, no resistance as he bent down to kiss her forehead, her eyes, and then her lips. With his hand around her waist, he had led her to his bedroom, and he had cleared away her things from the brass bed, and lifted her unto it.

That day, after they had made love, he told her that Plato said humans were originally created with four arms, four legs, and a head with two faces. But fearing their power, Zeus split them into two separate parts, condemning them to spend their lives in search of their other halves.

He had told her that they were very fortunate they had found each other, because they were meant to be one. He said, when they part, it will hurt them very much, because the oneness will be separated once again.

They had been apart for years. They had suffered. It was now time for their two halves to become one.

Melisande.

The *Pacifica* chugged on to the Bitter Lakes and then to the Red Sea. By this time, they knew their ship by heart: their first class cabin with its side table always stocked with Turkish delight and other delicacies; the smoking room where Samir chatted with the men; the promenade deck where they walked and gazed out at the ever-changeable sea; the women who fawned over Didier, their eyes sparkling at Samir as well. And there was the library where Didier scoured all the bird books; one afternoon, he appeared wide-eyed in front of his father to report that mynah birds could die from loneliness.

At the southern end of the Red Sea, they stopped at Port Aden where they caught a glimpse of the twin minarets of a mosque, then like a birthing, they passed through its gulf into the Arabian Sea. As he studied the wide expanse of the dark sea, Samir knew with certainty that Europe and the desert sands of Arabia were behind him. His throat had tightened when he considered that Melisande had been in these same waters after she left him—how could he have driven her to this distant place?

Melisande had always been in his thoughts. From the time he and Didier had boarded the train in Paris, he had tried to imagine the voyage she had taken a decade ago. He saw her on the ship's deck, in the dining saloons, the music hall, in all the port stops they made—there Melisande was, tall with her woman's figure and long curly red-brown hair.

Their next stop was Colombo, Ceylon, where they stared in awe at the modern General Post office and grand hotels. During their port stop, he bought a thumb-sized sapphire stone, violet-blue in color. That evening, he sketched a ring design for the gemstone, with Melisande in mind.

A few more days at sea and they arrived Penang in Malaysia where he saw an elephant hauling logs near a river. The air was more humid now, and the sun gleamed white, and the sky and sea were brilliant blue, and the palms and birds of paradise startling in their crayola colors.

Then one clear morning, after traveling for twenty-one days, the *SS Pacifica* made its way through the strait between Mactan and Ubec islands. The captain had warned them of their early morning arrival, but suddenly, Samir and Didier were unprepared, their things scattered in their cabin, Didier's books and toys lost in tight corners.

After packing the last of their belongings into their bags, Samir and Didier left their cabin and hurried toward the boat's railing to stare at the larger island, Ubec, a name they had only read, but which now held their future.

"Papa, are we here?" the boy asked, his voice quivering with excitement. He had on a white sailor suit, crisp and immaculate; it had been buried in the bottom of his suitcase, kept new for today.

"Yes, Didier." Samir held his son's hand tightly.

Samir's bravura had deserted him last night. He had peered out at the velvet darkness of the sky and sea and he had felt drained, afraid: He had left his work, his mother, Paris— his past. Had he done the right thing? Did Melisande have the capacity to forgive him? Would she be able to love this boy who was not hers? With Didier snoring softly near him, he had rummaged for her letter and had reread it for the thousandth time—she loved him still.

Didier swayed from left to right, straining to see more of the sea and the sandy shore with coconut trees and nipa huts; and the boy pointed at the lush green mountains that ran down the center of the island like a spine. Later, Didier's eyes fixed on some boys and girls who were playing in the water. "Papa, look, children." Didier waved at them. "Can I also swim in the sea, like them?" he asked.

"You have to learn to swim first," Samir said.

"I will, and I will also visit those mountains. I am sure there are many birds there, talking ones, like the mynahs." Didier became thoughtful before adding, "I wonder if the mynahs will sound like a phonograph."

Samir mussed the boy's hair. A feeling of well-being surged through him; he had not felt such happiness in a long time. "We'll find out when we're there," Samir said, his voice redolent of hope.

***

The City of Ubec loomed ahead, with its old Spanish fort and plaza, the stone churches, the sparkling white American buildings, and the myriad wood and stone structures that seemed strewn haphazardly. It was early morning in December, and the weather cool for the tropics. Ines closed the door to *The Ubec Daily* and hurried down Cristobal Colon Street toward Printemps. She knocked and opened the door. Melisande's assistants were not yet in and the shop was quiet. A long time ago, before Melisande had moved in, Ines had seen this place. It had looked like a warehouse then, rundown and dirty. Melisande had transformed it into a vibrant dress shop that the women of Ubec loved. The hanging dividers and mirrors gave a sense of space and light, which made visitors feel as if they were walking on air. A beveled glass showcase near the door displayed items that Melisande also sold: crystal bottles of perfume, alabaster pots of skin lotions and makeup, bed linens, tablecloth with matching napkins, lace handkerchiefs. There in the back section were two Singer sewing machines, silent this morning. A large bird cage and two mannequins wearing Melisande's haute couture faced the picture window. Ines hurried up the stairs to find Melisande in her bedroom. She was seated in front of her dresser mirror, studying her image while brushing her thick mass of hair.

"The boat is coming," Ines said, out of breath with excitement. She had in her hands sprigs of jasmine, whose scent filled the room. The jasmine vine outside her bedroom window had grown back thicker and healthier, filled with cascading clouds of sweet snow-white flowers.

Melisande moaned. "Oh Ines, I've gained two kilos since I last saw him. And my hair is so unruly today … and oh, my skin…" She reached for a pot with rouge which she lightly rubbed onto her cheeks, leaving her skin glowing pink. Melisande stared at her image and made a face. "Look at me, Ines. I look terrible."

"There is no time for that now. Felix said the boat is almost at the dock."

Melisande gasped. "And I haven't checked the shop." She quickly anchored her hair into a bun using combs and pins, and put some powder on her face.

"I'll make sure everything is in order." She found a vase, filled it with water, and arranged the spray of jasmine in it.

"But what if he notices that I've … grown old?"

"What does that have to do with their arrival?" Ines asked, perplexed.

The mantel clock chimed just then—it was getting late—and Melisande twirled around, threw her hands up in the air and laughed.

"Go, now!" Ines said.

Melisande picked up her purse and umbrella and she and Ines ran down the stairs. Melisande kissed Ines on the cheeks, blew a kiss at her mynahs who were half-asleep in their cage, then, taking a deep breath, opened the front door. She stepped outside and hailed a carriage. "To the pier, hurry!" she told the driver. "I have to meet the *Pacifica*," she added in a voice breathless with longing.

~END~

THE AUTHOR

Cecilia Manguerra Brainard is the author and editor of over twenty books, including the novels: *When the Rainbow Goddess Wept, Magdalena,* and *The Newspaper Widow.* She has edited books including the popular *Growing Up Filipino Stories for Young Adults* and its follow-up *Growing Up Filipino II. She also edited Fiction by Filipinos in America* and *Contemporary Fiction by Filipinos in America.*

Her recent book is *Selected Short Stories by Cecilia Manguerra Brainard* (University of Santo Tomas Publishing House 2021 & PALH 2021). She is collecting and editing *Growing Up Filipino Book 3: New Stories about Young Adults,* scheduled for release in 2022.

Cecilia's work has been translated into Finnish and Turkish; and many of her stories and articles have been widely anthologized.

Cecilia has received a California Arts Council Fellowship in Fiction, a Brody Arts Fund Award, a Special Recognition Award for her work dealing with Asian American youths, as well as a Certificate of Recognition from the California State Senate, 21st District. She has also been awarded by the Filipino and Filipino American communities she has served. In 1998, she received the Outstanding

Individual Award from her birth city, Cebu, Philippines. She has received several travel grants in the Philippines, from the USIS (United States Information Service). In 2001, she received a Filipinas Magazine Award for Arts. Her books have won the Gourmand Award and the Gintong Aklat Award.

She has lectured and performed in worldwide literary arts organizations and universities, including UCLA, USC, University of Connecticut, University of the Philippines, PEN, Beyond Baroque, Shakespeare & Company in Paris, and many others. She owns and manages PALH (Philippine American Literary House.)

She is married to Lauren R. Brainard, a former Peace Corp Volunteer to Leyte, Philippines; they have three sons.

Her official website is ceciliabrainard.com.

PRAISE FOR *THE NEWSPAPER WIDOW*

An old-fashioned novel isn't a bad thing when it's as well done as this one about people growing, loving, and rectifying past mistakes.
~*Library Journal*, July 2021

An intriguing mystery and also very much the story of the deepening friendship between two women of opposite temperaments, Ines and Melisande, and of the men in their lives who love and have loved them. Beautifully written. Evocative. A rich depiction of character, time and place that will live in a reader's memory.
~Eve La Salle Caram, Author of *TRIO, a Corpus Christi Trilogy*

Cecilia Brainard's deft hand for textured character and nuanced storytelling is on magnificent display in her latest novel *The Newspaper Widow*. What begins as a murder mystery transforms into something greater along the way, as love, loyalty, and friendship are tested and refined. Shortlisted for the inaugural Cirilo F. Bautista Prize for the Novels, Brainard's novel is a captivating read."
~ Dean Francis Alfar, Author of *Salamanca*

This is not your run of the mill 'who done it.' Matter of fact, about halfway through *The Newspaper Widow*, you'll be certain that the lawyer did it – or did he? But what this is, is Cecilia Brainard weaving her magic of culture, folklore and myth to produce a tapestry of rich Filipino history and that she remains one of its primary artisans."
~ James E. Cherry, Author of *Edge of the Wind*)

A must-read from a master storyteller, *The Newspaper Widow* promises not only to entertain but also to educate the reader about a critical period in Philippine history.
~ Herminia Meñez Coben, Professor Emerita and Author of
Verbal Arts in Philippine Indigenous Communities

The plot, that hinges on the quest for the murderer of the Spanish priest Zafra, involves many colorful characters, each with a personal history.

~ Paulino Lm Jr., Professor Emeritus and Author of
Requiem for a Rebel Priest

The Newspaper Widow by Cecilia Manguerra Brainard, treats readers to meaningful insights into historical events and life in the Philippines in the early 1900s. A work of fiction, it is more than a masterfully crafted and multi-layered mystery.

~ Lisa Suguitan Melnick for *Positively Filipino*